British journalist Yvonne Ridley has had a successful career in the media spanning four decades. The former Fleet Street reporter has written several books, but this is her first departure into the world of fiction.

Inspired by the dramatic scenery and surroundings of her remote Scottish farm and the rich but often violent history of the Borders, she created The Caledonians.

To those heroic people of Scotland, past and present, who have provided an eternal fountain of inspiration through courage, dignity, sorrow and hardship; all of which have been endured because of an overriding determination to be free.

Yvonne Ridley

The Caledonians

Mr Petrie's Apprentice

Austin Macauley Publishers™
London • Cambridge • New York • Sharjah

A CIP catalogue record for this title is available from the British Library.

ISBN 9781528926669 (Paperback)
ISBN 9781528964777 (ePub e-book)

www.austinmacauley.com

First Published (2020)
Austin Macauley Publishers Ltd
25 Canada Square
Canary Wharf
London
E14 5LQ

I'd like to thank my historical consultant, Andro Sillar, whose knowledge of Scottish history, culture and attention to detail were invaluable. A true Caledonian, he has proved to be as inspiring and mysterious as the erudite Mr Petrie, prompting me to wonder if our paths crossing were more than a happy coincidence. Great appreciation goes to the Lataoui children: Lamis, Lina, Yumna and Youssef, who spent a wonderful day with me immersing themselves in the world of Sweetheart and Mr Petrie, emerging from piles of paper with helpful feedback when it was most needed. Of course, family always plays a major role and influence, and I'm indebted to mine, especially my daughter, Daisy Jane, who injected a bit of technology and 21st-century thinking while my beloved husband, Samir, sat and listened patiently as the story of the Caledonians unfolded. His butter to my bread was the gentle words of encouragement he spread during periods of literary doldrums.

Chapter 1

"Spero Meliora! Spero Meliora! Spero Meliora!" raged the angry man in front of the assembled crowd. He beat the left side of his chest with a clenched fist held so tightly, his knuckles across his right hand were bleached white.

Again he roared the Moffat motto, this time in English: "For greater things." The hundreds of men who had gathered in the Lowland clan's building answered his cry, shouting back: "Greater things, great things!" The atmosphere in the vast barn was incendiary.

The barn usually held celebratory gatherings but tonight there were only tears of rage flowing for their murdered chief, Robert Moffat. This was probably the closest thing to a council of war and the clan was in crisis, so the most significant and powerful landowners of the Moffat family rallied to discuss who would become the next chieftain and what revenge would be taken.

The year was 1557 and the Moffat Clan was one of the most influential families in Dumfriesshire with a rich history punctuated by battle honours, royal and church support since the 13th century. The family gathering at the vast complex which included a stone tower, barmkin, animal pens, blacksmith's and brewery was the talk of the Annandale district.

A fire roared behind Fraser Moffat but the crackling noise of the tinder dry kindle hitting the flames was drowned out as he continued to rage, hissing and spitting his own fiery words. He carefully adjusted his leather jerkin before dramatically ripping off his cloak and throwing it by his feet to reveal his sword.

"I can almost hear the final words of our great father and leader, Robert, before he was laid to waste by the murdering, godless creatures who sought to cut his life so short. He may be gone and while his widow and children weep, I swear here and now to avenge his death on behalf of all the Moffats from the union of the Norse daughter of Andlaw and William de Movat Alto to those who fought so bravely at Bannockburn to the men who stand before me today."

The wife of the dead clan chief held her head high as she rocked the sleeping babe in her arms while her two young daughters sought to hide among the folds of her long woollen skirt. Aged seven and five, Helen and Marion were scared of the raw anger in the air and knew not why there was so much shouting.

Fraser had brought the widow of his brother and their children in to the room to add to the emotion of the occasion. Lost without their loving father, the girls couldn't understand where he was, since this was obviously an important meeting and he was always at the centre of any gathering.

But now their uncle was centre stage and they were frightened as he talked about blood sacrifices and death and destruction of the Johnstones. The historic significance bypassed the dead chieftain's daughters for they were unaware why the great and the good from this powerful clan had come together in their hundreds. They had yet to be told their father was dead.

Little did anyone know that this would be the last time for centuries that so many Moffats would be assembled under one roof. Among the generations were the greying elders, battle-scarred, weakened and weary from a lifetime of conflict standing alongside the swaggering young callants. Fraser Moffat held their admiring, youthful gaze and with each call to arms, their chests seemed to heave, swell and expand a little more.

Fraser was swarthy looking, nearly 6 ft. tall and appeared to be just as wide with powerful, muscular arms and legs that were the envy of most men who met him. His dark brown, curly hair was framed by loosely tied braids on either side of his strong, square face which was partially covered by an overgrown, red-tinged beard.

The smouldering, raging atmosphere had an almost hypnotic effect with most eyes focussed on the passionate speaker. His guttural brogue drowned out all other noises, making it easy for a group of strangers to move stealthily forward, unseen, down the several narrow paths leading through the courtyard to the barn.

A sealed entrance had been secretly left opened through some pre-arranged bribe which allowed the Johnstones..... in by the animal pens and blacksmith's corner. All were members of the most notorious of the Border Reivers, the Johnstones, and were certainly not invited or welcomed in these parts. The dried blood of the Moffat chief still clung to their dark weave cloaks and their very presence would have ignited the fury of the rival Moffats inside the barn.

It was an audacious raid and the element of surprise caught off guard a handful of men who were supposed to be on the lookout for trouble. The truth is none suspected such a brazened attack right in the Moffat heartlands and so focussed more on the plentiful drink which had just been brewed and served in a giant cauldron for after the meeting. As they talked and swigged the warm mead from the cauldron, they suspected nothing.

The Johnstones ambushed and overpowered the unsuspecting men by two to one, slashing their throats; the sickening gurgle and spluttering sounds they made as they bled out disturbed no one. It was full three minutes before the last breath of life left the corpses and it would be a few minutes more before they stopped twitching and finally lay still, drained of their lifeblood.

Carrying flaming torches more than a dozen of the shadowy figures crept around the building waiting for a signal to unleash their terror. The Johnstones were not seeking a truce or reconciliation for deeds done, and it was clear from the shouts inside the barn that neither were the Moffats. Tonight would end the centuries' old feuding once and for all, but the stakes were high and only one clan could emerge victorious.

Two of the raiders went to the large stone tower where the women and children had assembled. Quietly they sealed the entrances with several hayricks. Inside, a couple of older women toiled as they roasted a fatted calf over a hand turned spit. Red-faced from the heat, their corned-beef complexions were exaggerated by crisp white bonnets and high-laced, cotton blouses.

The woollen shawls tied loosely around their waists over long, heavy bum-rolled skirts exaggerated the size of their hips. One of the women nudged the other, pointing upwards to the thatched roof, as she went to pile more wood on the fire.

Watching them were the other clan women. Some of the widows openly wept for the murdered chief while the bewildered children looked on. Young maiden teenage girls who usually talked about the clan's potential suitors for possible future unions were sad and subdued and comforted each other.

Meanwhile, outside, cold sweat illuminated the brows of the Johnstones as a clear, cloudless sky carrying a full moon revealed their presence, but the only witness to the prelude of a massacre and the death of the gurgling guards was a short-eared owl. The silent predator perched in a nearby tree was ready to swoop on his next meal, a vole, but the tiny creature darted left and then right before bolting down a hole having being startled when the strangers overpowered the guards.

Unruffled at losing his next meal, the patient, unblinking, wide-eyed bird swivelled its head as if preparing to absorb and savour the whole ghastly spectacle which was about to unfold in the complex.

Back inside the barn, Fraser was making his final bid to become the chieftain by reminding those present of their glorious past and the future ahead. "Since the times of our forefathers, our people have made their mark and it will take a lot more than the bloody Johnstones to end our line; this is our border country which is why I've called you all here tonight, to bear true witness and testimony that we will not rest until the earth has been purged of such filth."

As if to emphasise his rage, Fraser threw back his head and gave a rasping, throaty sound which produced a glob of phlegm. He promptly spat out the thick mucus mass and as the gluey spittle landed by a couple of young boys, squatting underneath the table on which he stood, they recoiled in wonderment as the slimy spectacle gathered some loose dust before gluing itself to the earthen floor.

"Us Moffats have a proud history, drawn from all corners of the Lowlands. Our family is linked to brave and daring deeds. Anyone of us could step up and be a leader, for the blood which runs through our veins is that of fighting men born to lead.

"Robert was cruelly cut down, nay assassinated before his son has even come of age. The bairn is here tonight, swaddled in blankets unaware of the great destiny that awaits. Until he is old enough to pick up a sword, we must choose among us someone who can follow in the steps of his father and then we will take our revenge." With that, Fraser drew his sword and waved it wildly in the air, roaring once again: "Spero Meliora! Spero Meliora! Spero Meliora."

The rest of the clan began to echo his words in an ever-increasing crescendo when Fraser threw his head back for a final, dramatic roar and a call to arms but suddenly the whole spectacle was brought to a screeching halt as his eyes looked heavenwards and he became momentarily distracted.

A pall of black smoke was billowing in the open rafters and a couple of sparks dropped from the thatched straw roof. "Quick, get Robert's widow and bairns out, now!" he shouted and suddenly, in a heartbeat, the angry chanting had turned to unbridled panic as the words of revenge morphed into "fire, fire, fire!"

Within seconds, the flames could be seen more clearly and clumps of burning straw began dropping, but the choking descending smoke presented more of a danger as the overhead blaze sucked the oxygen out of the air.

On hearing the screams of "fire, fire!" the women and children ran to the doors of the stone tower but they refused to open blocked by the hayricks which had also been set alight. The intruders on the outside had made sure they were locked in tight and even the heaving mass of bodies pressing against them could not burst them open.

Suffocating smoke now filled both buildings and began to choke the already breathless occupants. Mass hysteria ensued as the frail were trampled underfoot and children left crying, detached from their mothers.

Fraser by this time had leapt down from his table and furiously punched and kicked a wooden side panel until it splintered and gave way to his aggression, revealing a jagged hole just large enough to save his dead brother's children.

He grabbed his screaming nieces, thrusting them through the gap but there was no relief or escape for little Marion and Helen as they hit the night air and ran. Cold steel sliced through Marion's waving arms as she tried to flee from the fire. She was no match for the powerful blows of the Johnstone swords – there was no mercy that night, not for the Moffat children, not for any of them.

"Can't we not just leave the bairns?" cried one young man as his sword hung over the head of a squealing seven-year-old Helen. An older man grabbed the sword from his hand and plunged it into the child's chest, hoisting her into the air like a chicken on a spit roast. "Little Moffats grow into big Moffats; the only good Moffat is a dead Moffat. Never ever forget that son."

When death finally came to flame-haired Helen, her little blonde sister Marion and the other fleeing youngsters, it was a relief. All had died in an orgy of blood and guts and a terror beyond their wildest imaginations.

The ground was so wet and clotted with the blood and guts of the families that some of the Johnstones slipped and fell as they wielded their swords, leaving their own flesh smeared in a ghastly cocktail of warm, sticky gore and mud.

Few Moffats escaped that night and those that did were left bereft and emotionally scarred as members of a headless family. It would be a full 426 years before they assembled again in 1983 to declare a new clan leader. Overnight, one of the most potent powerhouses in the Lowlands had been ethnically cleansed by their merciless enemies.

Mr Petrie's beady eyes twinkled and shone through his bushy salt and pepper brows as he scanned his open-mouthed, young audience, adding with relish: "Scotland's history, like its soil, is caked in the blood of innocents, especially in the Borders where the raiders and reivers slaughtered and murdered without mercy."

The history master's throaty brogue had rinsed out every syllable until it was bone dry, to maximise the dramatic effect to his attentive history class. As the last slide of the Moffat coat of arms disappeared, Petrie shouted: "Lights, McLeish!" and a pupil emerged from the back of the class to flick a switch transporting the third formers of Sweetheart Abbey boarding school back to the present day.

"Next week we'll be looking at the ballads that reflect the most active era of the Border reivers when robbery, horse theft, death and revenge were the orders of the day. For some light reading in preparation, may I suggest the history of the Battle of Otterburn and research on Sir Walter Scott's Minstrelsy of the Scottish Border?

"There's still thirty minutes to go before the bell, so I suggest you start right now. Clarkson, you're form head and so I'm putting you in charge and I expect you to report any unworthy behaviour and the miscreants to me," added Mr Petrie before he swept out of the classroom.

The Scottish History master was feeling rather pleased with himself. The demise of the Moffat clan was one of his favourite lessons because his class always paid attention to every minute, gut-wrenching detail. As he made his way to the car park, he was whistling to the strains of the Bonnie Banks of Loch Lomond.

"Finishing early, Mr Petrie?" enquired Dr Geraint Jones, the choirmaster, as the two passed in the staff car park. He looked up, slightly irritated and replied: "I have some pressing business in Stirling, a gifted scholarship candidate who has come to my attention. I used to teach his guardian and it seems the boy shows a lot of promise."

The Welshman's face illuminated as he asked: "Can the boy sing? I'm always looking for new talent for the choir." Mr Petrie shook his head vigorously in the negative, even though he had no idea if Duncan Dewar had an aptitude for music. He was extremely territorial and viewed the choir with some disdain as, apart from St Andrew's Day and Burns celebratory evenings, it was rarely pressed into service over matters Scottish.

With that, Mr Petrie jumped in to his pride and joy, an old black *Austin Cambridge* a former pupil had gifted him brand new. As he drove down the gravel drive, he looked anxiously at his watch and realised he might be a little late for his lunchtime meeting in Stirling.

***

Chapter 2

Gordon Buie loved the constant tick, tick, tick of his clocks. He was surrounded by them and the sound each one made resonated in such a way that he felt as if time itself was flowing smoothly and calmly around his workshop.

Not everyone was as appreciative on walking in to his workplace. For some people, a timepiece brought no such reassurance but merely served as a reminder of life slipping by second by second, each mechanical heartbeat signalling another step closer to the journey's end which awaits us all.

No such concerns for Gordon though. He was indeed a serene, peaceful man, troubled by little in life despite being forced to confront more than his fair share of unexpected sadness and sorrow. The death of his wife, Phyllis, was particularly painful, gone within weeks after cancer was diagnosed.

But the cruellest blow fate dealt him was the death of his only daughter, Moira, and son-in-law, Douglas, in a car crash leaving him alone to raise their baby son, Duncan. The saying goes that every cloud has a silver lining and the joy that came with the child proved to be the case.

Raising a baby there was no time for grieving or sorrow, not a second to be lost or a second regretted. Gordon made every moment with his grandson count and often wondered who needed who the most as they proved to be an emotional crutch for each other.

Being a clockmaker, he knew the value of time and as time passed in his workshop, wonderful memories were made and stored by the old man and his grandson who became almost as passionate as Gordon about the timepieces delivered for restoration and repair in the cluttered room at the back of their home.

Living in the medieval heart of the ancient city of Stirling also provided plenty of outside interest and amusement for the pair when they left their workshop to explore the old city, its castle and other historic buildings on their so-called 'adventure days'…

As Duncan got older, so did Gordon and this march on time began to trouble the old man. Age, he always felt, was just another number and while he slipped into his 50s with the greatest of ease, his advancing years were now becoming a problem especially after chest X-rays revealed an enlarged heart.

He knew he couldn't devote the time and energy his grandson needed to thrive and develop through his teens. Despite the huge age gap, and maybe because of it, the two rubbed along very well and spent most of their time, outside of school hours, in the old workshop where work and leisure combined seamlessly.

For a boy who came from the so-called X-Box Generation, Duncan loved nothing more than observing the intricacies of the tiny wheels and cogs that, combined together, produced a timepiece far superior to anything that could be flicked on with a switch or powered by a battery.

Duncan also found something soothing to be drawn from the sound of a clock's tick unlike the jarring electronic computer noises which screamed from old copies of Minecraft and Grand Theft Auto he'd bought on *Ebay*. He was so grounded in logic that the fantasy world of the gamer with all its violence, drugs and bad driving held no lure for him; if anything, they left him cold.

As a natural problem solver aged eleven years old, he found the storytelling and gameplay on his computer games barely believable and viewed the eighteen-age certificate with some disdain. 'Do adults really get pleasure out of this world of make believe?' he asked himself, almost giving an uncharacteristic sneer.

Perhaps it would have been different if he had brothers or sisters to compete against, but he didn't. Neither did he have many friends; forming relationships and bonding was difficult for him because he was not like most of the other kids from his school. Duncan was studious, a bit of a nerd, which earned him the nickname 'Geeky Ginge' by his contemporaries at Riverside Primary.

He excelled in maths, sciences and developed a passion for Gaelic too; it was a language Gordon Buie spoke and the pair would often spend their days conversing in it as they walked to the school from their home in the shadow of Stirling Castle.

It was a truly symbiotic relationship but Gordon Buie realised the time would come when out of love for his grandson he would have to let him go and find his own path in life. Repairing watches and clocks was no longer a lucrative business in a fast-paced, advancing electronic world.

This throwaway society was rapidly developing and seemed to hold contempt for non-electronic devices. However, power cuts brought about by the howling storms that periodically rolled in would often bring a wry smile and smugness as his tick-tock world continued to turn while those around him would be brought to a crashing halt.

However, he was wise enough to know he could not halt progress and by the time Duncan was old enough, there would be no business to pass on to his grandson. The horologist's art belonged to a different era.

When the decision about Duncan's future was finally made, it came rather suddenly by way of a completely unexpected visit from a familiar figure from Gordon's distant past. Walking into the workshop unannounced, the visitor declared: "I have an interesting wall clock which needs repairing but I feel its condition is too delicate to make the journey from Galloway to Stirling. I had some business at the castle and so I thought I would take a chance and pop in, Gordon. The door was open and so here I am."

The old man stared at Mr Petrie – a teacher from his old school – for some time. He recognised the voice straight away but thought his eyes were deceiving him as his history master from the 70s walked in to the workshop displaying the sort of familiarity friends held as though they'd only parted company the day before.

"Mr Petrie!" he exclaimed. "Well, I never. As you can see I have changed but you, why you look exactly the same as you did the day you told us the truth about Culloden?" laughed the clockmaker. "That shattered a few illusions among the English kids. Are you still at Sweetheart?" he enquired.

Mr Petrie nodded his head: "Oh, yes, and we no longer rely on funds from south of the border. We're international now. Students from all over the world, the Middle East, Far East, Russia, Europe, but we still take in local boys, especially gifted children with special aptitudes. So I'm happy to report that some of our standards and aims, anyway, are still being maintained."

After exchanging a few more pleasantries, he invited Mr Petrie around the corner in Castle Wynd for a 'wee dram' at the Portcullis pub. "And if you're hungry and want a late lunch, they do a great steak in Drambuie sauce," he said but Petrie waved his hand, indicating a drink would suffice.

As they sat down on wooden stools, the teacher enquired about his home life and soon learned Gordon had a grandson. "Duncan is a gifted child, right enough. I think he must have inherited his parents' genius," he reflected. "You know my daughter Moira and her husband were both brilliant scientists though I'm damned if I know what they did as it was all very hush-hush stuff.

"Something to do with space travel but beyond that they told me very little. Whatever they did, it was far beyond the simple world of a clockmaker, that's for sure. But I do know their laboratories were built underground, somewhere in Wiltshire. Moira reckoned if she didn't drag Douglas from the labs, they would never see daylight from one week to the next.

"It was pretty consuming work, and I thought once my grandson arrived, they would adjust but, wherever they went, he went too."

He then explained to Petrie how a double tragedy rocked his world in the worst possible way after a group of top government scientists were wiped out in a helicopter crash in the Highlands. "They would have flown there too, that was the plan. The whole damned lot were killed in a Chinook crash. I was so relieved when Moira telephoned to say she and Douglas were fine because they'd chosen to journey north by car instead because of the bairn. It was all over the news; great minds and top scientists all gone, no survivors and bad weather combined with a technical problems to blame.

"Then, twenty-four hours after the Chinook went down, the police arrived at my door to say there had been a terrible accident and my daughter was dead along with Douglas. At first I thought there was a horrible mix-up, you know with the helicopter tragedy, but the policeman was insistent this was down to a car crash. I couldn't believe it, overwhelming relief one minute that they were okay and then utter shock the next when I realised they had in fact been involved in a completely different accident; it was crushing.

"Apparently Douglas had been driving which, again, was rather strange as he only ever drove as a last resort. Moira was a confident driver whereas poor Douglas was always accused of being too slow and too cautious behind the wheel.

"I was devastated as you can imagine but then the police produced Duncan and the little fellow just reached out to me. We've been together ever since and in truth I think I need him more than he needs me, now."

As they walked down St John's Street towards his workshop, the pair went past the city's fifteenth-century church. "Moira and Douglas were married there, proudest day of my life it was as I walked her down that aisle. Never thought for a moment I'd be burying her and Douglas less than a decade later."

Mr Petrie looked over the wall and said: "Church of the Holy Rude, isn't it? That's where the King James VI was crowned as an infant. That Burgh kirk has seen some high days and holy days in its time."

He looked at Gordon who was wiping a tear from his cheek and put a hand on his shoulder, saying: "No parent expects he'll ever have to bury his own children. It's just not right but trust me, I know exactly how you feel."

Gordon Buie stammered: "I'm sorry, Mr Petrie. I was always under the impression you were a bachelor." But the history master held up his hand as if to stop him from speaking further. As they continued walking back towards the workshop, the grandfather added: "You know on the day, the very same day of the funeral, my home was broken in to and the workshop too. It was left in a right mess. Nothing was stolen, not even an antique Louis XVI ormolu-mounted clock I'd taken in a few days earlier from a regular customer.

"It was worth thousands which made me think some wretched kids had gone inside just for fun. A few days later, some government officials arrived and asked for any papers or files Moira and Douglas may have left behind. They even asked if they could search the place which I thought was a wee bit odd.

"I had to apologise as it was still in a bit of a mess because it was ransacked in the break in. Funny business, as I say nothing was stolen, not even my late wife or daughter's jewellery.

"Of course there was no cash lying around and if it was cash the villains were after, they'd obviously not done their homework. Otherwise they would have burgled the neighbour down the road; he's a scrap merchant and said to be worth a bob or two.

"The only thing I have of any value is Duncan and my memory bank up here," he said, tapping his large, bony forehead.

Mr Petrie nodded in agreement: "Yes, my friend. Our memories are priceless and they can keep us warm on the loneliest of nights and melt our frozen hearts on the coldest." He listened carefully as the grandfather's conversation then returned to his grandson and how the boy had developed an insatiable appetite for reading.

"As soon as the bairn could sit up in his cot, he grabbed a book. He absorbed everything and graduated very quickly from pictures to words, devouring each one as though it was a tasty morsel. He showed no interest in ball games, which is just as well at my age, but his great passion is reading and working out what makes things tick, literally. I think I've passed that on to him because he's very keen to help me in the workshop, especially when it comes to stripping down old clocks."

Educated or not, the truth is Duncan Dewar would have excelled at whatever he put his mind to because of his exceptionally high IQ and his sheer, natural ability in languages, mathematics and science.

And so, the idea of sending him to Sweetheart came about after some prompting by Mr Petrie. "It served you well over the years after you won a scholarship and could do the same for him. Bring him for a visit soon. He must be coming to an end with his current school and I doubt the local high school can offer anything near the facilities we have at Sweetheart. Think about it and call me next week.

"And when you do come, you can look at my old wall clock and see if you can save it from becoming a dust collector rather than a time piece."

***

Chapter 3

Two months later, Gordon Buie and his grandson Duncan arrived at Dulce Cor cottage in the grounds of Sweetheart Abbey School and sat silently in their car for a few minutes, taking in their surrounds. The old stone building had stood stoically in the centre of New Abbey village where it had been marking time for centuries in the shadow of the looming bulk of Criffel Hill.

The journey by car to the Solway coast in Dumfries and Galloway had taken a leisurely three hours and, as he opened the driver's door, Gordon Buie turned to his grandson and said: "This school could be the making of you. I want you to look upon today as the start of an exciting adventure, Duncan. You know how much I love you but I am getting on laddie and you need a better start in life than the one I can give you.

"Now remember, no one is expecting an answer immediately and it's not exactly the army these days, so if you don't like it you can say so. There's a perfectly good school waiting for you back at Stirling, but I really feel this one can give you so much more."

Duncan looked into his grandfather's eyes then stepped out of the car. The spindly youth was almost as tall as the old man who these days was slightly stooped and walked with the aid of a stick. "Grandfather, I don't want to leave you; you are all I've got and what about you? And this place looks scary, and I'm afraid."

The old man patted his grandson on the shoulder and said: "When your mother was alive, she rarely left your side. I'm told your Moses basket was perched in her laboratory next to the Bunsen burners, test tubes and glass flasks. God knows what Health and Safety monitors would've said. However, I know for a fact she would never have sent you away in a million years but what I do know is both of them wanted the best for you.

"And this is the best," he said waving his arm around. "The educational opportunities here at Sweetheart are really first-rate and I should know! Before you make any decision, and ultimately it will be your decision, lad, sit down and talk to Mr Petrie and see what you think."

The old man opened the rickety garden gate and the pair walked down the flower lined path. As Gordon reached out for the brass doorknocker, he paused momentarily. It was a menacing looking lion's head, but the door opened before he could lift it. There stood a welcoming Mr Petrie. Within minutes of introductions, some piping hot tea was being poured into china cups bearing the pattern of a Celtic-style cross. Traditional shortbread biscuits were neatly arranged on a lace doily over an oval plate with the same Celtic designs.

"So young Duncan, you're thinking of coming to Sweetheart Abbey then, following in your grandfather's footsteps, eh? A wise choice," said Mr Petrie. "I'm told you're a bright lad with a head for maths and science but what do you know about Scottish history?"

His eyes widened in horror as he was unable to utter a word having just taken a mouthful of shortbread; Duncan had literally bitten off more than he could chew and he froze as the piercing gaze of the history master seemed to penetrate through to his brain.

Without waiting for him to answer, Mr Petrie continued: "The trouble with the youth today, Gordon, is they don't know their history, who they are or even where they are from. They can all talk about Bannockburn and recite a little Burns and sing Flower of Scotland but there's more to this great nation than bagpipes, kilts and haggis; the land is awash with heroes and great martyrs and it is almost criminal they know so little about their heritage or the sacrifices made for future generations.

"Do you know I've had my own battle just to keep some of the history in the curriculum after complaints from parents and meddling governors that I have an anti-English agenda? Me? Anti-English? The trouble is, those south of the Border who send their children here to be educated want me to resort to an

Imperialist 'Rule Britannia' agenda, but I won't. We must tell it like it is, warts and all. That is my duty, and I won't deviate from it!

"I believe history should not just be written by the pen of the victors and our own Scottish story must be told. Otherwise pupils will leave here thinking we are all savages who guzzle Irn Bru, eat deep fried Mars bars, avoid green vegetables, paint our faces blue and get stocious every night on Buckfast and whisky."

Gordon Buie slapped his knees and roared with laughter: "After all these years, you still have a passion unrivalled; God bless you, Mr Petrie. You've reminded me about something I've long forgotten, the importance of our heritage, who we are and from where we came.

"I'm sure my grandson will shine wherever he goes but he's got his mother's very quiet, gentle nature and I don't want him pushed around by bullies. My life was made miserable by some of the thugs at Sweetheart back in the day. You must remember, Mr Petrie. You pulled me out of a few school ground scrapes but that was more than forty years ago.

"In truth I was surprised when you came to my workshop as I thought you would have retired long ago; in fact I thought you had…well, I wasn't sure you'd still be here. You don't seem to have changed at all, may be a few extra grey hairs, but…"

Mr Petrie jumped up and exclaimed: "Yes, well, we need to focus on the here and now and what young Duncan needs and wants. I'll look out for you, you can count on it, Dewar my boy," he said as he gave him a reassuring firm hand on his shoulder and then swiftly turned to point at an old wall clock near a bookcase.

"What do you think? Can you revive it?" Duncan ran over and shouted excitedly at his grandfather: "It's a mid-seventeenth century Lantern clock! Yes, we can fix that. I'm sure," beamed Duncan who suddenly seemed much more at ease. Everyone laughed and set about inspecting the antique silver clock. "She is a beauty. I don't think I've seen one in such good condition before. I didn't realise teachers were so well paid these days," remarked Gordon.

Mr Petrie laughed nervously and said: "It was a wedding gift. I think it was made around 1660 and is the forerunner to the grandfather clock, you know before the weights and pendulum were enclosed altogether to stop the pendulum being knocked accidentally."

Like a country doctor, Gordon never left home without the tools of his trade which he carried in a black leather Gladstone bag. Retrieving it from the car, he laughed: "My bare essentials." As he set about dismantling the clock, he said: "They're like human beings, you know. Each one sensitive and needy of love and attention. Clocks have been known to stop at very poignant moments, births, deaths and the like."

Duncan piped up: "Well, this one stopped just before 3 pm." Petrie's face began to fold inwardly as his eyes welled up and said: "Yes, you are right. The clock stopped just before my wife died and I've never been able to get it going since. She was its master and wound it up using this silver key." He handed over the key which was tied around a fraying and fading pink, silk ribbon.

There was an uneasy silence as the clockmaker stripped the timepiece lovingly, while Duncan meticulously cleaned each section and within two hours of painstaking work, it was back working again. The ticking sound was deep, rich and satisfying.

Refusing to charge a fee, he turned to his old history master and said: "Thank you for a very satisfying visit. We will be in touch. I think we might walk around the school grounds, if you don't mind, and I will recall my old school days with the lad." The men shook hands and then Mr Petrie turned to Duncan and used both his hands to clasp the boy's outstretched palm. "I will be seeing you in September. I'm sure."

As they walked back down the garden path, the old man turned to his grandson and said: "Did you smell something sweet in there? I got a vague waft of something, something from my childhood, but I'm not sure what."

"It was Parma Violets' granddad. The best sweets ever," replied Duncan.

"Nonsense, lad," he replied, laughing. "There's no way Mr Petrie would have Parma Violets in his house. He's more of a Soor Plooms man."

When the two got back to Stirling, they spent the evening and the next day checking the website of Sweetheart, reading about the traditions and past pupils. In the end, Duncan reluctantly decided this is where he would have his education. The prospect filled him with fear and dread of the unknown as well as being apart from his grandfather for the first time in as long as he could remember.

That September the fresh-faced youngster joined a host of other first formers at Sweetheart Abbey's Middle School. Wide-eyed and wary in their brand new navy blazers, V-neck jumpers, school ties and charcoal grey trousers, they sat cross-legged for their first assembly.

The headmaster, Andrew Collins, gave a hint of a smile as he addressed the new arrivals, most of whom sported short, tidy haircuts as though they'd been recruited for a military academy. "Welcome to Sweetheart Abbey. This will be your home for the next seven years and I want you to look upon the experience as one which will give you the best foundations from which to build your future.

"Education here is like an artist's canvas; it is up to you what landscape and image you want to create and it will depend on you the opportunities that are created from it. In other words, we will supply the paint but you are the artist who will use it to maximise your opportunities. So if you want to be a Van Gogh, Gauguin, Renoir or Monet, that will be your decision."

The boy sitting next to Duncan whispered: "I'd rather be a Banksy." To Duncan's horror, the headmaster stopped talking momentarily and looked down on Duncan and Ninian Swithers. "Sorry boys, is there something you want to share with the school?"

Both crimson-cheeked boys looked up at the grim-faced master and almost in unison shook their heads vigorously, too choked to speak.

Mr Collins continued: "Here at Sweetheart, we encourage you to think beyond and outside of the box and we will encourage creativity and innovation. We will work tirelessly to give you an education which will prepare you for the world outside.

"I and the rest of the teaching staff have an open-door policy. If you need help and advice, come and ask for it and we will do our utmost to deliver," added Dr Collins.

As Duncan Dewar sat and listened to Dr Collins, he could never imagine a situation where he would dare go and knock on the headmaster's door. The older boys had already regaled him with tales of how 'The Doc' as he was nicknamed by the pupils, used horrific psychological torture in order to obtain information of wrongdoing.

***

In the three years he'd been at Sweetheart, Duncan never tested Dr Collins' 'open door' policy and neither did any of his classmates. While he had lost some of the shyness and timidity since joining Sweetheart, he still maintained a lower profile than most of the other boys preferring to remain in the background.

Now he was a third-year student and a pupil at the senior school. He was still wiry in build but his short back and sides had changed into an overgrown mop of curly, ginger hair, thanks to a recent change in school regulations over haircuts being relaxed. He wasn't trying to be fashionable, far from it as Duncan didn't follow trends or fashion.

Today he was sitting at the back of the Scottish History lesson as Mr Petrie regaled the class with the horrific tale of the demise of Clan Moffat. Although recounted numerous times over the years, he never got tired of telling the story in all its graphic and gory detail.

Predictably, the boys recoiled in horror as they imagined the hellish scene as the Moffat men, women and children were locked inside burning buildings by their adversaries from the Johnstone clan. "Lights, Dewar," roared Mr Petrie as he concluded the bloody history of the Border family.

"Crikey! You'd think Old Petrie had witnessed the whole bloody thing himself. He can't half belt out a good story even if he is a pain," whispered Jacob Thornberry, son of wealthy industrialist Lord Thornberry.

"I'm only surprised he didn't blame the English. We get it in the neck for just about everything," retorted Crispin Sparrow, son of an eminent city lawyer whose clients included a sprinkling of European royals and aristocrats. Thornberry and Sparrow were typical of the privileged and elite who were enrolled at the exclusive sixteenth-century boarding school.

Ironically, the school was never meant for the rich and famous or privileged classes. Its honourable beginnings came about in 1585 when King James VI bestowed a grant and special status on what had been an old abbey. He endowed the abbey school with the intention of educating orphans and children from nearby farming communities, towns and villages.

A giant painting, depicting the occasion, hung in the grand reception room known as 'The Caledonian Suite', adjacent to the school's rather magnificent ballroom on the ground floor. Wearing very elaborate regalia, King James is captured in oils signing the charter while his more modestly dressed entourage look on.

It was a period when Scotland had grand ambitions to educate its children whether they were paupers or princes and as a result, nearly every town and village had a school which opened its doors to the poor and needy.

Sadly, dwindling funds forced this one, like so many others, to turn to the private sector by the nineteenth century and today only the very wealthy could afford to send their children to Sweetheart Abbey.

The school had produced several prime ministers, esteemed politicians, philanthropists and inventors as well as a handful of arms dealers and other equally shady businessmen. The elite favoured it above Eton simply because it wasn't Eton while others who wanted to keep alive their Scottish ancestry thought educating their sons north of the border would somehow achieve that.

In addition, the school had an internationally renowned reputation for academic excellence. Despite that, it still bestowed a few places every year to the under privileged and one of the 'freebies' as they were bluntly referred to by Thornberry and his posh friends was orphaned Dewar.

The tragedy of his parents' demise – both were killed in a car accident near the remote fishing village of Kylesku in Sutherland – cut him no slack or mercy from Thornberry or Sparrow. Duncan, barely a toddler at the time, was also in the car but had somehow miraculously survived after being thrown free from his baby seat before the vehicle went up in a fireball. A passer-by found him half-standing, half-crawling near the wreckage the following morning, distressed but otherwise unharmed.

***

Chapter 4

If Duncan Dewar found it difficult to make friends at his school in Stirling, he soon found it easy to make enemies once at Sweetheart. His quiet, unassuming manner made him a natural target for bullies and he immediately attracted the unwelcome attentions of Thornberry and Sparrow in his first year as a prep student.

They resented all 'freebies' and used the mocking term on Duncan. The youngster was initially wounded but took great comfort from the fact the same label had been given to his grandfather by the bullies back in his day.

"Stick and stones, sticks and stones, Duncan. Okay laddie, it's not a term of endearment but you should wear it as a badge of honour and let their insults wash over you," advised his grandfather when he told him about the verbal abuse.

However, over the next three years, life was tough at Sweetheart for the boy. His detractors, led by Thornberry and Sparrow, sneered at his lack of prowess on the rugby or football pitch, his inept inelegance at gymnastics and his abysmal performance on the athletics field while at the same time they resented being upstaged by him in the classroom as his natural academic excellence shone brightly especially in maths, languages and science.

The dislike was mutual and Duncan, after his first run in with the pair, resolved to keep out of their way as much as he could. He was so relieved when, after his prep years, he was sent to live in Plato House while his tormentors joined Pythagoras, nicknamed 'The Gores'.

The senior school had four different houses named after some of the founders and philosophers of classical education. The very English idea was introduced by a former governor's wife from London who in the 1950s wished to leave her mark of influence on the school.

Since her wish was followed by a very generous financial gift, no one complained other than Mr Petrie who thought the idea was ‘absurd’. However, more than half a century later, while Duncan Dewar could not recall the name of the governor’s wife, he was grateful to her idea since he was boarding in a different house to Sparrow and Thornberry.

At least this way their paths would hardly cross outside of the classroom. Tonight, however, presented him with a challenge since his roomie Ninian Swithers was celebrating his fourteenth birthday with a midnight feast hosted by the Pythagoras boys. It wasn’t an act of generosity but the winning of a bet in the schoolyard when a triumphant Swithers beat Sparrow in a game of bools.

Often used to settle disputes or old scores, pupils used the brightly coloured marbles to play against one another. One boy throws his first bool from a distance of a few yards away and the next must hit it with one of his own, or land within a hand’s span gap.

The boys resisted introducing electronic games to solve disputes in the combative arena of school duals, although some exuberant inter-house video games were played to let off steam after study and revision periods.

That evening, Duncan was still dwelling on the fate of the Moffat clan and, as he drifted off to sleep, he couldn’t help but relive the massacre as told so graphically by Mr Petrie. The terrible fate of Fraser Moffat and his family preyed heavily on his mind as he tossed and turned moving from the dark recesses of the twilight zone into the swirling mists of dreamland.

As the mist began to evaporate there, standing before him was none other than Fraser Moffat, dripping in the blood and guts of his family shouting: “Why didn’t you save us?! You saw them coming and you did nothing!”

Fraser Moffat moved towards Duncan and began shaking the boy’s narrow shoulders. “Save us, save us. We need your help.” The terrified schoolboy was frozen with fear and, unable to move, closed his eyes hoping he would disappear.

He was like a rag doll in Fraser’s massive arms. When he opened his eyes again, Fraser’s face was inches away from his, and he could feel his hot breath on his cheeks. He closed his eyes tightly and when he opened them again, Moffat's angry, twisted visage morphed slowly into that of Ninian Swithers. "Wake up, wake up. Hurry. Hurry, we're off to The Gores. It's my party. What the hell were you dreaming about, Duncs? You seemed terrified."

Duncan rudely propelled out of the world of nightmares, gave a massive sigh of relief, realising he'd experienced nothing more than a bad dream. As the Plato boys left their wing, they crept down the wood panelled staircase and into the courtyard, over to the Pythagoras House where one of the pupils had left a door in the stone archway off the latch.

Within minutes, they were in the Gores' common room where a whole feast of goodies was laid out. Sticky buns, chocolate bars, bags of crisps and even a Fortnum and Mason hamper were there.

"Oh yuk! Who would put salt in caramels? That's just sick!" shouted one of the boys, unimpressed by the contents of the luxury hamper from the Piccadilly department store. Moments later, there was a real buzz of excitement in the room as they were joined by the boys from Boethius House.

"Who's missing?" asked Ninian as he looked around.

"The Capella Crew, they're always late," remarked Plato monitor Robert Robson Roberts, known to one and all as Bobby Bob Bob. The son of a heavy metal rock star, he held a lot of kudos among the boys and excelling at rugby also helped make him one of the most popular in his year. Not even Jacob or Crispin ever felt tempted to sneer or mock him in the way they ridiculed everyone else.

It seemed in the parental pecking order at Sweetheart Abbey School the son of a drug fuelled rock star trumped minor royals, aristocracy and the offspring of a couple of Russian oligarchs and Chinese entrepreneurs.

Meanwhile back at Capella, Dr Gideon McKie had ten boys in pyjamas lined up in the common room. All eyes were staring at the wooden floor. Their heads were down looking grim as the housemaster marched slowly and deliberately in front of them.

"Nobody is leaving this room until I know where you were heading. Silence is not an option and, if you continue your ridiculously misguided all-for-one, one-for-all nonsense, you will be collectively punished, grounded for the weekend," said Dr McKie in his soft, lilting Lowland accent.

While the boys in Pythagoras House had promised Ninian Swithers a fourteenth birthday, he'd not forget this would indeed prove to be a memorable night for all the wrong reasons. As the party got in full swing, the feared master of Capella, Dr McKie, continued to pace up and down, slowly and deliberately in front of the assembled boys he'd caught attempting to sneak out of the house.

With each step, his military style polished brogues emitted a tortuous squeaking sound. It was a trademark of Dr McKie's, and while some saddle soap between the shoe tongue and the tied laces could have solved the problem, he seemed to delight in the obvious unease it caused those under his supervision.

He was the most despised of all the masters at Sweetheart; a humourless bachelor in his late 50s who, according to school gossip, had been jilted a week before his wedding. It was said he'd never cracked a smile in the thirty years since and carried the anger, humiliation and pain as though his heart had been broken just yesterday and not three decades previously.

There were plenty of rumours and speculation about why his fiancée had ditched him but most of these were dreamt up by the countless teenagers on detention as a result of incurring his wrath.

Having threatened the Capella boys with being grounded on Saturday and Sunday, James Darling decided to protest in what could be viewed as an act of extreme bravery or utter foolishness, depending on your perspective.

"But sir, it's rugby this weekend and if we don't turn up for training on Saturday, Mr Swain will exclude us from the team," cried James Darling.

"Silence, Darling, or I will personally see to it you are permanently excluded from playing rugby this term."

It was an empty threat as Darling was one of the best players the school had and if Dr McKie had attempted to ground Darling, Jon Swain would have intervened vigorously. Like all bullies faced with a formidable opponent such as Swain, a former Irish international, Dr McKie would have been forced to back down.

After another bout of silence, Dr McKie ordered all of the boys to hand over their mobile phones and said their parents would be informed. One by one they handed over their prized possessions in silence. Although angry and upset, not one of them dared to challenge the smouldering Dr McKie.

The stern-faced master readjusted his long black cloak and pushed his left, thin, bony hand like a comb through his mass of frizzy, white hair before dismissing the boys with a halfhearted wave of the same hand. They quickly returned to their rooms tired and subdued. Darling went underneath his mattress and pulled out another mobile and began furiously texting from under the covers. His roommate Willie Carmichael whispered: "How come you didn't hand in your phone. If Och Aye McKie finds out, it will be double detention, James."

James Darling poked his head above the sheets, grinning cheekily, saying: "My father always warned me to keep one step ahead and so I brought two phones this term in anticipation of this happening. I've texted the others just in case someone grasses."

As he pressed the 'send' button, Bobby Bob Bob's phone emitted a large bleep seconds later. The message read: "Och Aye on warpath. Capella grounded. We've been busted."

"Evacuate, evacuate, evacuate," hissed Bobby Bob Bob as he relayed the message to the assembled group. "It's every one for himself and remember, no one likes a grass. Keep schtum if any of you gets caught. Go carefully and in different directions because Och Aye is on the prowl."

The boys scattered while the hosts unplugged their Gameboys, hid their tuck and any signs of a midnight feast. In his panic, Duncan had run down the wrong corridor and in to a dead end. As he tiptoed back, he seemed to lose his bearings but he heard a familiar sound that sent a chill down his spine.

It was the squeaking leather soles of Dr McKie. In a panic, he scurried down a different corridor but on seeing another dead end looming ahead, he opened the first door he saw and dived in. He soon realised he was in some sort of broom cupboard from the waft of cleaning materials and polish.

He held his breath as McKie's footsteps approached. He seemed to falter outside the door and then continued past. As his eyes became accustomed to the dark, Duncan saw a small stone pillar and he quietly manoeuvred himself right to the side of it and continued to hide.

Again, he heard the return of McKie and this time the squeaking noise stopped abruptly right outside. Duncan took a huge breath and to his horror, the door handle twisted to open. A shaft of light entered the cupboard and he realised his hiding place was about to be discovered.

"Is anything wrong, Dr McKie?" The enquiring voice belonged to Professor JD McIntosh. Few knew what the *J* or the *D* stood for, and so the master was simply called JD by the boys. McKie nodded in the affirmative and said: "Capella were up to no good this evening and I foiled an attempt by them to sneak out to one of the other houses.

"I believe it was yours, Professor, and so I thought I would check, just in case."

Professor McIntosh, who taught maths, said in soothing tones: "You should have alerted me first. I'm not aware of any shenanigans and I've just checked their rooms. Trust me Dr McKie, all is well and there's nothing of interest in there unless you intend to do some spring cleaning. It's the broom cupboard."

McKie, realising he had overstepped the protocol mark by prying in to the affairs of another house, nodded curtly, closed the door and retreated. "It's after midnight, Professor. I thought you might be asleep. I do apologise for the intrusion."

As they walked together back down the corridor, the conversation became distant and muffled. A relieved Duncan let go of his breath and sighed. As he stood silently in the corner of the cupboard, he then overheard another conversation, but this time it was quite clear.

He looked up and realised he was standing below an old air-vent which led directly into Sparrow and Thornberry's room. He listened as the two talked about an end of term prank they would play on their nemesis, Mr Petrie.

"I'm telling you it's a classic. My father told me about how when he was here, Pythagoras boys kidnapped a sheep and planned to put the animal into Petrie's cottage. You know he lives on the estate, don't you?" said Sparrow.

"Unfortunately papa was caught red-handed and says Petrie gave him six of the best… You know they caned pupils back in the days when these bastards ruled by fear. Imagine that. Papa said he couldn't sit down for a week and he never forgave Petrie, so there's a bit of family honour at stake here, Jacob. Are you in?"

Jacob laughed, adding: "Yes, of course. Count me in, but I'm not going to kidnap a sheep. I think we can be more inventive and, at the same time, show our fathers how it's done.

"Funny, my old man never mentioned the sheep story, although he was in the same house as yours. Sad they only really became friends when they got to Cambridge, isn't it? I'll ask him about it when we next speak."

"He disliked Petrie as well. Reckons he looked ancient when he was here and thought he would have been dead and buried by now. How old do you reckon he is, Jacob?" asked Sparrow.

"No idea, but he must be nearing retirement. If he was ancient in the 70s, then retirement must be just around the corner. Whatever joke we play on him, I hope the old sod has a good ticker. We don't want to kill him off!"

Duncan didn't know if it was because he disliked Thornberry and Sparrow so much or because he had become very fond of Mr Petrie but he resolved to spoil their plans. While he was a bit in awe of the history master, there was something kind and reassuring about his presence that made him feel a strange, protective loyalty towards him.

Suddenly a harsh bolt of light came streaming in to the cupboard as the door swung violently open. "You can step out now," snapped the master's voice. Duncan had been rumbled but he almost breathed a sigh of relief to see that the one who stood before him was JD and not McKie.

"If you like Pythagoras so much, you are prepared to sleep in the cleaner's closet. I'm sure I can find you a place here, Dewar," said Professor McIntosh dryly.

"No, no, sir. Thank you, sir. I'm really sorry, sir. I took a wrong turn, I…I…"

But the professor interjected before he could finish and said: "Stop blethering and rambling, boy. Get out of my sight before I put you on detention and report you to your housemaster.

"Dr Wallace will not be best pleased if he finds out about this. If you're gone in thirty seconds, I will forget I ever saw you," snapped the professor who turned around and walked towards his study. He had a smile on his face and had known about the plans for the midnight feast a few days earlier.

Professor McIntosh was looking forward to this term and was excited about the promise Duncan Dewar had shown in his maths class. He was sure he could coach the boy to such a standard; he might enter him for the Scottish Mathematical Challenge, a problem-solving competition for individual pupils.

As Duncan crept into Plato House and back in to his room, Ninian Swithers shone a torch into his face. "Where the hell have you been? I had to roll up a pillow so Dr Wallace would think you were tucked up in bed. Apparently McKie caught three of us but I don't know who yet. I was beginning to think you might be one of the three."

Duncan told his roomie about what had happened and as Ninian listened to the story of the broom cupboard, he crammed his knuckles into his mouth to stop the laughter. They both agreed McKie was a nasty piece of work but that JD was a good sport.

Long after Ninian fell asleep, Duncan was still wide-awake because of the bursts of adrenalin that had pumped through his veins at various stages during the evening. As much as he disliked his posh adversaries from Pythagoras, Duncan was uncomfortable about being labelled a school snitch, so he knew if he was to stop Mr Petrie from becoming the victim of a cruel prank, he would have to be clever about how to tip off the old master.

Chapter 5

The next morning when Duncan woke up, he reflected on the events of the night before, the disastrous midnight feast and the conversation he'd overheard between Sparrow and Thornberry hatching a plot against old Mr Petrie.

He recalled when he first met Mr Petrie. It was in the master's home on the edge of the school grounds three years earlier. He realised now that both he and his grandfather had his best interests at heart and, despite the best efforts of Thornberry and Sparrow, he regretted not one day he'd spent at Sweetheart.

Duncan was staring at the ceiling when he narrowly avoided being hit by a wet flannel. "Hey, get up. No time for daydreaming in Sweat Shop Abbey," exclaimed Ninian Swithers. "Double maths to kick off Friday," he said with an exaggerated groan.

The prospect of double maths was seen as more of a treat by Duncan than a hardship, something which was not lost on Professor McIntosh. As the session that morning drew to a close, he told Dewar to stay behind.

Thornberry and Sparrow sniggered as they pushed past Duncan who was on his feet. One of them hissed: "Looks like the freebie's in trouble. Oh, what a joy!" While their reaction was entirely predictable, Duncan was mystified by the professor's request. He thought that he'd been given a free pass after being caught in the broom cupboard after Ninian's party.

He walked nervously from his desk at the rear of the classroom towards the teacher who was tidying his desk. McIntosh looked up, smiling and enquired: "So Dewar, how are you enjoying life in the third year at Sweetheart?"

Looking slightly puzzled, he responded slowly: "Yes sir, very much."

Nodding and smiling, the master announced: “I have a special project and I’d like to involve you but it will mean lots of extra work and little reward. You have a passion for maths, Dewar, and I want to encourage it. What you say?”

There was only one answer he knew he could give, and so he nodded and said: “Yes.” The maths professor told him the special project would involve giving up his Thursday evenings and sacrificing Saturday mornings if they were to achieve their goal. He wanted to enter him in a national schools’ competition which would bring kudos and prestige on the school if he won.

“So there’s no pressure, Dewar, is there? After all, it’s next year you are going to have to focus hard for your exams whereas this year you have plenty of time for the competition. So you are sure you are up for it?” Duncan nodded and the professor smiled and told him he could go.

As Duncan walked to the door and reached for the handle, the professor raised his voice and added: “You know I don’t like losing, don’t you, Dewar?” The boy turned around to look at the master but by then he was dusting down the blackboard, so he just pursed his lips and shrugged.

As he walked down the corridor towards Plato, Ninian jumped out and said: “So what did he want? Are you in trouble?” Duncan didn’t mention the competition but he said that the master thought he would benefit from extra tuition.

“Blimey, Duncs. This is payback time for the midnight feast!” declared Ninian as they walked across the courtyard. “I thought McIntosh was okay, but this is punishment above and beyond. One night a week and your Saturday morning?

“That will exclude you from rugby for the entire term. Tell him to get knotted,” he advised his roommate. The truth is Duncan was secretly pleased to be getting extra tutoring in maths from the professor and the more his free time was occupied, the less chance he had of bumping in to Sweetheart’s dreadful duo, Thornberry and Sparrow.

Forfeiting Saturday’s rugby was no hardship either as he disliked the sport and certainly wasn’t combative enough to survive the rigours of the rugby pitch. He seemed to spend most of his time running away from Thornberry and Sparrow who would try and punch, kick and knock him whenever the rugby master Jon Swain was distracted.

If anything, he was truly delighted, although he feigned dismay followed by a resigned sigh but as soon as Swithers left his side to relay the news to others, he clenched his fists and whispered 'yes' as though he'd just won a game of bools.

For the rest of the day, as news filtered out about his 'punishment', various pupils came over to offer their commiserations, making him feel unusually popular; boys he'd never spoken to patted him on the back as though he was some sort of hero who had sacrificed himself to keep everyone else safe. The story of Duncan's refusal to name names from the midnight feast was exaggerated with each telling.

He enjoyed his newfound popularity for the rest of the day and not even a chastising from Mr Petrie could deflate him. "Dewar, remove that silly grin from your face, lad. Give me the full names and titles of Brewster, Bruce, Buchanan and Burns in order of their dates of birth."

Starting off confidently with Robert the Bruce, King of Scotland born 1274, he moved to historian and scholar George Buchanan born in 1506, but then put the scientist and inventor Sir David Brewster, born in 1781, ahead of poet Robert Burn born in 1759.

"You've just earned yourself detention. See me after your final lesson and let's see if we can sharpen that lazy mind of yours," scolded Mr Petrie. As the clock struck 5 pm, Duncan Dewar tried to stifle a yawn but as he attempted desperately to keep a straight face, it was not lost on the sharp-eyed Mr Petrie.

"Bored, Dewar?" thundered the old history master. "Let's see how much has really sunk in to that numbskull head of yours. Before you give me a song of Burns, I want to know the context of Scots Wha Hae," he said in reference to the anthem widely regarded, alongside 'Scotland, the Brave' and 'Flower of Scotland' as the nearest thing Scotland has to a national song.

Nervously Duncan Dewar rose to his feet, initially stumbling over his words as he said: "Please sir, the year, the year was…erm…1793 and Rab, erm… Robert Burns was living in Dumfries. He had incurred the wrath of his employers, His Majesty's Customs and Excise, after a government spy reported that he was the head of a group of Jacobin sympathisers. He was put on a sort of trial when it was reported he had been singing the French revolutionary anthem *Ça ira* in a Dumfries theatre, rather than 'God, Save the King'.

"This was a huge blow because he faced losing his livelihood, and all of this at a time when he had a family to support, so he denied all the charges in order to keep his job. However in the same year, he continued writing in support of the revolution and that's when he wrote Scots Wha Hae, although it was published anonymously.

"It all coincided with the trial of Thomas Muir who was regarded as the most prominent Scottish champion of the French Revolution. Apparently Bruce's army marched to the tune while on its way to Bannockburn, or so Burns believed. His lyrics resemble a speech given by Robert the Bruce, before the Battle of Bannockburn in 1314. His words are an attack on tyrants and despots, and a call for liberty."

After an initial silence, Mr Petrie brought his fist down on his table, shouting: "Enough! Now give me a Burns' song and not Scots Wha Hae. Let's have 'A Man's a Man', Dewar." And so without a note of music, the boy performed Acapello with a gusto and passion that brought water to the rims of Petrie's eyes:

Is there for honest Poverty
That hings his head, an' a' that;
The coward slave – we pass him by,
We dare be poor for a' that!
For a' that, an' a'that.
Our toils obscure an' a' that,
The rank is but the guinea's stamp,
The Man's the gowd for a' that.

What though on hamely fare we dine,
Wear hidden grey, an' a' that;
Give fools their silks, and knaves their wine;
A Man's a Man for a' that:
For a' that, and a' that,
Their tinsel show, an' a' that;
The honest man, tho' e'er sae poor,
Is king o' men for a' that.

Ye see yon birkie, ca'd a lord,
Wha struts, an' stares, an' a' that;
Tho' hundreds worship at his word,
He's but a coof for a' that:
For a' that, an' a' that,
His ribband, star, an' a' that:
The man o' independent mind
He looks an' laughs at a' that.

A prince can make a belted knight,
A marquis, duke, an' a' that;
But an honest man's abon his might,
Gude faith, he manna fa' that!
For a' that, an' a' that,
Their dignities an' a' that;
The pith o' sense, an' pride o' worth,
Are higher rank than a' that.

Then let us pray that come it may,
(As come it will for a' that),
That Sense and Worth, o'er a' the earth,
Shall bear the gree, an' a' that.
For a' that, an' a' that,
It's coming yet for a' that,
That Man to Man, the world o'er,
Shall brothers be for a' that.

"You never fail in your endeavours, do you, Duncan Dewar? I'll make a Scotsman of you yet…may be even one day we will call you a Caledonian. Run along now. It's been a long day," said the master.

As Dewar grabbed his books and rucksack, he heaved a sigh of relief and hurried towards the classroom door without looking back. If he had, he would have seen a smile break out over Petrie's face and, as the door closed, he sighed, adding in a low whisper: "Well done, well done, laddie. You have the voice of an angel."

"I agree, Mr Petrie. That was quite a performance." The old master swung around, slightly startled by this unexpected interruption as a familiar figure moved from the shadows. The

Welsh choirmaster Dr Geraint Jones gushed enthusiastically: "I was quite mesmerised when I heard the boy's voice drift down the corridor, so I just gravitated towards the melancholy sounds and discovered they came from this room.

"You know I'm always looking for new talent to join the ranks of my choir and I am desperately seeking a treble. Why Mr Petrie, thanks to you my quest may finally be over. What's his name and whose house is he in?"

By now Mr Petrie was highly irritated at this unwelcome interest in his protégé. Reluctantly, he said: "He's one of the Plato boys, but Dewar is very unreliable and his voice will probably break any day now. I doubt he's worthy of your attention, Dr Jones."

Jones, a thickset man in his 40s with a full main of shiny black hair defined by a large widow's peak, looked at Mr Petrie in a slightly bemused way. Tilting his head to one side, he said slowly and deliberately in his Caernarfonshire accent: "Allow me to be the judge of that. I'll bid you goodnight."

Mr Petrie angrily picked up his books and notes placing them in to his briefcase. He began cursing and speaking to himself, expressing his frustration and anger. "That bloody choirmaster never misses a trick. Him and his damned choir, stalking the corridors like someone with a knife and fork looking for a piece of rump steak! The man is a flaming nuisance, a pest."

Like a few of the masters, Mr Petrie lived in the school grounds but while the majority had private bachelor quarters in the main stone building. He had his own quaint little cottage on the edge of the deciduous forest surrounding the school.

After leaving the classroom, he walked briskly over the gravel drive and down a side path towards his home. The architecture was gothic and with the many scary looking gargoyles and other mythical stone creations staring back at anyone who caught their chilling gaze, there was nothing cosy looking about the exterior of Dulce Cor. Someone once remarked it looked as though it could have come straight from the pages of a storybook written by the Brothers Grimm.

The exterior of the home invoked a feeling of unease, something unnerving, causing most passers-by to quicken their pace on observing its cold, grey stone architecture. However it only ever induced a feeling of contentment as Petrie opened the squeaky sage green picket gate to his home, the only home he had ever really known and it was here that his whole life revolved where treasured memories and secrets were jealously guarded.

It had been raining earlier and the last dribbles of water were spat from the mouths of the grotesques' spouts, making the gargoyles look even more demonic and wretched.

***

Chapter 6

The interior of Mr Petrie's home was more shabby than chic and while the study with its open fire had a warm, musty, bookish smell about it, the sort of odour that breathed wax polish and tradition, the rest of the house seemed to give off a cool, clean, almost odourless vapour, a bit like freshly laundered, crisp linen or chilled mountain air.

He walked through his lounge where he had served tea to Duncan and his grandfather some three years earlier. Passing the neat Sanderson print sofa on which they'd sat, he stepped down a couple of stairs standing on a worn and almost threadbare Persian rug, in front of a bookcase where the Lantern clock hung. It was still working perfectly well after Gordon Buie had performed his magic touch.

He gave the side of the bookcase a gentle nudge and it gave way to reveal the entrance of a dimly lit cellar and after a few more steps, the old schoolmaster turned left under a stone archway where he pushed open another secret entrance.

The view from this particular door never ceased to amaze Petrie and it always induced in him the ultimate self-satisfied expressions. There before him was a massive library where he was able to immerse himself in research. Shelf after shelf of ancient books, scrolls of papers and documents from his vast, personal archives beckoned.

The immense size spread far beyond the boundaries of his small home and after walking past at least ten rows of floor to ceiling bookcases, Petrie stood silently before a painting of a beautiful young woman by the celebrated Scottish artist George Jamesone whose work straddled the sixteenth and seventeenth centuries.

Delicate hands elegantly posed in front of her heart, she appears to be looking directly at the observer. The low cut bodice was extremely fashionable but the wearer chose to preserve her modesty courtesy of a diaphanous piece of fabric over the décolletage. The intimacy of the picture was profound and shared only between the artist and its commissioner.

Mr Petrie gently touched the side of the woman's face and ran his fingers around her rosebud lips before taking a deep breath as he pulled at the right-hand side of the gilt frame dated 1635. It opened to reveal a button embedded in the wall which he pressed gently.

The lights seemed to flicker ominously as a panel moved sideways revealing a steep, spiral stone staircase leading into a subterranean passage. A blast of cold air hit the old historian as he looked anxiously around him, as he always did before entering, and in seconds he was gone.

A path he had trodden many times before, he moved nimbly and with stealth for a portly soul, shining a small torch into the inky blackness of the secret passage. A few minutes later, an old timber door with a latch loomed large. He gingerly opened it to reveal a concave semi-circle of six passages, some more well-worn than others. Carefully scrutinising the ancient lettering above each one – Benyellary, Merrick, Kirriereoch, Tarfessock, Shalloch and Salar – he faltered before removing a couple of spider's threads and cobwebs lightly woven over the entrance marked for Salar.

Yes, it had been some time before Petrie had ventured through this underground chamber. Tonight, armed with various papers and ancient documents, he continued on his journey.

Moments later, Petrie passed through another creaking, carved oak door and suddenly the gloom was gone as he crossed into a dazzling, golden glowing space. He appeared to be standing in a grand throne room of white and gold marble, its opulence almost excessive and blinding. Every section of the floor shone as though it was brand new, every knob, bauble and tassel whether glass, gold or gilt shone with a recency that was barely credible.

And like a rock star emerging from the mists of a smoke machine, a tall, slender figure draped in flowing white gowns appeared. From head to perfectly manicured toe, Salar towered at a majestic six feet in height with a luxurious main of sleek, platinum white hair swept to one side and threaded into an intricate and magnificent braid draped over the right shoulder.

"What troubles you, my friend? Our meetings are less frequent, yet the world is more treacherous place than ever," said Salar in a smooth, lingering tone which seemed to gently carry an echo which resounded in the grand chamber where both stood. "Perhaps you have grown weary of being a Guardian, Mr Petrie?"

He nodded and bowed his head out of respect for the luminous presence which seemed to hover before him. "Weary, yes, the centuries have dulled my enthusiasm for a noble job in which I thought I could change the course of history. Alas! I am nothing but a mere mortal as you well know and while you have gifted me with extraordinary powers, I continue to be exasperated by the limitations of my brief.

"As a man of history, I could change the world but instead the changes you allow me to make change nothing but perhaps a few lives. I am beginning to wonder if the gift you have bestowed upon me is more of a curse."

Salar's large almond brown eyes, framed by the longest curved eyelashes, flashed angrily in Petrie's direction; with a sharp turn to the left, the long white robes swished and flowed as if in slow motion. Salar, silently and elegantly glided across the room, while constantly staring at Petrie and, with a voice slightly elevated, said: "Such ingratitude is not a characteristic I've witnessed in you before and such negativity threatens to dull the harmonious atmosphere we have carefully created here.

"I am most perplexed why you bothered to come this hour and seek my counsel. Join me in my private chamber where we can relax and talk so I know what has exhausted your mind and then you can tell me all your troubles." Petrie looked at Salar quizzically.

"Oh come, Mr Petrie. There are no secrets here, which is why we have always enjoyed a mutual understanding. I know what you are thinking even before you have spoken; you were originally chosen because of your principles and integrity, although of late your dull outlook has given cause for concern with the rest of the Council of Anam Cara.

"I spoke recently with the members, Benyellary, Merrick, Kirriereoch, Tarfessock and Shalloch, and I can tell you that you are creating a wave of consternation Mr Petrie and in these precarious times, that is not a good thing."

If Salar was threatening Mr Petrie, he did not appear to show any fear. Salar was right. He was tired of his role as a Guardian of Anam Cara but when, as a young scholar of history, he gratefully and enthusiastically received the Guardian role, he was becoming jaded by an increasingly corrupt, violent and treacherous world. Far from making a difference, he felt that over the centuries, he was on the losing end of a battle between good and evil.

The secret Council of Anam Cara had promised him special powers which would enable him to travel through time so he could make changes. His sacrifice in turn was to reject all worldly goods and possessions and was forbidden from exploiting his special status for personal gain.

The young Petrie relished the opportunity and with a guaranteed immortality, he felt the world belonged to him, except it didn't. He watched helplessly as his first and only love Clara grew old, withered and died. He outlived his children and their children until the last line of his seed expired due to plague. Unable to travel back in time and change the course of history in order to save them, his family left him one by one.

If the cursed portrait of Dorian Grey soaked up the burden of age and infamy, allowing Grey to stay forever young, the reverse could be said of Petrie who by now bore the angst and deep lines of a man burdened by life's dark soul and character.

The Guardians of Anam Cara only allowed him to make changes for some but Petrie was forbidden from changing the lives of others that might, in turn, threaten the future events of history, and so he felt the little good that he performed as a Guardian made barely a ripple in the history books.

As if already reading his mind, Salar dramatically waved a long, lily-white arm with outstretched fingers around the elegant, private chamber. "Look around you, Petrie. You contributed to a lot of the items here. I've no doubt some will be priceless in your world while others will be of little monetary value but precious in other ways.

"For instance, look at this dossier. If their contents had been allowed to circulate to the wider public, we might not be here now. You saved us and for that we are all entirely grateful," said Salar after pulling out the heavy grey file from between other documents and ancient scrolls.

Petrie leant forward and took it, smiling gently and nodding in agreement as he opened the folder and looked at the distinctive signature of the Rt Honourable Margaret Thatcher, British Prime Minister on the first page. The date of the document was 29th November 1990, a full day after she had resigned; it was never made public and its contents remain unknown till this day.

The top-secret file had been prepared for a select gathering of government ministers scheduled to meet on the Thursday and contained the details of controversial plans to drill deep into the rounded dome of Mullwharchar, one of the most remote Lowland summits in Scotland.

Government scientists had found unusual rock formations which they felt would provide an ideal, safe area to store nuclear waste. It was top secret and, apart from a handful of scientists and a couple of Thatcher's most trusted advisers, no one knew of the existence of the dossier or its contents.

There had been rumours about government plans for Mullwharchar linked to Britain's nuclear weapons programme, but angry environmentalists and peace activists had worked hard to make sure test drilling in the 1970s was stopped before it started, except it hadn't. Some handpicked experts, who had previously signed the Official Secrets Act, were told to continue investigating the possibilities of gutting Mullwharchar and draw up a feasibility plan.

All of their relevant files and notes were classified and would remain sealed for at least ninety years and only two copies of the dossier were in existence; one was with Thatcher's personal secretary in a locked draw to be copied for Thursday's cabinet meeting and the other was in the Iron Lady's study.

Around 4 am on the morning of Margaret Thatcher's final hours as PM, the special powers bestowed on Mr Petrie had enabled him to walk into Downing Street undetected and in to Thatcher's personal assistant's office. He removed the first file from Cynthia Crawford's desk which, as far as he could establish, had yet to be copied and then went into the PM's study to retrieve the second and last file.

"Damn, damn," he whispered under his breath. The door was locked, but where would the key be? Petrie looked at the ceiling and shook his head in disbelief. He realised he would have to try and find Thatcher's handbag in her private rooms upstairs and hope that the keys would be inside.

After opening a few doors, he finally found the master bedroom and saw a burgundy wool twill suit by Aquascutum, with velvet lapels and covered buttons draped over a wooden valet butler stand. This was obviously the outfit she had chosen for her last day as PM.

The occupants of the bed were fast asleep and as he looked around there it was – the Thatcher trademark, a black leather Launer handbag sitting perched on the dressing table. Petrie deftly picked up the bag, twisted the catch to look inside and was shocked by the contents or lack of them. Apart from a lace handkerchief, a compact mirror and a Waterman ballpoint, there was nothing else. He lifted the compact and gave a sigh of relief.

There at the bottom was a set of keys – he removed the one most likely to be her office key and turned quietly to tip toe out. "MEEEE-OWWW…" As screeches go, it was voluminous and bloodcurdling. Petrie looked down and removed his right foot from the tail of Number Ten's chief mouser.

The black and white feline shot out of the room with Petrie following close behind. "Bloody Humphrey. I shan't miss him," groaned Denis Thatcher from under the bedcovers. Margaret Thatcher by this time was sitting bolt upright surveying the room with her beady blue eyes but all seemed as it was when she had retired less than three hours earlier.

Meanwhile Petrie was back downstairs unlocking the door to the Iron Lady's study, closely followed by his nemesis Humphrey the cat who seemed strangely attracted to the Downing Street intruder.

Within minutes, he found the file and his mission was complete; he was soon gone along with all traces of the dossiers – it would be as though Operation Mullwharchar had never existed. Deeply suspicious of incriminating computer files, Thatcher had ordered the dossier to be typed on a 'trusty Rimmington' and so all traces of the highly controversial and secret operation were now in the hands of Petrie.

Thatcher's demise had happened so quickly; he was counting on other events pushing Operation Mullwharchar to the back of her mind but just to make sure, Petrie locked the study door again and put the stolen key into his pocket.

His instincts had served him well, for a few hours later, just before 9 am, Thatcher was tiptoeing down the staircase to head for her inner sanctum for one last look. If she had planned to take the file with her, she was stopped in her tracks, unable to open her famous study because it was locked. She looked inside her handbag but when she pulled out her key ring, there was one key missing.

She would later record in her memoirs The Downing Street Years: "Wednesday 28th November was my last day in office. The packing was now all but complete. Early that morning, I went down from the flat to my study for the last time to check that nothing had been left behind. It was a shock to find that I could not get in because the key had already been taken off my key ring."

Slightly shaken and wondering who in her presence had removed the keys from her bag, her eyes welled with tears as she realised she was no longer the most powerful woman in the western world.

"Yes," laughed Petrie. "I felt a bit like James Bond that day. Those tears in Thatcher's eyes may well have been down to me, although I think she suspected someone in her security team of removing the keys. Oh, how the mighty fall along with their wicked plans!"

Salar responded: "The Council of Anam Cara is eternally grateful, Mr Petrie. If that nuclear drilling had gone ahead and waste had been stored, it would have put us all in danger. The source of our power could have been discovered and destroyed and the powers of the ancient stream diminished forever. You certainly made a change that day.

"But let's move on to less dramatic events; tell me what has got under your skin, to make you feel so troubled?" asked Salar. "You're not usually given to such wasteful emotions."

Mr Petrie looked up at the ceiling, grandly painted in the style of the Sistine Chapel by the artist Michelangelo. "I remember when I found Michelangelo for you; he had such vision and such style and a passion I'd not seen in many other artists but above all he had human frailties and faults often exposed in his drive for perfection.

"While his work has stood the test of time, I'm afraid my self-worth and value as a Guardian is rapidly diminishing."

Salar looked at the old man thoughtfully and said: "I will communicate with the other members of the council to see what we can do. There are very few Guardians left in the world today, Mr Petrie, and we don't want to lose you.

"There are troubled times ahead and a storm is brewing and we will need you more than ever once we have established the full threat," said Salar mysteriously. "However, let's address today's dilemma. Perhaps it is time we gave you an apprentice; someone who could help and assist you. What do you think?" asked Salar.

***

Chapter 7

Mr Petrie's thin red lips pursed, making them almost invisible as his eyes sunk back into the sockets above his raised, ruddy cheeks; the pained expression created an exaggerated effect of someone in extreme discomfort.

Salar, the enigmatic head of the Council of Anam Cara, had offered him an apprentice, someone who he could work with on the missions he was expected to carry out for 'the greater good'. But exactly who could fill the role and, indeed, could Mr Petrie work closely alongside someone he would need to trust hundred per cent?

He looked anxiously at Salar and thanked him for the offer but added: "I'm not sure. I've never worked alongside anyone before nor shared the secrets of the Council of Anam Cara, not even with my late wife.

"Allow me to percolate the idea in my mind; it is a huge ask and sacrifice to make and while I was only fourteen years old when I leapt at the chance of becoming a Guardian, I never fully appreciated the true cost of agreeing to undertake such an appointment," said Mr Petrie.

"And, of course, much as I respect the wisdom of the Council of Anam Cara, I would prefer to choose my own man," he added. "Or woman, Mr Petrie. You should know by now there is no gender discrimination here. We do not assign anyone on something as primitive or base as gender. Until the human being is above such matters, it will continue to dwell in a primitive condition."

With that, Salar beckoned a diminutive figure from the shadows who had stood by patiently. A pale blue-skinned, almost skeletal creature stepped forward taking instruction before being dismissed. Although almost human in shape, the creature, no more than four foot high, moved silently across the room.

Having large round eyes but no mouth or nostrils, one might wonder how the skelwarks, as they were known, managed to communicate, eat or breathe. The heavy fragrance of Parma Violets seemed to linger in the air after they'd exited a room.

Turning to Mr Petrie, Salar said: "We have always trusted you to use your knowledge wisely but you must remember your oath to the Council and remember your duty is to protect the Council first and foremost.

"I cannot pretend to understand the human condition of love but I've watched you over the years sink into a swamp of despondency following the demise of your wife, Clara. I know you couldn't understand why we failed to give her the gift of immortality, but we must all make sacrifices for the greater good."

Mr Petrie gripped his thumbs and held them tightly within the palms of his hands until the pain almost made him wince. The love he felt for his wife was as deep and as sharp as the day she had died many centuries earlier. No one had come close to replacing her in his heart, not that he had ever allowed anyone to get close to him again.

He sighed inwardly as Salar added: "Know that you are valued and your work is important. Changing someone's life may seem small in the grand scheme of things but the satisfaction it brings others can be dramatic and meaningful.

"There are dark forces at play and the task of wiping out all evil is an impossible one. However, we can but try and get some to see the folly of their ways. Despite all our efforts, and those of The Guardians, wars continue to erupt and famine and hunger move forward relentlessly in a world where some humans are obese and others are starving.

"Your initiative over the fate of Dr William Brydon was indeed a valiant effort but we cannot legislate for the stupidity of man nor his refusal to learn from history," added Salar. Mr Petrie nodded sagely as Salar touched upon what he regarded as one of his biggest personal failures and a period in which history would record the greatest defeat ever inflicted upon the British Army by an Asian enemy.

The year was 1842 and on January 6th, a 4,500 strong army of soldiers plus another 12,000 in support marched from the Afghan capital Kabul in the belief they would be given safe passage to the city of Jalalabad, but one week later all were dead having been wiped out by merciless Afghan warriors.

It was Mr Petrie's idea to go back in time and save the life of one man who could then recount the tale of what would turn out to be incompetent military leadership combined with a mix of Afghan intrigue and complex politics on the ground. "Just one cautionary tale would have, I believed, stopped military forces and foreign powers from ever invading Afghanistan again and meddling with their politics," he said.

Posing as an administrator from the British East India Company which had a huge presence in the region, Mr Petrie appeared in the military quarters or cantonment where Dr William Brydon was preparing for the British retreat from Kabul. There was a state of general confusion as senior officers supervised the packing of goods, valuables, clothes and food on to horses, camels and anything else with four legs.

"This is a fine chestnut," said Mr Petrie as he stroked one of the ponies near where Dr Brydon was standing. The assistant surgeon, sporting a magnificent bushy moustache, looked over to the stranger and said: "Aye. He's one of six ponies I've managed to assemble to carry me and my servants out of here. I'm afraid they're all spoken for," he added, anticipating that Mr Petrie was about to make him an offer.

"Don't concern yourself, sir. I have my own plans in place for tomorrow's departure. I just heard your voice and it's always heartening to hear a fellow Scot. Progress will be slow tomorrow as more snow is expected and it's already a foot deep on the ground."

Once Dr Brydon realised he was in the company of another Scot who was not after anything but good conversation, he relaxed. He was even more delighted when his new friend offered him some food for supper that evening. "I've a little business to do and then I will return with a good, hearty meal which will already have been prepared and cooked by my own servants," said Mr Petrie.

The two met up later that evening after Dr Brydon had tended to his patients. "We are going to have to leave some behind in the cantonments because they are too sick to travel. We've been assured of a safe passage and that the men will be cared for but there are ugly rumours circulating that we have neither protection nor friends here."

Mr Petrie leaned forward in earnest and said: "William, we're both Company men, so may I talk frankly? The moment you leave this cantonment, you will come under fire and the Afghans are in no mood for anything but slaughter. It is their intention to kill everyone and there are thousands waiting in the hills for the entire route.

"The military command is incompetent and Shah Shoojah is a man who stands alone, a king without an army but an army of enemies waiting to cut down every last British soldier on the road to Jalalabad. Keep your wits about you and take this." Mr Petrie handed him a large sheepskin coat, warning him that the freezing weather conditions would prove treacherous, if not fatal for those exposed to the elements.

Dr Brydon looked at his fellow Scot and said: "What of you? You'll need this coat more than me. I can't accept this gift. We barely know each other."

Mr Petrie smiled and responded: "Promise me one thing, William. Promise me you will write an account, leaving out no blame and names, when you arrive in Jalalabad.

"It is vital the world beyond Afghanistan gets to know the truth so that no other men in uniforms will follow into the folly of military misadventures in this godforsaken land. Alexander the Great could not conquer these people and neither could the Mongol hoards, and we must not let history repeat itself again."

As the two men stood up and bade farewell to each other, Dr Brydon shouted back: "Mr Petrie…you left this behind in the pocket. It's a magazine…"

But before he could finish the sentence, his new acquaintance responded: "Read it, enjoy it and then put it in your helmet for insulation. It will prevent your head from feeling the cold." With that, he walked away as the surgeon shouted back: "See you in Jalalabad!"

Mr Petrie's warning proved to be right, for only moments after the Kabul to Jalalabad, retreat began shots were fired and men were killed even before they'd left the cantonment. The long, painfully slow convoy was looted, animals slaughtered and thousands died on foot over the next seven days. If they were not killed by the Afghan warriors, they succumbed to the sub-zero temperatures and atrocious blizzards which caused snow blindness.

There were times when Dr Brydon feared for his own life and a week in to his terrifying ordeal his fears were realised when a scimitar wielding Afghan tried to kill him. He would later record in his journal: “I was pulled off my horse and knocked down by a blow on the head from an Afghan knife, which must have killed me, had I not had a portion of a Blackwood’s magazine in my forage cap.”

Two days after that attack, and having endured several more equally violent encounters, he did reach the fort in Jalalabad with wounds to his head, shoulder, arms and leg. He also survived to tell the story and fulfilled his promise to Mr Petrie to write a full and frank report. The contents made chilling reading as he regaled, in detail, the many ambushes and massacres by a formidable enemy.

He submitted the report to superior officers in Jalalabad but it would be more than thirty years before its contents were ever published, and even then they only appeared as an appendix in a retired general’s account of his own forty-three years serving in India.

“There was a cover up by the British Establishment and the East India Company. That whole exercise proved to be futile. Even now I feel angry and frustrated,” recalled Mr Petrie.

Salar sighed: “The intentions were good, if not a little naïve, although I’m sure the family of Dr William Brydon and his descendants will be forever grateful.”

A half-hearted, half-exasperated smile crossed Mr Petrie’s face. “He was a very clever man, as skilled in writing as he was in medicine and I thought if he could just record events as they unfolded then any army would think twice about the folly of going in to Afghanistan.

“He did survive. He did write a report; it was a truly graphic account not only exposing military incompetence but the terrifying, unpredictable and brutal nature of the Afghan warrior. Sadly the powers in force at the time made every effort to stifle its contents.

"All that effort and today, even now in the 21st century, foreign forces are still waging a losing battle in Afghanistan. All that innocent blood wasted, lives lost and sacrificed…it's all such a tragedy," reflected Mr Petrie. "They say the pen is mightier than the sword and, indeed, if only Dr Brydon's journal and notes had been published immediately, who knows the good it could have done?"

"What was the title of that magazine?" asked Salar, almost baiting Mr Petrie but the old man just 'harrumphed' and bemoaned 'man's inhumanity to man' referencing a Robert Burns quote. "I did visit Dr Brydon at his family home in Fortrose on the Black Isle to find out why his manuscript never saw the light of day.

"Of course he was too loyal to say anything or genuinely did not know; either way he could enlighten me no further. The man was worthy of a medal for the courage he displayed and with, or without my help, it was still a miracle he survived but dark forces were at play," concluded Mr Petrie.

"If only humans could learn from the follies of the past. However, Mr Petrie we must keep trying, and without our small efforts, please know that this world would certainly be a much darker place. Being a Guardian does not guarantee success even with your prowess and the special powers we give you.

"Without your intervention, Dr Brydon might not have survived and, although his report has yet to be given the full recognition it deserves, you did not fail in your mission that day. You saved a man's life and that is a priceless gift. Let's meet soon and further discuss the issue of an apprentice."

Mr Petrie nodded and bowed his head respectfully towards Salar before walking backwards to the door but before exiting, he said: "Blackwood's Edinburgh Magazine."

Salar smiled and said: "Ah yes, of course it would be, wouldn't it?" The history master looked over his half-moon glasses and raised his eyebrows, giving the hint of a smile at the same time, before exiting.

He trudged wearily through the long passage and emerged from the tunnel which led him back into his vast library. Feeling slightly less despondent, he turned to close the sliding panel and gently placed the portrait to its original position.

The old man paused as he lifted his hand falteringly towards the painting. "Oh, Clara, how I miss you, my love," he whispered in an uncharacteristically, hesitant voice. She was indeed the love of his life and his love for her never did ebb even as the years passed.

Saying goodbye to the woman who had grown old while he remained immortal was one of the most heartbreaking episodes of his life and the pain was as sharp as ever nearly five hundred years later. It was a cruel blow to watch the ravages of time transform his beautiful bride into middle and old age while he remained a robust and healthy figure of a man.

Petrie returned to his small study and began to ponder the offer Salar had made. A young apprentice, he mused, but who could he trust and also, more importantly, who could he burden with the status of Guardian?

Expecting a youthful aid to keep such a burdensome secret as the work of a Guardian would, indeed, be a heavy load to bear, but if he could find the right person, then it would make his job much more bearable. 'When there's no one to trust or confide in, that's when you realise how lonely life can be,' he reflected.

After pouring himself a modest glass of whisky, he picked up a half open book of poems by Robert Burns on his side table and, by the dim light of his table lamp, he flicked through the book, searching for a particular prose.

"Aha, yes Robert Burns, my friend. You knew all about the power of loneliness, didn't you, lad?" As he mulled over the words of one lament, Mr Petrie drifted off to sleep in his armchair and began dreaming of his wife, Clara. Soon his arm dropped along with the book of poems and he was fast sleep. The frown on his face melted away and there was almost an uncharacteristic smile threatening to lift the permanent gloomy look which usually weighed so heavily on his visage.

The next morning, Mr Petrie was annoyed to discover the entire third form history class had been diverted to the school clinic for their MMR vaccination jabs against the diseases measles, mumps and rubella. "I'm really sorry. It was my fault. I simply forgot to inform matron and then the vaccines arrived this morning, Mr Petrie," said Jennifer Hunter. I also forgot to book additional nursing staff, so I'm going to have to roll up my sleeves and help out in the clinic," she added, smoothing down her neat auburn fringe.

Miss Hunter, the normally super-efficient headmaster's PA seemed unusually flustered, so Mr Petrie decided not to make matters worse by complaining to Dr Collins. "Well, just send them back to my class and we'll do some revision today instead," he said.

The boys stood in a queue with the right sleeve rolled up as the matron prepared to administer the vaccine. Miss Hunter told the matron: "I'll take down their details in the adjoining room, so if there's anything else you need Matron, just ask."

The school matron Alice McDonald was irritated and flustered. She liked everything to be orderly and was both puzzled and annoyed that the normally efficient Miss Hunter had forgotten to inform her about the vaccines arriving. As each boy received his injection, he then went and submitted his personal details to Miss Hunter.

"It's Duncan Dewar, isn't it?" said Miss Hunter as he entered the room. She closed the door behind him and asked how he was. "Yes, Miss Hunter. I'm fine, thank you." She enquired if anything else was troubling him and he responded: "Well, I do have a pain in the back of my neck just here," he said, pointing his finger to a reddish spot.

"Oh, we'll let matron see that," she said. The boy waited outside until the last third-year pupil had been vaccinated and then matron called him back in to her room. "Okay, young Dewar, what am I supposed to be looking at? Get that ginger mop out of the way so I can see this teenage plook, then."

Miss Hunter busied herself putting the vaccination paperwork in order while the matron inspected Dewar's neck. "Ha-ha! My Timmy has a raised pimple just like that," she said as she prodded and poked the inflamed piece of skin. "Is that your son, Matron?" he asked.

Again she laughed and said: "Goodness sakes, no! He's my wee sausage dog and I had an implant tracker put in the back of his neck in case he went wandering off. Dewar, you are a teenager and teenagers get all sorts of spots and pimples. Don't be such a baby. Now be off with you."

"I didn't realise you had a dog, Matron," said Miss Hunter. "How long have you had him? I've always wanted a little dog.

Tell me more about him." The two women talked for about half an hour after the clinic which surprised the matron as the headmaster's PA seemed unusually chatty. She'd always thought of her as quiet and reserved and quite aloof.

Chapter 8

Duncan Dewar had somehow crossed the rubicon from classroom geek to being the uber-cool kid and everybody's friend. No longer the ginger kid, he was the edgy red head with a bad boy reputation.

Had the other boys known the true agendas of Professor McIntosh or that of Mr Petrie, they might not have held Duncan Dewar in such high regard but as far as they were concerned they saw him in a new light. The fact that the teachers appeared to be gunning for Dewar since the ill-fated midnight feast served only to elevate his status in their eyes from school swot to dangerous rebel after 'taking one for the team'.

He'd never experienced popularity before and as he sat down for breakfast, fellow pupils patted him on the back, sympathised over the extra maths and asked his opinion about all manner of things. Pupils who he'd never spoken with suddenly began to catch his eyes and smile in his direction. Only Thornberry and Sparrow continued to look on him in complete disdain for as far as they were concerned 'the freebie' would always be beneath them.

"So, Duncs, are you up for another midnight feast?" laughed Bobby Bob Bob. Dewar could feel a warm blood rush to his cheeks as the most popular boy in the school had actually chosen to sit next to him for breakfast. He looked around nervously and it seemed as though all admiring eyes were focussed on the pair.

"What do your parents do then, Duncs?"

The boy looked at Bobby and said nervously: "They died in a car crash when I was nearly fifteen months old. I guess I never really knew them."

His new companion drew back and said: "Oh, I'm sorry. I really didn't know. Gosh! I just can't imagine life without mine as embarrassing as they are at times. That must have been hard for you to deal with."

Still flushed and red Dewar nodded and said: "Yes, it has been hard but I've still got my grandfather. Do you mind if I ask you a personal question? Why were you christened Bobby Bob Bob?"

Delighted that the conversation changed direction, he threw open his arms and then grabbed the corkscrew curls on his head before dropping his hands on the table. "Well, you must know I have the most dysfunctional parents in the world, a mother called Chrystal Rox and my father is Mickey Grunge, drug-addled genius and front man par excellence for the band Molten Iron?" Without waiting for an answer, he continued: "When I was born, my old man went on a seven-day bender, snorting, sniffing, injecting anything he could get his hands on by all accounts and the media circus went wild.

"So this showbiz reporter from The Scum, oops, *The Sun*, turns up at the doorstep with his snapper for a pre-arranged photoshoot and this big story is done, see? Mum did most of the talking as Dad was apparently off his head but all went smoothly.

"He got the press off his back, enabling him to continue his bender. They got a nice story and my mum got some peace. The band's PR machine was happy as everything fell into place, ensuring more record sales, nice pictures and headlines.

"It all went swimmingly until the old man was seeing them off the premises when the journalist asked what name had they chosen for me. Instead of saying nothing he tried to remember the name mum had chosen and said out loud Robert…erm…Robson…mmm…Roberts. The next day, Mickey Grunge's son – me – was introduced to *Sun* readers as 'Bobby Bob Bob'. It kinda stuck."

Duncan laughed, declaring: "Blimey, that's a great story. So your name is Robert Robson Roberts Grunge, then?" His new best friend looked at him sideways, saying: "No, you muppet. Mickey Grunge is a soubriquet. All the blokes in Molten Iron have stage names. My real name should have been Royston Sydney Roberts after my mum's father in Yorkshire, so I reckon I had a lucky escape. Bobby Bob Bob's not too bad when you get used to it. It has a sort of rhythm to it and Mum's just about forgiven the old man now," he mused as he tapped out a drumbeat on the old oak table where they were sitting.

"It's also useful because the teachers hate shouting it out in class, so I rarely get any questions. Look, it's great flexin' with you but I've got to split. See you later," and with that, Bobby Bob Bob was gone. Duncan couldn't imagine what it must be like to have rock star parents, especially ones who were rarely out of the headlines for behaving badly but he thought his new BFF was handling it all very well.

He began to wonder about his own parents and could vaguely remember a smiling, oval-shaped face peering into his, as one of his earliest memories. The face was always smiling and framed with long, wavy red hair, sometimes loose and sometimes tied back. He was sure this was the earliest memory of his mother but wondered if it was a false one he'd created from the only photographs he had of her and his father, a serious looking, bespectacled man with thinning blond hair and a long face.

He was just thankful his parents were at another end of the morality spectrum compared to Chrystal Rox and Mickey Grunge.

Suddenly he was shaken out of his deep thoughts by a claw-like grip on the back of his neck. The pain was unusually sharp, causing him to wince and as he turned to see the source of this rude interruption, he caught the dark brown glower of the choirmaster bearing down on him. "Mr Jones, sir," said Dewar, as he rubbed the back of his neck.

"Ahem, so you already know my name, boyo? Well, that's a good start. I want you to come and see me after lunch today. Nothing to worry about but I'll be in the chapel annexe, so don't keep me waiting."

He was puzzled. He had never really met Mr Jones before but knew who he was as the pupils nicknamed him Drac as in Dracula because of the enormous widow's peak which looked as though it had been dreamt up by Central Casting for a vampire movie.

"Crikey Duncan, I thought old Drac was going to bite your neck and suck the life out of you then and there. What the flip did he want?" asked Ninian Swithers. His roommate hunched his shoulders, pursing his lips: "I was wondering the very same thing. He wants to see me after lunch in the Chapel annexe, though."

Withers emitted one of his theatrical squeals: "Well, take some garlic and a wooden cross. OMG! Maybe he fancies a bite this afternoon and you are on the menu." The pair left for classes, pushing and joshing with each other but privately Dewar was troubled. What could the choirmaster possibly want with him?

After lunch, Duncan Dewar walked towards the school's chapel where Sunday worship and other significant religious services were held during the Christian calendar. Some boys went every week but others, like him, were uncomfortable about religion and so opted for other activities on Sundays instead.

The annexe was also used for other religions and there was a multi faith prayer-room available for those students including the growing number of Muslims. As he walked towards the annexe, Dewar wondered how anyone had the discipline to pray five times a day. Just then, he saw fifth former Ali Reza walk out of the annexe, and smiled.

"What's got you so amused, Dewar?" Buoyed by his newfound popularity and growing in confidence, he responded: "I was just wondering how anyone finds time to pray five times a day and then you appeared."

Ali Reza, who was Iranian by birth, smiled and said: "Well, I'm a Shia, so we can bunch up our prayers in one go if it's really necessary but don't let Mo hear me say that, as he believes differently being a Sunni," he said, referring to Saudi-born Muhammad bin Al Wahid bin Awad bin Aboud.

"What's the difference then between Sunni and Shia?" he enquired. "Oh well, one's homicidal and the other's suicidal; just make sure you don't upset either," laughed Ali Reza walking off, leaving an even more puzzled boy behind.

Duncan carefully opened the door into the chapel annexe. The autumnal air was so chilled inside; he could see his own breath vaporise before him, as he looked around the bare room lined only with stone floors and stonewalls with a few chairs for choir practice. Another Muslim student was finishing his prayer and began to lift a rather ornate prayer mat from the stone floor.

As he left the annexe, a side door swung open from the chapel and in walked the Welsh choirmaster who took a few slow and deliberate steps, as though he were leading a funeral procession. He came to an abrupt halt about five paces in front of the nervous looking pupil.

"Dewar, I was supervising some boys who were being held back for detention the other evening when I heard a sound, not an unpleasant sound either. In fact it was almost haunting and melodic. So I followed the direction of the tones drifting down the corridor and imagine my surprise when I discovered the source of this Heaven-sent voice came from you – such a scrawny, puny little thing and yet such a powerful God-given voice. Are there many singers in your family?"

Duncan looked confused and wondered where this conversation was going. He was unsettled by Drac and felt deeply uncomfortable in his presence in the same way as a mouse would when confronted by a cat.

"I'll cut to the chase, boy. I don't like dilly-dallying around. I want you for my choir, you and your treble voice, which means two nights a week rehearsal and I will personally coach you on Saturdays. Mr Petrie says your voice is about to break and that you're an unreliable scoundrel, is that true?"

He looked up at the tall master as all his newfound confidence seemed to abandon him in a heartbeat. "I'm, I'm not sure what you mean. I've never really sung anywhere and as far as I know, there's no history of singers in my family. I'm, I'm an orphan, Mr Draaa, erm…Mr Jones."

The choirmaster grabbed Dewar by the throat and swooped his head down to his level. Pressing his face closely to his own, the boy could feel the master's hot breath on the side of his neck. By now he wanted to scream and imagined at any second Drac would sink his fangs into his neck, draining him of every drop of Dewar blood.

Whispering in his ear, the choirmaster asked in a demanding manner: "Have your vocal cords changed? Does your voice box sound louder and do you squeak and croak flipping between low and high notes?" Loosening his grip on the terrified boy, he turned to face Dewar who used every ounce of composure he could find to respond to the question.

"I, I haven't noticed anything strange, sir. No, but I'm already committed to extra maths tuition on Saturday mornings, sir, as well as…"

Before waiting for him to finish, the Welshman swung around and swooped down to eye level with the boy, saying: "Don't concern yourself. We can meet after lunch on Saturdays. That'll keep you out of trouble. We'll start this Saturday with the scales.

"Oh, don't look so worried, boy. I only want your precious voice. I'm not after your soul…not yet, anyway! Now run along and we'll meet at 2 pm sharp every Saturday until further notice."

Duncan Dewar didn't know whether to laugh or cry. When he sang before Mr Petrie the other night, he didn't realise he had a special tone or talent and now he had the scariest master in the school taking an interest. When he caught up with Ninian Swithers in their bedroom and told him, he emitted another of his trademark shrieks!

"I'm telling you, one minute you'll be singing 'I'm walking in the Air' and the next moment, he'll be sinking his fangs into your neck faster than you can say 'snowman'.

"You're doomed, doomed Duncan my boy," said Swithers in a grossly exaggerated Gorbals twang.

"You may as well bequeath me your entire supply of Jethart Snails now," he said, tugging on a large brown paper bag of peppermint-flavoured sweets. They had become a firm favourite of Duncan and his grandfather's after the pair stumbled across them during a weekend visit to the borders town of Jedburgh.

The distinctive boiled peppermint candy was moulded in to the shape of a snail using a twelfth-century recipe of sugar, butter, cream of tartar and peppermint and seemed to last for ages. To the boy's delight, a bumper delivery of snails had just arrived at Plato House courtesy of his grandfather.

Well, it looked as though weekend outings with his grandfather would now be cancelled until the end of term, he mused, since both the maths and choirmasters were going to occupy his Saturdays.

Grabbing a few of his sweets, he and Ninian wandered into the Common Room but just as they entered someone shouted:

"I blame the Bogofs! Let's get them!" A group of Plato boys leapt upon a pair of twins, bringing them down before piling high on top of them – Alexei and Andrei were identical and even their mother had a job trying to tell them apart.

Duncan was relieved he had arrived after the horseplay had started as he hated this sort of hands on rough and tumble and whispered to Ninian: "So why does everyone keep calling them the Bogofs when their family name is Volkov?"

His roomie turned around laughing and said: "Bogof! You buy one and you get one free. You buy one you get one free. B-O-G-O-F… Flippin' hell, Duncs. Do keep up, for a swot you're sometimes a bit slow off the mark."

The Volkov twins originated from Rublyovka, a suburb for the super-rich in the west of Moscow. While many of Russia's oligarchs and elite chose to live in Europe, most of the boys' family had remained in the Russian capital which is now home to more billionaires than any other city in the world.

Considering just a few decades before the turn of the 21st century, Russia had no millionaires, let alone billionaires, there were question marks over how families like the Volkovs had accrued their wealth in such a relatively short space of time.

However, it was one question no one chose to ask either of the Volkovs who both represented Sweetheart in martial arts and fencing events. And there were certainly no such questions asked when the twins' proud mother, Svetlana, bestowed a £250,000 gift towards the development of the school choir when her beloved sons were recruited for Sweetheart's baritone section.

"I had no idea a windfall would follow after I brought the Volkov's on board and, in truth, if they sang like two tomcats screeching on a tin roof, I would have grabbed the money and smiled and hoped for the best, but the reality is those Russians have voices of the richest, smoothest velvet," confided Mr Jones to headmaster Dr Andrew Collins when Svetlana Volkova's generous cheque arrived.

'The pair made unlikely choirboys,' mused Duncan Dewar as he watched the two use sheer brute force to power their way up from the Plato common room floor. Back-to-back, they emerged through the pile of twisted arms and legs and completely overwhelmed their would-be attackers. Triumphant, and still back-to-back, they began shouting the old Red Army battle cry: "Urah! Urah! Urah!"

The Volkovs, light olive skinned, robustly built and with thick waves of tousled hair punched the air triumphantly. Only fourteen, they looked much older and cut quite a picture with their Hollywood matinee looks, finely carved jawlines, dazzling white teeth and perfectly-shaped noses.

They could have been created in a Hollywood cosmetic surgery, but in fact the boys inherited their mother's natural beauty which was just as well as their father was not as blessed. He was a short, stocky man with enormous shoulders and a square head exaggerated in shape by a fierce-looking crew cut.

One of the twins grinned broadly as he spotted Duncan Dewar in the corner of the room and shouted: "Hey, Shrimp. Come here!" He then lunged forward and seized Dewar in a bear hug, lifting the scrawny thirteen-year-old off the ground in his giant arms. Feeling feeble and helpless, he just had to grin and bear the humiliation as there was nothing he could do to resist or repel whichever twin it was who gripped him so tightly and spun him wildly around the room.

By this time, everyone seemed to be shouting the battle cry: "Urah! Urah! Urah!" and stamping their feet on the ground, but in all the excitement, no one noticed the common room door swing open. Dr Liam Wallace, the Plato House Master, stood there and surveyed the scene for several seconds before roaring: "Put Dewar down, now." The short, portly Plato House Master was also the school's head of geography and known by pupils, rather irreverently, as Bacchus, after the fattest of the Roman gods.

Andrei Volkov clicked his heels and stood to attention like a soldier who'd just been given a military order. His arms automatically dropped by his side, causing Dewar to collapse in an undignified heap on the wooden floor but if he expected help or sympathy from Dr Wallace, he was getting neither.

"Pick yourself up, Dewar. Nobody likes a victim just as no one likes this sort of clodhopping tomfoolery. Volkov, see me before breakfast and I want an explanation…and bring Dewar with you." As he walked away, Alexei Volkov taunted the master by enquiring in a sneering tone: "Dr Wallace, which Volkov do you want? Andrei or Alexei?"

There were a few muffled sniggers which ended abruptly when the Plato head stopped in his tracks, paused and without turning around, said: “I’m in no mood for your buffoonery and for that you can both accompany Dewar to my study in the morning.”

“Ouch,” said Ninian as the door closed: “I think that’s what is meant by double bubble and poor Duncs is collateral damage, yet again.” While the boys in Plato remained in a boisterous mood, there were more serious issues being discussed elsewhere as the governors held their annual meeting.

Chapter 9

Today, Dr Andrew Collins was chairing the annual gathering of the governors which was always a test of his mental stamina and navigational skills as he steered the good ship Sweetheart through the choppy, if not stormy waters of internal politics and petty grievances.

He was the consummate diplomat but the school's head was certainly no pushover. In fact most people who encountered him knew within seconds not to take him for granted. Head for twenty years, he was a tall, imposing man who instilled fear into every pupil and their parents. He was neither loud nor aggressive, quite the reverse, and that's what made those around him slightly wary, because for two decades he had remained an unknown quantity.

His academic standing was beyond question, having read Classics and French at Pembroke College, Cambridge, graduating with a Double First. It was his unnervingly peaceful nature that gave rise to wild speculation from pupils, who nicknamed him 'The Doc', speculations that he had trained as an MI6 spy in interrogation techniques and had some sort of inbuilt lie detector.

As the governors, drawn from all walks of life and spheres of influence sat down with school heads, deputies and other academic representatives Collins wondered how the meeting would progress. Inwardly, he dreaded it as this gathering had the potential to turn in to a very combative arena where all sorts of agendas would come into play from the registrar's office to the bursars, competing for funds from the other welfare and trust departments involved in the running of the school.

There was much excitement as Dr Collins announced that Svetlana Volkova had donated quarter of a million pounds and as various heads of departments poised to swoop and make a bid for a slice of the money, they were visibly crestfallen at the news every penny would go towards regenerating the school choir.

Dr Geraint Jones sat at his place around the oval table looking like the cat who'd got not only the cream but a lifetime's supply as well. Grinning from cheek to cheek while trying to keep a straight face as the announcement was made proved extremely difficult. To say he was self-satisfied was an understatement. Not daring to catch anyone's eyes or envious glances, he kept his own firmly fixed on his papers in front of him.

Ironically, the contents of the school curriculum were rarely challenged with the exception of one area and that was usually the Scottish History department – a euphemistic reference for Mr Petrie. His particular focus on all matters Scottish frequently gave rise to questions from governors via concerned parents who felt Mr Petrie's views were distinctly anti-English.

Surprisingly, this time the subject was absent from the agenda. Furthermore, once it was established, there would be only one department to benefit from Mrs Volkova's cheque, the remainder of the meeting seemed to move quickly towards a peaceful conclusion.

However, there was just one more hurdle – any other business. The dreaded AOB always provided one of those moments reminiscent of the wedding service where the priest asks: "If anyone can show just cause why this couple cannot lawfully be joined together in matrimony, let them speak now or forever hold their peace." After a few seconds' silence, Dr Collins surveyed the room with the same angst as a guilty bridegroom in an episode of a TV soap drama.

As he looked around for any potentially disruptive participants planning to unload an unexploded 'bomb' to the headmaster's utter dismay, Retired Royal Navy Rear Admiral Sir George Beauchamp began to stir and clear his throat as the question was asked: "Any other business?" Sir George raised his right hand in an abrupt and forthright manner as if to illustrate the gravitas of his concerns.

"I want to raise the issue of the Scottish history classes," he bellowed.

"Oh, not this old chestnut again," sighed Collins under his breath, as he sank despondently into his chair. Beauchamp continued: "It's that chap of yours Putti, Petrey, erm…well, whatever. It's just not good enough. He's filling the boys' heads with a stuff of nonsense and claptrap that's frankly dangerous as well as anti-English. Anti-English, I tell you.

"Some of the parents have approached me over his latest interpretation of the Battle of Otterburn claiming the English army was forced to surrender to a gooseberry bush. It's outrageous, outrageous I tell you, making a mockery out of our own heroic history; and this is just one example of his subversive, anti-English rhetoric.

"Another cause for concern is his view on Culloden. Everyone knows it was a great English victory. Look, we are already in danger of losing the union and if those young minds are bombarded with this sort of piffle, God alone knows where it's all going to end."

Collins sat perfectly still for a minute considering this typically ill-timed outburst from Sir George. Instinctively, he wanted to ignore it and move to close the meeting saying the issue would be itemised for discussion on the next agenda, but even he knew this would be frowned upon. He also knew that Sir George's pronouncements were sometimes wide of the mark and on this occasion about the Battle of Culloden, he was indeed short on fact and detail.

Collins, briefly raising his eyes to the ceiling as if to summon the help of some unseen force, turned to face the Rear Admiral. "You know, Sir George, one can say many things about our Scottish history master, but promoting historical inaccuracies, I am glad to say, is not one of them.

"Where would Sweetheart be if I accepted teaching methods like that? Now, Mr Petrie may have strong views on certain subjects and embrace rather eccentric teaching methods, but I have never had cause to fault him on the breadth, depth and accuracy of his knowledge. Indeed, I know he has inspired and informed not only the boys, but some of the other teaching staff over the years."

The Rear Admiral looked wounded. He wasn't used to being challenged in such a public arena. In fact he wasn't used to being challenged at all. After an uncomfortable silence, the meeting was concluded to almost everyone's relief with the more social gathering to follow.

They were gently ushered in to The Caledonian suite, a grand reception room where the portraits of various Sweetheart luminaries hung. Liveried staff moved effortlessly around the room serving wines and offering appetisers before the formal dinner.

However, if the head thought the subject of the Scottish history classes would have been left in the committee room, he was to be disappointed. Sir George was a tenacious character and as Mr Collins walked by he said: "Well, you have your views, Headmaster, as have I, but I won't have a man in such an important and influential position spinning tales… I won't have it, I tell you, I…"

The headmaster gently, but firmly raised his hand to object and, turning on his heels, he looked his adversary directly in the eye and said: "Sir George, let's settle this through the basic examination of the particulars of the Battle of Culloden. In short order, it was a dynastic struggle, the last gasp of the struggle between the exiled Stuarts and the Hanoverians sitting on the throne in London.

"Yes, much of the troops fighting for Prince Charles Edward Stuart were Scots, but they were Highland clans and in the main Catholic, reviled in much of the rest of Scotland and indeed Britain. Many clans fought on the Hanoverian side and Lowland Scots regiments lined up to face the Jacobites across Culloden Moor. An English battle against the Scots it certainly was not."

Sir George, red-faced and angry, blurted out: "Yes, well, they were all bloody traitors as far as I am concerned, bloody traitors, I tell you," boomed his loud and petulant voice. The quiet murmur of conversation in the room ceased and all eyes turned towards Collins and the Admiral who by now was rather flushed; a distinct ruddy colour had crept from his collar line to his already weatherworn cheeks while the veins which threaded across his face and congregated around his red, bulbous nose were almost deep purple.

"That's as maybe, Sir George, the facts speak for themselves," said the unruffled Collins, maintaining his trademark calm and soothing tones. "There was great cheer amongst the lowland protestant Scots at the defeat and in northern English Catholics a great sorrow. Come now, these events did take place some time ago. I'm sure we can agree the events form part of Scotland's rich and varied history," he added giving Sir George's huge arms a reassuring, friendly squeeze.

The bluff and bluster of the retired seaman seemed to run out of traction as he said in a slightly crestfallen tone: "It's the thin end of the wedge, the thin end of the wedge, I tell you. When I went to school, I was told we had an empire and the sun never set on it, so vast and powerful it was.

"Every part of the map under our command was painted pink, pink I tell you, and the world map was dominated by pink. But if it was up to your man Putri, Petrie whatever, why then they'd think all sorts of dangerous notions. It's one thing celebrating Burns Night and Hogmanay, but should we be celebrating the defeat of the English army? No, I say. No, we should not. Where will it all end? Are we going to rewrite World War II to appease any German students who enrol here?"

By now, the small group which had gathered around Sir George and the headmaster had dispersed, leaving only the rather deflated Rear Admiral with his long time RAF chum Dr Godfrey Rogers, affectionately known, by his closest friends, as Wing Nut. Sir George looked exasperated, but just then his attention was diverted as a silver platter of tasty seafood headed in his direction.

He only had time to pop one crab pastry into his mouth, and to his annoyance, the tray of delicacies had gone. He looked around and, catching the eye of another waitress, beckoned her over, although when she put her platter in front of him, he frowned, becoming rather irritated and perplexed by the gourmet Asian salad served on a delicate china soupspoon.

This trendy twist on classic food fare did not impress. "If you can't jab the bloody thing on a stick, what's the point, Wing Nut?" he asked. Fellow Governor Dr Rogers was equally unimpressed by this culinary innovation and shrugged his shoulders in dismay. And so, as the merits of finger foods and falling British culinary standards consumed Sir George, the

subject of Sweetheart's Scottish history lessons were momentarily forgotten.
However, another governor, the tenacious Dame Sylvie Cole, raised the issue again with Collins. A major lawyer in London's financial Square Mile, Dame Sylvie had her own agenda having been fully briefed by legal colleague George Henry Sparrow to push the issue of Mr Petrie's lessons within the curriculum.

She was pleasantly surprised and pleased that bumbling Sir George had conveniently served up the subject for discussion and now she would attempt to move it along further. Sparrow, she imagined, would be impressed at her initiative, and who knows where that might lead as he was extremely influential in city's legal circles?

However, unknown to Dame Sylvie, the Mayfair lawyer was using her as a useful idiot in a long-standing grievance against Mr Petrie going back to the 1970s when he was a Sweetheart pupil. On discovering through his son Crispin that Mr Petrie was still teaching, it ripped open old wounds and a determination to seek revenge.

A chance conversation with Dame Sylvie enabled him to capitalise on her new status as school governor and he persuaded her to raise the issue of Sweetheart's Scottish history in the curriculum.

Sparrow was a petty, vengeful man who bore grudges and found it virtually impossible to forgive or forget anyone who crossed his path. He certainly never forgave Mr Petrie for caning him and every time the master's name was mentioned, his buttocks automatically adopted a clenched position.

"So how was your first governor's meeting, Dame Sylvie?" enquired the headmaster. She smiled, nodding approvingly and then said: "Gosh, that was quite an eruption from the Rear Admiral. I must admit I was a little disconcerted when he expressed his concern that the Scottish History master was dangerous and a subversive…erm, has he been here long?"

The headmaster was annoyed that the subject was being raised again but he didn't show his displeasure. Instead he smiled, raised his eyebrows and tilted his head towards the new governor, stating clearly for everyone in earshot: "Mr Petrie is many things but a dangerous, subversive…well, I think not. You may not be aware, Dame Sylvie, but his status at

Sweetheart is unique as he's not on the teaching staff as such. The position he holds was created back in 1585 when King James VI bestowed a grant and special status on the abbey.

"In it was a protected bursary set aside purely for the teaching of Scottish history, over the centuries the role has continued to be protected and while masters come and go, the role of Scottish History Master will remain."

"So there will be plans to replace him in the future, then?" she enquired. "I understand he must be reaching retirement soon. I imagine he'll be looking forward to hanging up his cap and gown and it would certainly give you the opportunity to recruit someone with perhaps a more progressive attitude," added Dame Sylvie.

Collins smiled and nodded in the affirmative, assuring her the matter would be looked in to. What he didn't reveal was the matter had been looked in to some years back by the Human Resources Department but discovered the teaching records of all staff prior to 1980 had been destroyed by floodwater.

Getting hold of Mr Petrie's original paper contract was proving difficult, if not impossible, and the old master had prevaricated and obfuscated successfully ever since. Furthermore, Collins liked Mr Petrie and admired his teaching methods and loyalty to the school and, out of all the staff members, he seemed to cause the least amount of disruption and never quibbled over his budget, housing or modest allowance.

Since most of the senior teaching staff was expected to join the social gathering, there was a heightened interest when Mr Petrie made his entrance. Rather predictably the effect on the Rear Admiral was like a red rag to a bull; striding over purposely to the short, portly master, he rushed straight in to the conversation: "Look here, Putri. Petrie, what's this nonsense about the English being forced to surrender to a gooseberry bush at Otterburn? I'm not having it, man. I tell you, I'm not having it."

Mr Petrie looked up at the red-faced Sir George and said: "Why sir, I don't blame you. What an outrageous thing to say! Fascinating battle though as the Scots were outnumbered three to one by the English army.

“It was the first time ever warfare was conducted during the night, you know?” Sir George seemed to relax a little as the masterful Mr Petrie drew him in with the skill and stealth of an experienced fly fisherman stalking a giant salmon.

“Really? How fascinating! I never knew that.” The old master nodded sagely, adding: “The battle in August 1388 was conducted by moonlight and the Scottish leader, the 2nd Earl of Douglas, was mortally wounded. He was worried that his death would encourage the enemy, and so he told his men to hide his body beneath a bush so nobody could see it.

“The men continued fighting, unaware their leader had expired but they triumphed in the end and when the English offered to surrender, they were taken to where the Earl of Douglas lay. And that is why it is often said that the Battle of Otterburn was won by a dead Scot and the English surrendered to a bush.

“But you are quite correct, Sir George. It certainly wasn’t a gooseberry bush. I believe the English surrendered to a bracken bush. It seems you have been misinformed and I do wish these boys would pay more attention in class to the detail…that’s where the Devil is, in the detail. Oh, and by the way my name is Petrie, not Putri,” smiled Mr Petrie before raising his glass to an open-mouthed incredulous Sir George.

“More wine for Sir George, please,” advised Collins to a waiter. “His glass appears to be empty and we can’t have that, can we? Now Sir George, please tell me about your time in the Falklands when you engaged the Argentinians. What was your role in the Task Force?”

Collins once more gritted his teeth and smiled. He knew that the old salt liked to talk about his own triumphs at sea and this would take his mind completely away from Mr Petrie, the Battle of Otterburn and the vexatious subject of the Bracken bush. It was a self-sacrifice but the price, he reflected, was worth paying.

Dame Sylvie who had silently observed the verbal dexterity of Mr Petrie from a safe distance studied his profile in detail, trying to work out his age. She was standing just below a large oil on canvas by the late 16th century Flemish artist, Paul Van Somer, depicting King James signing documents confirming

Sweetheart Abbey's special status watched by a group of admiring courtiers.

Had she turned around and scrutinised the painting in a similar forensic manner, she may have noticed one of the courtiers portrayed by the artist looking over the king's shoulder bore a remarkable resemblance to none other than Sweetheart's Scottish history master.

Instead, she decided it was time to speak to Mr Petrie herself and she moved across the room towards her target just as he looked towards her and smiled, half bowing his head in acknowledgement. "Aha, the ubiquitous Mr Petrie! Allow me to introduce myself…" But instead of waiting, he picked up her hand, kissed it and remarked: "Dame Sylvie Cole. I know, your reputation in the world of finance is second to none.

"I'm sure the school board is richly enhanced by your presence. But look, your glass is empty. Let's see if we can find someone to charge it," he said as he looked around for one of the wine waiters. "White, isn't it?" Dame Sylvie was quite taken aback at the charm which seemed to ooze from her intended quarry. He was certainly very disarming and this disappointed her as she had wanted a more combative response to her opening line.

They paused their conversation as a waiter arrived to fill her glass while another one came bearing red wine to replenish Mr Petrie's. "Just half will do," he advised. As the waiters walked away in search of other needy recipients, Dame Sylvie adopted a mildly flirtatious tone and asked: "I see your glass is only half full, Mr Petrie, or perhaps you see it as being half empty?"

He looked down at the beautifully crafted Persian carpet on which they stood and smiled before returning Dame Sylvie's gaze, responding: "A glass can never be half empty or half full. Full and empty are absolute states which are impossible to half or modify so technically, neither is true.

"Now, had you asked me if I was a pessimist or optimist, I would have said the latter. I prefer to live in the sunlight of transparency and not lurk about in the shadows. What about you?"

"Forgive me, Mr Petrie, I had no idea you were quite the philosopher. I can see I have underestimated you." As she finished her sentence, she raised her arm and touched his, only for a second and very lightly, but the movement raised his hackles.

If her tactile approach was meant to put him at ease, it had the reverse effect. Mr Petrie liked neither to be patronised, trifled or teased, and Dame Sylvie had deployed all of her female armoury to try and make a lasting impression. It was an error of judgement from which it would be difficult for her to recover in order to gain his respect or trust, and inwardly she admonished herself on realising the serious miscalculation. Mr Petrie, unlike most men she encountered, appeared to be completely impervious to her feminine wiles.

"Please excuse me, Dame Sylvie. I've a rather pressing engagement to attend before dinner. No doubt our paths will cross again." She smiled as Mr Petrie left the room, for she had already arranged to make sure her seat was next to his for the banquet.

Once again she had underestimated him, for while she continued networking, Mr Petrie was altering the table plan ensuring that he was, in fact, sitting opposite her on the grand dining table. Not only that, he swapped his place card with Admiral Beauchamp before slipping back in to the room presenting what can only be described as a self-satisfied expression.

***

Chapter 10

Excitement was growing by the day at Sweetheart Abbey as the winter holidays approached, for it signalled the end of term which meant the annual inter-house cross-country race, a trip to Edinburgh's Christmas Market and the traditional Carol Concert attended by parents, friends and supporters of the school.

The general chatter in morning assembly was at a slightly higher volume than usual but it ceased abruptly as headmaster Dr Andrew Collins rose from his seat on the school stage. The passing of each year presented both a mixture of sadness and relief and, as he walked towards the wooden plinth to address the school, he adjusted his master's gown and gave a reassuring pat to his school tie.

"These final two weeks promise to be extremely hectic but I would urge a little moderation in all things from you, boys. Surveying the room, he continued: "Remember each and every one of you here today is an ambassador for Sweetheart Abbey, so let's try and maintain a modicum of decorum.

"No running in the corridors for instance, Swithers," chided Dr Collins who was nearly knocked off his feet when the excitable Ninian ran headlong into him on his way to assembly a few minutes earlier.

"If you have ambitions to be a prop forward for the school's team, go and ask the rugby coach Mr Swain for a trial."

There was a frisson of exaggerated laughter at the head's comment, especially among the first and second-year prep boys who sat cross-legged in front of the school stage. It was always a relief to laugh at someone else's expense. Their beaming, fresh faces swivelled around to try and spot the embarrassed

Ninian Swithers who by this time was squirming in his chair in the front of the third-year rows.

Duncan Dewar, sitting next to his roommate, struggled to keep a straight face and avoid the laser-like stare of the headmaster who had, by this time, locked on to his scarlet-complexioned friend with the electronic precision of a guided missile.

The dramatic moment was only interrupted as Collins' side vision detected a slow, deliberate jaw movement nearby; it was the telltale sign of a piece of chewing gum being sloshed around in a pool of saliva in the mouth of Timothy West. With his eyes still fixed on Swithers, The Doc lifted his arm slowly and deliberately, clicked his fingers and pointed in the direction of the unsuspecting West: "Remove that gum at once and see me after assembly, West. You know the rules," said the headmaster who by this time had darted his eyes to the right focussing on West.

Dr Gideon McKie tilted his whole body slightly towards Dr Liam Wallace and, in a schadenfreude-laced whisper, said: "Not a good day for Plato House." Wallace, whose lips were pursed tightly, was barely able to disguise his displeasure.

"I've also received complaints from the village of boisterous behaviour outside The Abbey Arms Hotel on Sunday afternoon," continued Dr Collins. "So will the pupil who performed circus stunts on his bicycle in the hotel car park present himself to me at 10 am in my study?

"The festive spirit is much in evidence with all four houses making a great effort, I'm told, in producing eye-catching nativity scenes. As usual, there will be a prize for the most outstanding. However, today's judging has been suspended after housemaster Dr Samuel Shinwell informs me that someone has stolen the Baby Jesus from the Boethius crib and left a ransom note. I want him returned by tea time today before serious consequences are set in motion."

After assembly, the boys headed to their various classrooms speculating who could have stolen the Baby Jesus from Boethius and who was doing wheelies in the hotel car park.

"Old Shinny's on the war path because he is convinced someone is trying to sabotage our entry," said Ali Reza as he prepared some equipment in the chemistry laboratory. "But it was rather funny to find a ransom note in the crib, almost as funny as you knocking 'the Doc' down in the corridor, Ninny!"

Ninian Swithers scowled: "I didn't knock him down, Ali, and I got the bigger fright. Imagine hurtling in to the Doc and now I've got to go to his blasted study in thirty minutes to hand myself in for doing a wheelie outside the hotel. Life is so unfair. I wonder who grassed me up. It'll be that awful manager, I bet.

"I was showing off to some girls at a wedding and one asked me to do some tricks, so I did a wheelie and landed right in a puddle. How was I to know the bride's mother would pop out for a fag and stand in the wrong place?! That'll teach her to smoke even if it was one of those perfumed e-cigarettes.

"Today's turning in to a nightmare and it's not even 10 am!" he exclaimed. "What else can go wrong?" As if to answer his question, a flame from his Bunsen burner singed his shirt cuff. Poor Swithers was exasperated and excused himself from the chemistry lesson so he could change into a clean uniform before his encounter with the eagle-eyed Doc.

He ran through the courtyard and into Plato House to the room he shared with Duncan Dewar but as he approached the door, a furtive choirmaster emerged looking startled as Ninian came into view. "Can I help you Mr Jones, Sir?" enquired Ninian cautiously but he just grunted, shaking his head in the negative and walked off.

"Bloody hell!" exclaimed Ninian under his breath: "I wonder what Drac wanted?"

The room looked largely undisturbed and then he remembered his meeting with the headmaster so quickly changed and headed for Mr Collins' study. By the time he got there, Capella boys James Darling and Willie Carmichael were also standing outside the head master's door. "What are you two doing here?" enquired Ninian.

Darling explained: "Both Willie and I were in New Abbey on Sunday afternoon on our bikes. We're stymied, see, because Collins didn't give a name of who was doing the wheelie and since we both did, we thought we may as well hand ourselves in. And you?" Ninian shook his head in dismay: "Well, this is a to-do for sure. I thought it was me. Maybe I should go."

Darling grabbed him, saying: "You can't, what if it is you?"

Unknown to all three, John Russell from Boethius House was already inside the dreaded study as Dr Collins sat behind his Victorian desk, gently tapping his forefinger on the tooled green leather inset as though he was knocking out a Morse code while simultaneously making notes on a yellow post-it note. Russell stood quietly in front of the desk as he completed the paperwork.

The room was deadly silent apart from two noises, the ominous tick-tock of a grandfather clock behind him and the irritating scratching sound of the head's fountain pen as it travelled across the paper on which he was writing. Then there came a third noise. It was the beating heart of Russell which seemed to be pounding inside his head rather than his chest.

His mouth went dry and his palms became damp as he continued to stand nervously in front of Dr Collins. Russell tried shifting the weight on his legs when the noise of the scratchy pen stopped without warning. "Right, Russell. Tell me what you were doing to incur the wrath of the locals in New Abbey, then?" he asked.

Russell cringed as he explained how some girls in the hotel car park had goaded him in to performing acrobatics on his mountain bike. It would be a variation on a theme the amused headmaster would hear three more times, for Russell, Swithers, Darling and Carmichael had all performed wheelies at some stage during the day in the hotel car park.

The young girls were guests at a wedding and, bored by the proceedings inside, had gone into the car park in search of a distraction by way of local boys. To their delight, a string of 'posh 'uns' from Sweetheart Abbey crossed their path on their way to the cake shop.

After listening to all of the evidence, he realised the original guilty party was indeed Ninian Swithers who had inadvertently splashed the mother of the bride when one of his bike stunts backfired. "I'd just done a track stand and was trying to perform a nose wheelie when I ended up pile driving myself and, then…"

Dr Collins interrupted him: "You may as well be talking in Swahili. I did not understand a word of that Swithers and nor do I have any desire to know about the intricacies of such trivial matters. Suffice to say I want all four of you to return to here at 4 pm when a suitable punishment will await."

"More sweating, more nerves. I tell you that man must have trained under the Gestapo or whatever was around when he did his training. I've aged about ten years today," Russell told his three co-defendants as they speculated the nature of their punishment.

This time, all four were called into The Doc's office together. "Each one of you brought the school into disrepute with your hubris and misguided self-importance, and so I have decided that the village will be off limits to all cyclists until the end of term."

Darling began to heave a sigh of relief but was interrupted before he could fully exhale as Dr Collins added: "Furthermore, I want a thousand-word, handwritten essay from each one of you on the consequences of narcissism and the dangers of excessive interest in or admiration of oneself in the presence of the opposite gender.

"You can submit your work collectively tomorrow at 4 pm. Dismissed."

As the boys turned to leave, Dr Collins coughed and said: "I imagine you will need to copy this... It's the title of your essay but I am warning all four of you now, that beyond the title I do not expect to see any repetition from any of you. In other words, no collaboration, conferring or duplication."

Ninian reached out and took the yellow note. Crestfallen, the boys returned to their various common rooms as word spread about the 'wheelie punishment' and the bike ban in the village, which everyone agreed appeared to be excessive. "One thousand words and I don't even understand the question," moaned Ninian as Duncan walked in and offered him a Jethart Snail to chew.

Duncan then fell back on his own bed but felt something alien underneath the quilt. He pulled back the covers and exclaimed: "Jesus!"

His roommate turned round and said: "What do you mean, 'Jesus'?"

Exasperated Duncan repeated his words: "Jesus! It's bloody Jesus, the baby. It must be the one taken from Boethius, but who would plant it here?"

Ninian stood up and gulped for some air but then started flapping around and panicking. "What? What is it, Ninny? For God's sake man, spit it out!" shouted Duncan who was getting highly irritated by his friend's overly theatrical antics. Then he suddenly realised this was no game; in all of the excitement, Ninian was choking on the Jethart Snail which had lodged in his throat near his windpipe.

Duncan smacked his friend on the back several times using the flat of his hand before opting for abdominal thrusts to get rid of the boiled sweet. He tried several times without success as Ninian hammered his fists against the wall.

His eyes began to roll and he felt his body becoming weak and almost limp. Duncan tried one last time but the effort resulted in both him and Ninian crashing against another wall causing a maths book to fall from the bookshelf in the neighbouring room shared by the Volkov twins.

"What the hell is going on?" bellowed one of the Russian twins who stuck his head round the door to complain about the noise.

"Help. Help me. He has a blocked airway. I'm trying to do that Heimlich Manoeuvre thing and it's just not working!" shouted Duncan.

"Out of the way Shrimpy, watch me," said Andrei Volkov. Moments later, he lifted Ninian off the ground and with a sudden squeeze, the offending sweet shot out of the boy's mouth enabling him to breathe again.

"You saved my life, Alexei, or is it Andrei? Anyway thank you, thank you," rasped Ninian.

"Well, I tried to save you as well. I just couldn't get your diaphragm to work properly but I would've got there in the end," said Duncan defensively.

"At your service. Any time you need help, just call for me. I'm like a Russian superman," boasted Andrei as he pumped up his arms and posed, before he left the two boys alone.

Just then, Duncan remembered the Baby Jesus and exclaimed: "I'm really sorry if I startled you but it still doesn't solve the problem over who planted this in my bed."

Ninian tugged on Duncan's arm, still rasping he said: "I think I know. That's why I leapt up and the bleedin' snail shot to the back of my throat. I was trying to tell you that when I came back from assembly to change into a clean shirt, I caught Drac coming out of our room.

"He looked well dodgy and shifty and when I asked if I could help, he sort of grunted, brushed me aside and disappeared." Duncan was mystified and neither of them could work out why Drac would plant the Baby Jesus in his bed, but if it wasn't the choirmaster, then who was it and why? Why frame Duncan?

"So what are we going to do, Ninny?" asked Duncan. "We, where does the 'we' come in to this? Have you seen the title of the essay I have to write for The Doc? If I don't get this finished tonight, he'll have my guts for garters, or something even worse.

"Let's work something out tomorrow and steer well clear of Boethius in the meantime. Trust me, the lesson I've learned today is that volunteering information can backfire and honesty is not the best policy. Handing Jesus over to Old Shinny will get you some vile punishment," advised Ninian in unusually sombre tones.

Duncan wrestled with the problem for a while but felt uncomfortable leaving the nativity figure in their room. It could be incriminating but where to hide it? If it was found in Plato, then there would be collective punishment, so he decided the best and most fitting place would be the chapel.

If the choirmaster found it, he wouldn't dare report where it had come from without revealing the part he had played in planting the baby in Duncan's bed in the first place, reasoned the schoolboy. He picked up the life-size infant which was swaddled in a checked Falkirk Tartan blanket. The black and white tartan, also known as Border Drab, was the theme adopted by Boethius for their nativity scene.

Duncan slipped out of Plato with the baby and headed for the chapel, keeping as close to the garden foliage as possible en route. It was a clear night with a full moon and the star-studded sky overhead was the best he'd ever seen.

As he crept inside the chapel, the hair on the back of his neck prickled and stood on end, causing him to rub his nape and the familiar little pimple or raised birthmark which cradled in the centre.

Duncan was not a particularly religious boy but as he walked towards the lightly illuminated stable and nativity scene, he looked upwards and whispered: "Please forgive me but I don't know what else to do."

And with that, he squeezed the tartan-swaddled baby into the already occupied crib. The eyes of the Virgin Mary seemed to follow Duncan and when he looked back, he pondered momentarily if twins might have been changed the course of Christianity.

He looked around to survey the chapel and its intricate woodcarvings and walked over to the stalls where he would sit with the choir for the carol service. He was feeling slightly nervous about the whole affair because he was to perform solo a version of Silent Night.

Towards the rear, he saw a spiral of stone steps leading to what was rumoured to be a crypt, all sorts of myths and legends telling stories of weird goings on were fuelled by the fact the entrance had been sealed for as long as anyone could remember.

Duncan, feeding his own curiosity and taking advantage of the moment, inspected all the nooks and crannies the 16th century chapel had to offer, and then he walked over to the pulpit made of oak and began to scrutinise five panels which defined its hexagonal shape.

Inside each panel was an androgynous looking being. It was almost impossible to determine the gender but in the absence of wings, Duncan concluded they couldn't be angels. He pondered they might be saints and then he saw each panel bore a name; in an instant he recognised Benyellary, Merrick, Kirriereoch, Tarfessock and Shalloch.

They were the names of peaks in the South West of Scotland that make up Galloway's so-called Awful Hand, an area known well to hill walkers and mountaineers. As he looked at the staircase leading into the pulpit, he noticed a sixth panel, again with a carved figure and stepped up to take a closer look.

Like the other images, it was human in shape but appeared to be neither masculine nor feminine. There was a word below but he didn't recognise it at all and said out loud: "Salar." His voice echoed through the chapel just as the rear door opened.

He immediately went down on his hunkers and crept inside the pulpit where the priest traditionally stood to give the sermon. Cursing his own curiosity, he heard metal-tipped footsteps heading down the aisle towards him but, mercifully, they faltered and stopped short of the pulpit.

***

Chapter 11

The mystery visitor sat in one of the front pews normally reserved for VIP guests and other respected visitors, unaware that Duncan Dewar was only a few yards away hiding in the pulpit.

Suddenly, the tranquil atmosphere of the chapel began to echo to the familiar twenty-first-century sound of electronic bleeps from a mobile phone keypad as the user appeared to be checking and responding to text messages.

Duncan Dewar remained crouched down wondering how long he could maintain this uncomfortable position as a familiar burning and tingling sensation began to creep into his left leg; the telltale signs of pins and needles filled him with dread as he tried to silently squeeze his calf muscle to repel the onset of the painful condition.

He winced in pain as his leg muscles tightened and gritted his teeth, pulling a bizarre facial expression which would have won any gurning competition. How long he could have remained like this will forever remain as one of life's imponderables as something quite unexpected happened, causing him to forget his own pain.

The mystery person began to shuffle and move in their seat before making a throaty straining sound. It was followed by a familiar noise which shattered the silence and ripped through the air. Far from an electronic bleep, this was the sound produced by the high velocity of gas being expelled through an extremely tight sphincter muscle which in turn produced a series of impressive farts!

Duncan's eyes popped wide open and he let go of his painful leg, ramming both his hands into his mouth as his shoulders rocked silently and tears rolled down his face. There was nothing like a good dose of flatulence to induce hysteria and laughter in any thirteen-year-old schoolboy. He was in complete agony, unable to make a sound or movement for fear he'd be discovered.

However, he was able to deduce from the high-pitched noise that the person in the chapel must surely be a man as he recalled how his friend Ninian had reliably informed him that girls don't suffer from flatulence like boys. "My sister Veronica told me girls can't fart, no wonder they're so weird and miserable," he said with the seriousness and wisdom of an old sage when the subject came up after an evening of self-induced farting by the chugging of carbonated drinks and dried fruit.

A few seconds later, the mystery man made another familiar sound – the rapid wafting and fanning of air to dilute the odour produced – in this case, the purveyor of flatulence enlisted The Common Book of Prayer to assist him.

Duncan was sure he caught the most unfragrant whiff of bad eggs and mused about the chemical content of the gas of the mystery man. He recalled somewhere that a typical fart is composed of about fifty-nine percent nitrogen, twenty-one percent hydrogen, nine percent carbon dioxide, seven percent methane and four percent oxygen but foods like cabbage and cheese can increase the hydrogen sulphide content, thereby increasing the intensity of the pong.

Not sure when he would ever be able to use this information again, he was quite pleased with himself at being able to recall such details. However, amusing as this unexpected interlude was, the respite it gave to his pins and needles soon disappeared and he was forced once again to try and stretch and massage his calf muscles.

Moments later, the heavy metal clunk of the chapel door reverberated through the building followed by the sound of more footsteps coming down the aisle. Unlike the flatulent occupant of the front pews, these sounded more like the crisp staccato beat of a pair of high heels echoing off the stone floor.

A furtive conversation then began between a man and a woman but that was all Duncan could discern from the whispers other than their words, which were in a foreign language, possibly Russian.

He sat there and pondered about the conversation but shook his head suddenly as he could've sworn he'd just heard his name being uttered. He listened in earnest and picked up on Andrei and Alexei and there it was again, his name among a list of other names. He recognised most of them as being in the choir, but he wondered what the conversation was about.

When the clandestine meeting concluded, there was some shuffling as the couple stood up. Duncan couldn't see a thing from his hiding place inside the pulpit but he could distinguish the grating metal heel sound of the man's shoe on the chapel floor again.

However, to his frustration, he realised the woman remained behind, leaving him to wonder how much longer he'd have to conceal himself. Once again the door opened and more footsteps could be heard but Duncan recognised them in an instant as belonging to the choirmaster.

"Dr Geraint Jones," said the heavily accented female voice, echoing in the cavernous chapel. "Ah, Mrs Volkova, always a pleasure but I am mystified as to why you would want us to meet here. It's certainly a very chilly night and I fear we may soon be in the grip of a snowstorm. The white stuff has just started to descend from the Heavens as I arrived."

Svetlana Volkova responded huskily: "We Russians do not feel the cold. It is our friend, Dr Jones. I arrived in Edinburgh last night but wanted to meet you in advance of the carol concert to make sure that you have everything you need."

Dr Jones smiled broadly: "Since your generous gift, any problem we may have encountered has been overcome. The equipment for the school orchestra has all been upgraded and this has certainly been reflected in the sound of music as you will discover on the evening of our concert.

"The school's tailor has ordered a special weave of Falkirk Tartan for the choir's kilts; it's more commonly called Shepherd's Plaid or Border Drab, as it was originally worn by shepherds in the border's area between Scotland and England. This is a sample of it," he said removing a black and white wool scarf with a distinctive check. "A small gift for you."

Svetlana looked at the weave, singularly unimpressed as he handed it over to her. On seeing her lack of response, he added enthusiastically: "We will also be announcing your generous donation and the setting up of a prize in your name, Mrs Volkova." After giving the scarf another cursory look, she held it to the side of her face, serving to highlight her perfect cheekbones and almond-shaped green eyes.

The emerald colour they radiated had the choirmaster entranced as she said: "It's not really necessary to mention my name. We do what we have to do for the benefit of the school and the boys. However, I have some exciting news and I wanted to tell you to your face, just to watch your expression."

Dr Jones looked intrigued as Svetlana fluttered her eyes at him. The school choir, she said, would be invited to sing in Russia's cultural centre of St Petersburg but at a special performance in the Church of the Resurrection of Jesus Christ. The historic building is more commonly known in the old imperial capital as the Church on the Blood as it marks the spot where Alexander II was assassinated on March 1881.

"It is a great honour and while Christmas is probably the most important day of the calendar for people in Western Europe, in Russia we attach more importance to the New Year and that is when the concert will be. Tell me Dr Jones, what do you think?"

He stood before Svetlana almost dumfounded but wide-eyed with excitement until a look of doubt crossed his face. She could read him like a book and added: "Naturally all costs will be covered and my husband has agreed to let us use his private jet to transport the choir."

Dr Jones looked overwhelmed and then said: "This is indeed an honour and unbelievable generosity from you and Mr Volkov. I think most of the boys would be delighted to come, although it is extremely short notice."

Looking mildly concerned, Svetlana added: "As long as the majority of the choir can make it and, erm, especially the boy Duncan Dewar. The twins tell me you discovered him and his voice is exceptional."

Nodding enthusiastically, he said: "It's true. I'm giving him a solo spot at the carol concert. The boy has an incredible voice but for how long is anyone's guess. I only hope it doesn't break between now and the New Year. He's at an awkward age, you know.

"I can't think he'll have anything planned for his holidays. He comes from a rather humble home and lives with his elderly grandfather, although I'm not sure he'd be prepared to travel without his grandfather over the festive period."

Svetlana pulled on a lock of blonde hair from beneath her fox-fur hat and, twisting it around her right hand, something she always did when she was nervous, she said: "Yes, well, the old man can travel with us. I expect you'll need at least two chaperones or responsible adults for the choir anyway."

Duncan was bursting with excitement on hearing the news but was forced to contain himself in the pulpit as he continued to eavesdrop on the conversation between Mrs Volkova and the choirmaster.

As the pair got up and walked back down the aisle, Duncan could only catch certain words. He strained his hearing but he did catch one thing. It was an expression of surprise by the Russian woman on noticing two baby figures in the Nativity crib.

Dr Jones boomed: "I know exactly where this young chap has come from but I've no idea how he got here, Mrs Volkova. Let's call it high jinx or japes by some of the boys.

"I will return this to Dr Shinwell at Boethius House. I'm sure he will be relieved," said Dr Jones who turned to look back around the chapel before he escorted Svetlana through the chapel door and out into the snowy night. Offering his left arm, the choirmaster walked her safely to her chauffeur-driven car.

He retraced his steps through the crisp, white snow to the chapel to lock it for the evening. Stopping short of the entrance Dr Jones moved his head to one side as he examined the outlines and number of footprints. He could account for his own lumbering size-elevens and Svetlana's dainty stilettos but there was another set of smaller footprints which could only have come from the chapel a few moments earlier.

"How strange," he said out loud to himself. "It seems Mrs Volkova and I had company. Well, we'll just have to solve this mystery by following the footprints." The choirmaster tracked the steps in the snow with the furtiveness of a wolf stalking its prey. They led him towards Plato when the choirmaster's concentration was rudely interrupted by a flying snowball which smacked him on the forehead.

“Oops, sorry sir. I didn’t see you coming,” said Ninian Swithers. “A few of us were just letting off some steam, sir, when…”

But before he could finish his sentence, Dr Jones snapped: “Enough.” Like frozen statues, a handful of Plato boys stood rooted to the spot as he looked in despair at the ground. The lying snow had been ploughed up by more than half a dozen different shoes of similar sizes making it impossible to continue his search.

“I know one of you Plato boys stole the Baby Jesus from Boethius but I’m not prepared to check shoe sizes in this weather. I’ve bigger fish to fry but I will be reporting you sprats to Dr Liam Wallace and he can deal with the lot of you.

“Dewar! Come here! Give this to Dr Shinwell with my compliments and tell him I will catch up with him tomorrow. Good night,” growled Dr Jones before turning once again towards the chapel to lock the door. As he walked down the footpath, he shouted: “Don’t even think about it, Swithers!”

Ninian looked shocked and dropped the snowball he’d just made. “Has he got eyes in the back of his head?” Duncan’s heart was beating quickly as he realised how close he’d come to being caught. He was also mildly amused to be left holding the baby again and looked down at the figure, saying: “What do I have to do to get rid of you?”

Later that evening, the Baby Jesus was safely back in his crib at Boethius after Duncan handed over the swaddled figure to a relieved Dr Shinwell. Swearing Ninian to secrecy, he told him what had happened after he went to the chapel.

Ninian was already on a high after finishing his ‘wheelie’ essay and escaping punishment for landing a snowball on Dr Jones, but Duncan’s night in the chapel surpassed everything, especially the farting episode. “OMG,” he exclaimed. “So who was Johnny Fartpants, then?”

Duncan jumped on his friend: “Ssshhh!” He hissed as he tried in vain to silence his roomie with a pillow. Seconds later, there was a full blown pillow fight which only came to an end when the Volkov twins next door hammered on the wall, telling the two to stop larking about.

The next day at 4 pm, James Darling, Willie Carmichael, John Russell and Ninian Swithers stood before the headmaster with their essays in hand. 'This is going to be excruciating,' thought Swithers, who had reflected on his traumatic day before which started with running into the headmaster and ended in a snowball fight resulting in his unfortunate encounter with 'the Drac'.

Similarly, the other three stood there grim-faced, waiting to have their work scrutinised word by word by The Doc. After several minutes' silence apart from the tick-tock and the sound of a scratchy nib on paper, Dr Collins looked up and said: "Pass me your work." Each neatly, handwritten essay was placed on his desk and they were then asked: "Has this proved to be a worthwhile exercise, boys?" All nodded vigorously in the affirmative, so the head rose to his feet and, collecting the essays, walked over to a machine in the corner of his office.

It made a whirring sound when he switched it on and then, one by one he fed the essays into the machine without reading a single word. The process took around two minutes and with each sheet of paper fed in to it, the boys watched their work emerge in hundreds of tiny strips in a Perspex collection bin at the other end of the shredder.

Once it had finished, Dr Collins switched it off and said: "That'll be all boys."

The four retreated in complete silence and waited until they'd reached half way down the corridor before Ninian groaned out loud: "He didn't even read a bloody word. We could've written complete gobbledegook and he read not one word. I sweated blood and tears. I'm telling you he is evil."

The others muttered in agreement and Darling was in tears. "It's probably one of the best essays I've ever written. I even footnoted and referenced each section. The bastard could have at least had the courtesy to mark it. What a waste of time!"

***

Chapter 12

The starting pistol was fired by Jon Swain who roared encouragement as around one hundred and twenty boys from all four houses set off on the annual cross-country festive run. Waved on by their housemasters and most of the teaching staff and a few pupils not taking part, it was a highly competitive event regarded as one of the highlights in the school's sporting calendar.

Entry was purely voluntary, however since all entrants would earn points for their house regardless of their finishing position, this was an incentive which spurred so many to sign up. Duncan Dewar normally avoided such outdoor activities if he could but, having being cajoled by the rest of the boys in Plato, it was difficult to resist such peer pressure.

He looked on in envy as the likes of Bobby Bob Bob, James Darling and the muscular Volkov twins tore off at a fast pace to lead the front of the group while he was destined to be one of the 'tail-end Charlies' with the equally sluggish Ninian Swithers and Little Mo who earned his nickname because of his diminutive figure plus few could recall the Saudi's birth name in full: Muhammad bin Al Wahid bin Awad bin Aboud.

Duncan was particularly uncomfortable with his lowly position because the rump also included Jacob Thornberry and Crispin Sparrow who were both useful runners, and yet on this occasion they chose to sit in behind the slow coaches. As they headed towards the woodland skirting the village, the pair kept jostling Duncan, calling him 'freebie' until Darling told them to 'pack it in'.

Quite why Darling had slipped so far behind after his blistering start wasn't immediately obvious but Thornberry and Sparrow were a bit wary of the lanky, streetwise boy. Apart from being 'new money', they thought he was a bit rough around the edges and therefore far more likely to sort out differences physically rather than opting for a game of bools.

Darling was the extrovert son of a wealthy, self-made Glaswegian entrepreneur who had built up a nationwide car cleaning empire after starting off with a soap and bucket. Class snobs Thornberry and Sparrow regarded him as a bit of an unknown quantity as he did have a reputation for running fast and loose with school rules, authority and discipline, yet somehow managed to evade being caught.

“Like trying to nail jelly to the wall, a real slippery creature,” observed his housemaster Dr McKie to the headmaster over a recent schoolboy prank in which some foaming liquid had turned the Sweetheart fountain into a giant bubble bath. Darling was the Number One suspect but despite all of his investigatory powers and skill, ‘Och Aye McKie’ could not pin the crime on him.

The evidence was indeed incriminating after an empty industrial-sized liquid container of car-cleaning soap wash was found discarded under a bush near the fountain. It could only have come from a car wash operation deduced McKie but when the house master called Jimmy Darling and put the evidence to him, he was severely admonished by the aggressively rambunctious Glaswegian.

Mr Darling was not a man to be messed with and he made that very clear to the increasingly obsequious McKie in colourful language and dialect drawing on metaphors that made the old master blush. Despite his dogged pursuit of Darling junior, an exasperated Dr McKie finally threw in the towel telling the culprit: “Your denials are neither plausible nor convincing. From now on, I am going to be watching you like a hawk, Darling,” he said after the incident which became commonly known as ‘soapgate’.

While most pupils would have kept their head down and lowered their profile for the rest of term, Darling continued to showboat and the annual cross-country run gave him a chance to exhibit his man bun. Naturally, he attracted several disapproving looks from onlooking masters as he tore off at a blistering pace; the bun was a style not many fourteen-year-old boys had the confidence to pull off.

"I thought the Alice band was bad enough last year, so God alone knows what Capella can expect from him next year…a blue rinse perm, perhaps?" said Dr McKie wistfully to Boethius head Dr Shinwell who responded: "It's ever since the rules over haircuts were relaxed, standards have slipped. Sometimes I feel as though we're trapped on that film set Shampoo with Warren Beattie!"

Even the po-faced Dr McKie sniggered at this comment: "You're showing your age, Dr Shinwell."

Darling's ears should have been burning but ten minutes after verbally subduing class snobs Sparrow and Thornberry, he was sitting in the village cafe enjoying a hot chocolate drink crammed with miniature marshmallows.

"I know what you've done, laddie. You're going to wait until they come back this way for the final mile, aren't you?" said the woman behind the counter. "Oh please, don't grass me up, Betty. You know I look upon you like my big sister," protested Darling.

The old woman who had served generations of Sweetheart Abbey pupils laughed and said: "Away with your flattery, I'm old enough to be your great granny. You might fool the masters up there but you don't fool me and you're certainly not the first to pull such a stunt but here's a tip: Don't be the first past the line, come in around eighth place and that way no one will question you."

Meanwhile, as the main body of runners splashed knee-deep through the freezing cold waters of the New Abbey Pow, some of the other boys diverted in preference to crossing the river upstream courtesy of an old fallen oak bough.

Duncan and Ninian opted for this route rather than 'freeze off our bollocks in the Pow' as Ninian bluntly remarked. "Come on, Duncs, there's only seven more miles to go and we'll be back at Plato for a hot shower. You know we are probably going to be last but at least Thornberry and Sparrow have gone and I'm not quite sure where Darling or Little Mo are. I didn't see them pass us."

The two slowed down as the magnificent root system of the giant fallen oak loomed large on the river's edge as if it was some tentacled monster rising from the ice-cold waters.

Carefully clambering over the root network, they gingerly made their way across the ancient bough.

"You go first, Ninny," urged Duncan who thought if there were any hidden hazards his clumsy friend would find them first. His instincts served him well as his left foot crunched through some rotten wood near a hollow in the trunk.

"Yikes!" he squealed, and after a precarious moment he managed to pull his balance back and leapt with some satisfaction to the bank side turning to Duncan to hurry up. Just then he looked over his shoulder, convinced they were being watched. He was certain he'd heard some muffled laughter, but then dismissed it as his imagination while grim-faced Duncan made the journey across the gnarled, rotten tree.

As he prepared to make his final step, something caught his right ankle and he lost his balance plunging headlong into the fast moving water, screaming as he fell. Ninian gasped as he saw his friend being swept away. Again he was sure he heard the sound of laughter. Seeing two figures running away, he thought he'd spotted Sparrow with his distinctive blond hair, but wasn't entirely certain. Looking back at the section of the trunk from where Duncan had fallen, he saw a piece of twine and realised his friend had been deliberately tripped.

To add to his shock and anger, he looked around for Duncan but he had disappeared and he couldn't see anything other than the fast moving, swirling water. Panicking, he ran down the river, shouting his friend's name and calling for help in between.

Little Mo appeared on the other side of the river. He had fallen so far behind; he was contemplating throwing in the towel when he'd heard Ninian's cries. The pair followed the river until Ninian caught sight of Duncan's limp body being carried downstream. Thankfully, the current swept his lifeless friend into a shallow stretch of the rock-strewn river.

Both boys clambered in and waded to where Duncan was floating face down. Using all the strength they could muster, they dragged him out of the water. He wasn't moving and the boys noticed he had a smudge of blood on his nose and ear.

Remembering their first-aid class, Duncan was gently put into the recovery position. They were shocked to find blood on their hands after adjusting the position of his head. "Do you think he's still alive?" asked Ninian.

Little Mo hunched his shoulders, adding: "If he's dead, it is the will of Allah," on hearing that Ninian charged back through the water and scrambled on to the opposite side of the riverbank before sprinting towards the village to raise the alarm.

He burst into the teashop and told Betty what had happened and she called the emergency services. As he caught his breath, he noticed a sheepish looking Darling peeping up from behind a table where he'd being hiding after Ninian had burst in. Seeing how distressed he was, James volunteered to go back with him.

Within minutes, they were at Duncan's side with Muhammad. All three used their bodies to keep him warm until the ambulance crew arrived. On seeing his injuries, the paramedics strapped the unconscious boy into a stretcher and advised a medical team to be on standby at Dumfries and Galloway Royal Infirmary for a potential serious head injury case which was complicated by the onset of hypothermia.

Local police called to the scene as a matter of procedure took the three remaining boys back to their school as the ambulance drove off. They explained to Dr Collins what had happened and he, in turn, advised Dr Liam Wallace to go to the hospital until Duncan regained consciousness.

As news swept the school of the accident, Dr Geraint Jones waved down the Plato head's car and said: "I'm coming with you. That boy means a great deal to me. He's supposed to be singing solo in less than forty-eight hours at my carol concert. Dr Wallace nodded tersely and the two set off down the gravel drive.

"You might want to show some concern for the boy's welfare when we arrive. Otherwise the medical staff might think your only interest on the boy is based on your bloody carol concert Geraint," said Dr Wallace.

Ninian, James and Muhammad were hailed heroes while the school matron advised all three to get showered immediately and into warm clothes. As Dr McKie escorted his boys back to Capella, he pulled Darling aside to enquire as to why he was not as wet and bedraggled as the others. "Well, one of us had to remain on the riverbank and help haul him in." The suspicious schoolmaster was not convinced but he also knew he was unlikely to get to the truth of the matter.

Meanwhile, since the hospital was less than ten miles away from the school, Duncan was soon being examined by a medical team of head and spine injury specialists. Dr Liam Wallace and the choirmaster paced up and down in the accident and emergency department awaiting news of their pupil. About an hour later, a consultant from the trauma team emerged to brief the two teachers.

"The boy has been very lucky and undoubtedly the quick action of those around him saved his life. He is suffering from the side effects of hypothermia and he has an enormous swelling and deep cut on the back of his head but fortunately all the damage is superficial and not internal.

"As far as we can ascertain, there's no lasting damage. Although since he's taken quite a hefty knock, we will be keeping him overnight for observations. He's a little drowsy, a combination of medication and the accident," added the doctor.

As the two listened, Gordon Buie burst in through the entrance doors and walked quickly over to where the two Sweetheart masters stood. The old man was distressed, breathless and almost hyperventilating as the news was relayed to him. In tears, he said: "I thought you were going to tell me he'd gone. It's brought it all back, the death of his mother, my daughter, nearly twelve years ago.

"Can I see him? Is he awake?" The doctor put his hand on the old man's shoulder and advised him to take a few deep breaths. He then said: "Can you tell me, has he suffered head trauma before requiring surgery or…"

Gordon Buie responded: "No, never. He was in a car accident in which his parents died but he thrown clear of the wreckage before the whole thing exploded. It was a miracle he survived, but no. He didn't have any broken bones or anything, a few cuts and bruises. Why do you ask?" he enquired in a trembling voice.

"Oh, don't concern yourself. It's just that we picked up something on the X-ray. Not much bigger than a grain of rice, really. It looks like a piece of metal in the nape of his neck, maybe something from the car accident. I suppose we could remove it, although I'm sure it will pop out in the passage of time. It's not unusual for car accident victims to carry minute particles inside them for years without problem as seems to be the case here."

Gordon Buie looked at Dr Jones and Dr Wallace and said: "What do you think? Should they remove it?" Dr Jones shook his head vigorously: "Oh, no. Best leave it where it is. It's not even worth mentioning to the boy since it obviously doesn't bother him. Let's go and see young Duncan and make sure he's fine and well…"

"And no doubt well enough to sing, eh?" interjected Dr Wallace testily.

Duncan opened his eyes and was trying to focus. His head was pounding and he seemed to be in a bright, white room. A black spectre loomed into his vision and as he attempted to concentrate an indistinct, threatening shadow bore down on him giving him a start.

"There, there boy," said the choirmaster. "You've had an accident but you are fine now and the doctors say you'll be well enough to go back to school tomorrow and take part in the concert."

Dr Wallace pulled the teacher aside and said: "Damn it man, let the boy see his grandfather. He doesn't want you hovering over him like the Grim Reaper."

"There lad, how are you? You gave us all a start but now you're fine, thank God," said Mr Buie. Sitting on a seat by Duncan's bed, he told him how he'd received a call from the school about the accident and thought the worst. Without mentioning how he was deliberately tripped, he told his grandfather about the run and falling off the old trunk into the water banging his head on a rock as he was swept away.

"I thought I was going to die. My life just flashed before me."

The old man laughed: "Well, that must have taken all of twenty seconds then! Listen, I've got some exciting news, although I'm not supposed to tell you," he whispered in Duncan's ear. He repeated what Dr Jones had told him about the St Petersburg trip and said: "I know you've had a knock on your head but I thought you'd be more excited and surprised."

Of course Duncan already knew about the trip to Russia after his dramatic evening hiding in the pulpit. Feigning surprise, he said: “Sorry it took a while to sink in. Does Dr Jones want you to go and can you come?”

His grandfather nodded and the boy smiled. “You know I have a solo part, too? This is going to be our best holiday ever.”

The two continued talking and he was told about the ‘grain of rice’ in the nape of his neck. Wide-eyed, Duncan said: “I knew it. I knew there was something there and it causes me pain if someone grabs me on the spot. I thought it was some sort of weird birthmark. So what do you think? Should the doctors remove it?”

“Well, Duncan, it’s been part of you for more than a dozen years now. Personally speaking, if it doesn’t bother you, I would just leave it.” The boy nodded in agreement with his grandfather and on being told, Dr Jones also breathed a sigh of relief. It looked as though his carol service and Duncan’s solo spot would go ahead after all.

As all three left the hospital, Dr Jones faltered. “I haven’t told him about the Russian concert yet. Maybe I should go back.” Dr Wallace lost his patience and grabbed, rather brusquely, his colleague’s arm, saying: “Come on Geraint, back to the school. I think that young man has had enough excitement for one day without you filling his head full of St Petersburg, private jets and the mucilaginous wife of a billionaire Russian oligarch.”

Dr Jones furrowed his bushy black eyebrows and determined to look up the word mucilaginous in the dictionary; it didn’t sound like the sort of adjective his generous patron Svetlana Volkova deserved, he mused.

Chapter 13

"So Duncan, if you remember anything else, any detail no matter how small, be sure to let me know," said police officer Jane Rooke. "You know, if there's anything on your mind or anything troubling you, you can trust me. A problem shared and all that."

Duncan was sitting on the edge of his hospital bed and feeling decidedly uncomfortable. He had already told Officer Rooke that he couldn't remember anything from the fall but he hadn't been entirely truthful. The last thing he could recall before plunging headlong in to the river was being tripped by a cord or thin line as he tiptoed across the old bough.

"Here's my card. You can call me any time," she said and with that she left the room. Once in the hospital car park, she called the station to speak to her supervising officer.

"Seems he can't remember a thing Sarge but I get the feeling he's holding something back. I'm going back to Sweetheart Abbey just to tie up a few loose ends but unless we get more information, I can't take it further."

Constable Rooke stood there patiently as her sergeant responded and once he finished she protested: "It's not my imagination. Some things don't add up and I did find a piece of twine dangling from the bough at the scene. And sir, just for the record, I resent being called Miss Marples," added the policewoman.

Jane Rooke was frustrated. Her sixth sense was telling her this was no accident but her sergeant thought otherwise. Back at the station, as he put down the phone, Sergeant Donald Gilchrist told colleagues: "Rooke is trying to turn that schoolboy's accident into an attempted murder case. She's a bloody nightmare, fresh out of probation and trying to fast track to detective. And now she's just told me off for calling her Miss Marples. The last thing I need is some politically correct PC!"

As the young policewoman finished her conversation with Sergeant Gilchrist, she saw Dr Geraint Jones pull into a pick up bay in the distinctive Sweetheart Abbey school mini bus. "It's Dr Jones, isn't it?" she said, extending her hand as he stepped out of the vehicle. "I'm Constable Rooke. I've been assigned to the case involving your boy Duncan Dewar."

Dr Jones looked surprised. "Case? What case? It was an accident, wasn't it?" Rooke, realising she had over-stepped her brief, pulled back immediately and said: "Oh, nothing to alarm you, sir. I'm just tying up a few loose ends, protocol and all that. He's a nice lad and I'm just glad he's fine and well. Have you come to collect him?"

"Yes, I have. He's doing a solo performance at the school concert tonight. Look here constable, why don't you come along? There's a small reception afterwards and I'd like to show my appreciation – here's a couple of VIP tickets for you and a friend." Dr Jones reached back into the car and pulled a couple of tickets from the glove compartment and gave them to the officer.

After a few more pleasantries, he headed towards the hospital and went to the room where Duncan was ready and waiting. "Feeling better, Dewar?" And without waiting for a response, Dr Jones continued: "We've got a hectic day ahead with rehearsals, timings etc. Somehow you've got to fit in some rest. Oh, and your grandfather is heading for Sweetheart this afternoon and will stay at Mr Petrie's cottage on the estate."

As the pair drove towards the school, Dr Jones excitedly told Duncan about the trip to St Petersburg in more detail adding: "Now I don't want to put you under any pressure but you have a solo spot singing 'Walking in the Air'. You must have heard of it…it was written by Howard Blake back in 1982."

Duncan looked slightly overwhelmed: "You mean The Snowman song? But I don't know the words. I've never sang it…I…I…"

"Ssssh, don't concern yourself boy. I'll get you through the rehearsals but your focus will be on tonight and then we can work out a schedule over the Christmas that'll suit everyone.

The patron wants you to sing it and so that is what you will do. Svetlana Volkova calls the shots, young Dewar. And you know what they say: He who pays the piper calls the tune!"

As the minibus pulled up outside the gravel car park, Dr Liam Wallace emerged to greet Duncan. "How are you, Dewar? I'm told you must try and rest before your performance at the concert tonight, but before you go to Plato, the head would like to see you. Oh, and Mr Petrie is expecting you to take tea at his home when your grandfather arrives."

Duncan was glad to be back in familiar surrounds but was apprehensive about seeing Dr Collins. As he walked to the head's room, his PA, Miss Jennifer Hunter, smiled and offered him a seat. "I'll call the head and let him know you are here. He's anxious to see you and find out how you are."

Never before had he received such a warm welcome on walking in to the head's office but he was still apprehensive. Moments later, Dr Collins appeared and ushered Duncan in to his room. "Well, you certainly gave everyone a bit of a start yesterday morning, Dewar. Excuse the pun, but run me through what happened."

Duncan sat there and recalled events exactly as he had told Constable Rooke. Again he omitted how he suspected he was deliberately tripped as he stepped over the old bough. As he reached the end, Miss Hunter knocked on the door and interrupted: "Sorry, but you did say I had to remind you to get these signed off today before the afternoon post."

She handed him a series of letters which he carefully read through and signed, adding handwritten comments with his fountain pen where appropriate. As a fellow ginger, Duncan marvelled at Miss Hunter's hair bob as she leant over the headmaster's shoulder and wondered why it always fell neatly back in to place when she straightened herself. The silence in the room was, as usual, interrupted by the familiar sound of the ticking of the clock and the scratching of the pen nib.

To this day, Duncan still does not know what emboldened him, but as Mr Collins concluded his business and his PA left the room, the schoolboy said: "I notice your pen nib scratches on the paper, sir. I think this is caused by the flow of ink which lubricates the pen's journey. So if the quick movement of the pen outpaces the lubricating flow of the ink, then it will make a noise.

"I believe your pen is moving faster than the ink flow can support, so maybe the nib's tines need readjusting, sir," he concluded.

Dr Collins was rarely lost for words but this observation by Dewar left him aghast and, if he dare admit it, slightly guilty because he had deliberately adjusted the tines on the nib of his pen so it would create the irritating scratching sound which so jarred with pupils who had the misfortune to be summoned to his office for a misdemeanour.

Hundreds of boys had been forced to sit silently in worried anticipation while enduring the 'scratchy nib treatment' in Dr Collins' office. Today though the headmaster had been busted by the third former but he wasn't sure if the boy was deliberately playing him or had made the observation in all innocence.

After an embarrassing silence, the usually unruffled Dr Collins said: "Thank you for that observation, Dewar. I see that bump on the head has not affected your analytical and observational powers. Good luck with tonight and I look forward to seeing and hearing you this evening. Do try and get some rest."

Duncan was almost shaking as he left his office and shook his head in disbelief, wondering what had come over him to say such a thing. He wondered if it was the painkillers or other medication given to him at the hospital. Ironically, the very same thoughts entered Dr Collins' head as he sat and wondered what had just happened.

When he walked in to the Plato common room, he was immediately overwhelmed by well-wishers until Dr Liam Wallace boomed: "I'm under strict orders to make sure Dewar gets complete rest and he can't if you lot bombard him with silly questions. There'll be plenty of time for that later. Swithers take Dewar to his room and make sure there are no visitors for at least the next two hours."

"Flippin heck, Dunc, I'm so glad to see you. You do know it was Thornberry and Sparrow to blame, don't you? I told that Rozzer," blurted Swithers once they got to their room.

“You did what?” asked Duncan. Ninian Swithers sat down his roommate and told him how he was sure he had heard some laughter when he fell into the river.

“When I looked around, I saw a flash of white blond hair streak past. It had to be Crispin Sparrow and wherever that minger is, Jacob Thornberry is not far behind. They had it all planned; that’s why they hung back when we set off.” Duncan raised his eyebrows and added: “Yes, but you’ve got no real proof, mate. Not unless they admit it.”

Ninian sighed: “I know that’s what that policewoman said.”

Duncan grabbed his friend by the arm: “You told the cops? I knew that policewoman was on to something. She was like a terrier this morning. She wouldn’t let go.” He then told his friend how he felt some twine around his foot causing him to fall.

“You see, I knew it. Let’s report them,” urged Ninian but Duncan added: “It still doesn’t amount to proof and unless this becomes an episode of CSI I hardly think the local force is going to set up an incident room and send crime scene investigators to find the rope that could hang those two bastards.

“By the way, Ninny, you are right about one thing,” smirked Duncan. “That policewoman is a bit of a babe, isn’t she? And she gave me her card as well. Look, here it is Constable Jane Rooke and, more importantly, her telephone number!” Ninian looked both delighted and shocked at his roomie since he’d never expressed any interest in the opposite sex before.

“So my friend, Duncan. You have an eye for the laydeees, especially blonde chicks, eh?” The two boys fell onto a bed in a heap of giggles as they made more inappropriate observations about the young female constable. After a moment’s silence, Ninian sat up and said: “You know I went to confront Sparrow and Thornberry.”

Duncan expressed amazement and surprise at his friend’s courage as Ninian was never one to go looking for trouble. “Oh, worry not, Duncs. I bottled it at the last minute but I did find out something interesting. Those two are planning to set up old Petrie and I think I know how.”

Ninian explained that in a burst of anger he went to Pythagorus' House to confront the two suspects over his friend's accident. "I really didn't know if you were dead or alive, mate, and something inside me just snapped. But by the time I got to their room, I bottled it. However, the door was slightly ajar and I did overhear them talking. Instead of bursting in, I just earwigged and this is what I heard."

He then regaled his friend with the details and afterwards Duncan said: "I've got to lie down and take all of this in. This needs some careful thought though and there's not much time if it's going to happen tonight. Okay, let me have a nap. We'll speak later." Duncan stretched out on his bed and rolled over as Ninian went to leave. Just before he opened the door, the exhausted schoolboy said: "Oh, by the way, Ninny. Thanks for saving my life. You're the best friend ever." Ninian grinned and then left the room so that his friend could rest.

***

Chapter 14

Duncan was shaken out of his deep sleep by Dr Jones. "Gracious boy! I thought you'd passed out or taken the wrong medication. We have to do the dress rehearsal for tonight's show. It's nearly 2 pm and you're on at 6 pm.

The over-exuberant master half dragged the drowsy youngster off his bed and out of Plato House into the square. Once the fresh autumnal air hit his face, he began to wake up properly and remembered the story told to him by Ninian about how Jacob Thornberry and Crispin Sparrow had hatched a plot to set up Mr Petrie.

Duncan pulled against Dr Jones and said: "I'll come to the chapel but I must use the bathroom first, sir. I'll see you there are soon as I can." The choirmaster looked exasperated but he knew the worst thing a singer could be afflicted with was a full bladder, so reluctantly let him go. "I'll see you in the chapel and don't be long."

As soon as he disappeared from sight, Duncan ran in the other direction towards Dolce Cor cottage and once there, he hammered on the door loudly. Mr Petrie appeared: "Gracious Dewar! I was expecting to see the Four Horsemen of the Apocalypse you made such a racket. I'm glad to see you've made a full recovery but your grandfather's not yet arrived."

Breathless, Dewar said: "I've come to see you, to warn you. Can I come in, sir? I think I need to sit down. I feel slightly dizzy." Mr Petrie stepped aside, ushered in the boy before looking around to see if anyone else was watching and then he closed the door.

After drinking a glass of water, the third former sat and told Mr Petrie the whole story from beginning to end including Ninian's suspicions about Thornberry and Sparrow and about the plot he'd overheard to humiliate the old master.

Mr Petrie did not seem the least surprised but he added: "You were right not to tell the police without any firm proof. Suspicions are one thing but none of what you said would stand up in a court of law although, in truth, I believe you were targeted by those two aristocratic ne'er-do-wells.

"As for their plot, it's not the first time I've been targeted by a Thornberry or Sparrow. Leave this to me and say nothing to anyone else. Best tell Swithers to keep his own counsel as well. One thing is certain, laddie, tonight is going to be interesting."

As he left Dulce Cor, Mr Petrie said: "Thank you for this, Duncan. It means a great deal to me that you see me as a confidant and someone who is also prepared to watch my back." The boy stared back at the history master in slight wonderment as this was the first time ever he had called him 'Duncan'.

He looked at his watch and it was nearly 2:30 pm. Without a moment to spare, he headed for the chapel where, within fifteen minutes of his arrival, he was standing by the pulpit decked out in a kilt of Border tartan complete with sporran and a Bonnie Prince Charlie jacket, vest and winged shirt. "We'll do the bow tie later, just sing boy, sing," said Dr Jones.

Duncan opened his mouth as the music began but was suddenly overcome by a fit of giggles as he saw Dr Jones fanning himself with a music sheet. The unexpected wave of hysteria was probably a combination of being overexcited, tired, weary and the thought of the mystery flatulent visitor performing the very same actions.

Whatever caused the outbreak of mirth, it was infectious as soon the orchestra descended into more laughter to the consternation of Dr Jones. After a few loud claps from his hands and calls for order, everyone seemed to calm down and Duncan sang.

Afterwards, the choirmaster went over to Duncan, lifting his lapels and then patting them down while saying: "Perform like that tonight and I will have no complaints. Now please, please go back to your room and rest. This is a big night and we cannot afford for anything to go wrong."

Duncan left the chapel just in time to see his grandfather's car roll up the drive. He went running over to give the old man a hug but resolved to tell him nothing of what may or may not have happened as he crossed the river with Thornberry or Sparrow.

"Well, aren't you The Caledonian?" marvelled his grandfather as he looked at his kilted grandson. "I've never seen you in traditional clothes before but you wear it well, laddie. I've brought my own Highland dress too. I'll be flying the flag for the Buie clan tonight."

"Great to see you, Gordon. Your grandson cuts a fine figure, doesn't he? Why Dewar, you are a sight for sore eyes. Shoulders back lad and don't forget to swagger." Mr Petrie was beaming as he joined Gordon Buie and his grandson on the gravel drive.

"I've a feeling tonight is going to be a night to remember for many years to come," said the history master as he gave a most uncharacteristic wink in Duncan's direction.

By 5:30 pm that evening, most of the parents and friends of the school had arrived and were being ushered by first form pupils from the car park to the chapel where outdoor heaters had been strategically placed to combat the chilly night air. There was a fine sprinkling of aristocracy, industrial leaders, politicians and businessmen sitting alongside other parents with less remarkable careers or privilege.

The first formers had decided that the prize for the most flash motor went to the Darlings of Glasgow who arrived in a silver turbo-charged *Porsche 911* with gull wing doors. Jimmy Darling was more than six feet tall with a long, thin face dominated by a bony nose which looked as though it had been broken several times. There was a scar just below the left side of his bottom lip and another just above his right eyebrow. He looked like a man who did not take kindly to being challenged.

Mrs Shona Darling, a hairdresser by trade and the mother of third former James, was once described as pint-sized by *The Daily Record* tabloid newspaper after she won a wet t-shirt competition promoted by her husband's carwash business. The Darlings were very much 'new money' but held no pretensions about their humble origins.

You got the feeling that whatever hand life had dealt them, the Darlings would have met each other and come together. Despite their tempestuous relationship, there was a bond borne out of adversity that the two enjoyed. Their common love and source of pride was their son James who had all the roguish charm of his father and the fashionable flair and style of his mother but like most ambitious parents, they wanted more for their son.

The prize for the most expensive car was more challenging and was a toss-up between the parents of Muhammad bin Al Wahid bin Awad bin Aboud and the Volkov twins – both arrived at the school in chauffeur driven *Rolls Royces* of similar years and models but the first formers suspected the Russian oligarch's car took the edge because it appeared to be both bomb and bulletproof.

Saudi Sheikh Al Wahid bin Awad bin Aboud emerged from his car dressed in a conservative dark suit tailored in Jermyn Street with his wife, Amina, who wore a simple Chanel navy two-piece with matching emerald green accessories. In terms of style, elegance and fashion, she was only rivalled by Svetlana Volkova who looked equally stunning in a Ralph Lauren navy dress coat with fuchsia accessories topped off with an extravagant white fur hat and wrap.

The Thornberry family arrived in a Bentley Mulsanne and the school caretaker directed it into a space next to Mr Petrie's old Austin Cambridge. Lord Thornberry, accompanied by Lady Jemima, a former top photographic model, stepped out with their younger daughter Cecilia, a rather unfortunate-looking child with a plump frame, big round cheeks and braces.

Moments later, they were joined by George Henry Sparrow and his wife, Eugenie, in a *Range Rover* having driven there from their weekend country retreat overlooking the Mull of Kintyre. "Gosh, it's becoming more of a fashion parade these days instead of a religious service," said Eugenie in sneering tones.

Inside the chapel, there was an air of excitement and expectation as news had begun to filter out some days earlier that one of the Russian parents had donated £250,000 to the school choir. "I think it's a vulgar display of wealth, quite frankly," hissed Eugenie in her husband's ear.

Svetlana Volkova looked even more diminutive as she sat next to her husband, Viktor, who was so broad that he must have taken up to three spaces on the front row pew. He leaned in to his wife and asked: "How much did we give the school choir?" She sighed and opened her order of service, replying tersley: "Why is it always about the money, Viktor?"

The Russian looked up at the wooden beams overhead and smiled. He didn't often smile. He was a very serious character. "My mother used to say that all the time Svetlana when we had nothing, not even a kopek to scratch our…" Svetlana coughed and urged her husband to mind his language in church. Again he smiled.

Meanwhile outside in the car park, another *Range Rover* pulled up with blacked-out windows and, as the door opened, a billow of smoke followed. "Will you put out that bloody spliff and remember where you are and why you're here? Tonight is not about you, Kevin. It's about our Bobby and not making a show, Okay?" It was of course pop star Mickey Grunge and his partner Chrystal Rox.

"How many times have I got to say it? Don't call me Kevin outside of the house!" demanded the singer.

Laying on a thick Yorkshire accent, his wife replied: "Eee, but our lad, that's your name, innit? When I met thee, tha name was Kevin Grimshaw, not Mickey Grunge, and you were the local potman down at the pub in Keighley." The pop star pulled his long hair behind his ears and said: "Okay, okay. I get your drift but if I'm Kevin Grimshaw that makes you, my love, knicker factory machinist Gladys Braithwaite, so think on."

Chrystal Rox sniggered: "Okay, point taken. Just be on your best behaviour. We can manage that for one night only, surely. And take off those bloody sunglasses. It's night time!"

The parents of Bobby Bob Bob wore their most understated clothes and sat towards the back of the little chapel. Minutes later, the teachers and pupils filed in to the reserved rows down one side of the building. They were followed by Constable Jane Rooke who had just finished her shift and was still in police uniform.

She slipped in to the cloakroom at the rear to add some lipstick when a suspicious-looking Crispin Sparrow followed behind. Speaking in a furtive manner he said: "You must be Rooky, yes?" Jane turned around slightly disconcerted at this young man's informal approach and use of her nickname but she nodded in the affirmative.

"You're a bit early, aren't you? Here, take this. Let's call it a modest donation for your police fund in appreciation of duties performed." The pupil glided a brown envelope stuffed with £20 notes by her handbag and was gone before she could respond.

Sparrow nodded across the aisle on spotting his parents as he returned to his seat next to Jacob Thornberry. He leaned over to his friend, while grinning and looking around, and hissed: "We are going to have some fun after the concert. Power Five, Jacob?" The pair laughed, giving each other a fist bump. This certainly was going to be a night to remember.

Just then the lights lowered and a hush descended in the little chapel as a spotlight fell on the Boethius House nativity scene at the front of the altar. The choir rose to its feet and gave a haunting rendition of Once in Royal David's City.

As the evening progressed, the headmaster read a festive lesson and announced Svetlana Volkova's donation and bursary to the school. A ripple of polite applause swept through the chapel but when it hit the Volkov twins, the noise erupted into a thunderous response as the popular brothers encouraged their classmates to show louder appreciation.

Dr Jones followed with the news of the invite to the choir to sing in St Petersburg before making his own special announcement. "We have enjoyed some of the finest choral offerings anyone will hear in this festive season but I am especially excited to introduce our grand finale featuring a young man who has the voice of an angel. Please welcome Duncan Dewar.

Not a noise could be heard as the air filled with nervous anticipation when the lights dimmed into darkness, leaving only a spotlight to search the altar area until it finally landed on Duncan Dewar. He looked nervously around but could see nothing other than the spotlight penetrating his eyes and then he heard the opening bars.

Duncan closed his eyes and began: "Silent night. Holy Night. All is calm. All is bright…" By the time he reached the final chorus, the choir joined in and as he opened his eyes, the lights came back on. There sat his grandfather by Mr Petrie and both men had tears streaming down their faces.

With the exception of a predictable few, there wasn't a dry eye in the pews; even Mickey Grunge was struggling hard to keep a straight face but it was a losing battle as some remnants of eyeliner began to run and streak down his face. The ever-attentive Chrystal rectified this with a clean tissue.

Mr Collins returned to the lectern next to the nativity scene and said: "I think we can all congratulate Dr Jones for this truly wonderful concert and I think many of us will treasure the memory of Duncan Dewar's choral debut.

"While everyone deserves to be credited for tonight's performance, what many of you don't know is that yesterday Duncan had an accident during the annual cross-country run which resulted in him being rushed to hospital, unconscious. As you can see from this evening's performance, he has made a remarkable recovery.

"A large part of that recovery is down to three boys whose brave actions should be rewarded with special certificates of bravery. Please step forward Ninian Swithers, James Darling and Muhammad bin Al Wahid bin Awad bin Aboud. Your life saving skills and tenacity will be rewarded with scrolls of courage, extra points for your houses and £50 book tokens."

This was a most unexpected interlude. Ninian Swithers looked around for his parents as he stepped forward. Both Thomas and Elizabeth Swithers who served in the diplomatic service, normally kept a low profile but they stood up and applauded their son along with their younger daughter Veronica as he received his scroll – the school's highest honour.

James Darling was beyond shame and threw his arms in the air like an Olympian as he walked towards Dr Collins to receive his scroll. Jimmy Darling stood up and shouted: "That's my boy!" And then he looked around and urged other parents to cheer him on, which they did with gusto rather than inflame him.

Muhammad was last to receive his award and his father, sitting in the front row, looked on approvingly but in a more dignified and less exuberant manner than the carwash entrepreneur who was still on his feet, urging parents to cheer.

As the boys sat down, Dr Collins said: "Can I now invite all of our guests to partake in a little sherry and festive fare in the main school building? Our pupils from the first and second years will escort you to the building but please be careful how you go. There's ice on the ground and while we've salted the pathways, conditions are still challenging."

***

Chapter 15

As the parents filed out of the chapel, uniformed police constable Jane Rooke sat on the aisle side of the last pew smiling at everyone as they walked by. She couldn't help but notice her presence had an unsettling effect on some including celebrity couple Chrystal Rox and Mickey Grunge.

"What did you do with my spliff?" he asked his wife as they got out of earshot.

"I put it inside my beehive. It'll be safe there but if you have anything else on you, you'd better go straight to the bog and flush it. We can't get busted at Bobby's school, he'd never forgive us."

Jimmy Darling was also slightly perturbed and revealed to his wife: "I didn't have time to tax the new motor. Do you think that's why she's here? The last thing I want is the Old Bill sniffing around in front of all those posh folk trying to make a show of us."

She tutted and said: "I knew we should've just come in the *Mercedes*, but no, Jimmy Darling wanted to play the big man and show off.

"We can't impress this crowd, Jimmy. We're not like them and they're not like us. That flaming Lady Whatshername looked at me as though she'd just spotted some dog dirt on my Manolo Blahniks! It doesn't matter how much money we have, those lot will never treat us as equals. I couldn't care less, love, and you should be the same. Stuff 'em. Stuff 'em all."

Jimmy Darling looked down at his feisty wife and said: "What the frig has Barry Manilow to do with this?"

Looking at him, she said: "Manolo, Manolo… Manolo Blahniks, my bloody shoes you noodle."

Her husband looked down seemingly unimpressed at his wife's feet, adding: "Very nice."

Meanwhile, Svetlana Volkova nudged her husband on spotting the policewoman and whispered: “I hope you are not carrying Viktor.” The big Russian looked uncomfortable as he felt inside his suit jacket and reassured his wife that ‘our PSS friend is in the glove compartment’.

“For goodness sake, Viktor, nobody is going to try anything in Sweetheart Abbey. We are safe here,” said Svetlana.

Dr Jones hurried down the aisle swatting away a couple of first formers, so he could personally escort Svetlana and Viktor to the reception. He couldn’t entrust his benefactors to anyone else but as the three walked towards the door, Jane Rooke stood up and waited for them to pass. Then, to the consternation of Viktor Volkov, she tapped him on the shoulder and said: “Just a moment of your time, sir. Have you mislaid something?”

The broad-shouldered Russian tensed as his wife began pulling on a strand of her blonde hair. They both slowly turned around and looked puzzled as the policewoman waved something white in front of them: “Your handkerchief, I presume? It is initialled VV?”

Svetlana broke the uneasy silence and smiled, saying: “Thank you, officer. Viktor show your appreciation.” He pulled out a money clip stuffed with £50 notes and Jane’s eyes widened: “Really, there’s no need. It seems everyone wants to give me money tonight.”

She then handed over the silk handkerchief to Viktor and walked towards Dr Jones. “Thank you for giving me a ticket for tonight’s performance. I really enjoyed it, although apologies for still being in uniform. I didn’t have time to change. Otherwise I would’ve been very late.”

“But the night is not yet over Constable. Please do come and join us in The Caledonian Suite. Now that you’re off duty, I’m sure you could have a wee dram, as we say in Scotland,” said Dr Jones. And with that, the group headed towards the main school.

Jane Rooke was secretly pleased. She wanted to solve the mystery of the brown envelope and was fascinated by the assembled group of parents, an eclectic mix of people many of whom seemed to have something to hide. ‘What are their guilty secrets?’ she mused as she walked towards the main building.

Once inside, she went over to Duncan Dewar who, by this time, was standing next to his grandfather and Mr Petrie. "My, you all look a picture in your kilts. Duncan, I was enchanted by your voice – who knew you had that inside of you?"

Duncan could feel himself blushing. "How are you feeling after the accident?"

Duncan stammered: "Yes, yes, I'm fine. I'm glad you liked the performance. I didn't know you were coming tonight," he commented.

"No, me neither. It was a spur of the moment decision but I'm glad I did."

Gordon Buie chimed in: "I'm glad you came too, my dear. I just wanted to thank you and the other emergency services team for saving my grandson's life. If everyone had not acted so quickly the outcome could've been so different. Please pass on my appreciation to your superiors. I will be writing anyway but now that you're here, let me get you a drink."

The clockmaker and his grandson headed towards the informal bar leaving the officer with Mr Petrie. She said: "For a moment, I thought I was going to be offered more money. It's been quite a night of donations," she laughed.

Mr Petrie moved his head to one side and said: "Really? Please do expand." And so, she told him about the pupil who gave her an envelope in the chapel cloakroom 'as a show of appreciation for your police work' while Mr Volkov produced an eye-watering wedge of cash after she found his handkerchief.

His curiosity now aroused, he prompted her: "What did the boy in the cloakroom look like? Maybe I can help solve the mystery." Looking around the room, she said: "Well, he was very distinctive. He had a shock of blond hair and I'm sure he'll be easy enough to spot. In fact there he is," she said nodding in the direction of Crispin Thornberry.

"Ah yes, Crispin, the future Lord Thornberry destined to be head of one of the most influential families in the UK. How public spirited of him!" he said with an enigmatic smile.

A few yards away, Jimmy Darling was chastising his son James over the so-called 'soapgate' affair. "How many times have I told you not to get caught?"

The boy looked at his father and protested: "But I didn't get caught. Och Aye McKie only suspected some wrongdoing and he tried to call your bluff but I understand you kicked that in to touch because you're far too smart for him."

Mr Darling was about to start grinning when he noticed a steely look from his wife: "Yes, well, it could've backfired. Don't put yourself in the frame again because people like that master get obsessive and before you know it, they're there, around every corner waiting for you to slip."

Shona Darling interrupted: "Let's talk about nicer things. I was so proud of you, James, when I heard you'd saved that boy's life, so proud. Tell me what happened and don't spare the detail. I want to enjoy every wee scrap." James smiled awkwardly and skipped the fact he'd been loitering in the local cafe when Ninian burst in to raise the alarm.

After he finished his story Shona went off to the cloakroom to reapply her lipstick when Jimmy Darling leaned down and said in his son's ear: "You've made your mum proud but I'm not as gullible as she. I've given the police enough statements in my life to know when someone's telling porkies. I don't want to know son, either. That's another of life's lessons: Keep people on a need-to-know basis only but I'm telling you now that story has more holes in it than a Swiss cheese and is ten times smellier.

"I hope that copper over there isn't here for any reason other than she likes a good Christmas Carol followed by a wee dram and small talk. Stay out of her way and keep that shut," he said, pointing to his own mouth.

James looked up at his dad with an overwhelming sense of pride. He might not have been blessed with a great education but he reckoned few in the room could outsmart his old man.

"What I want to know is why you're not in the choir? I've heard you singing around the house, son, and you've got a great voice," said Mickey Grunge. "Well, Dad, it's like this. You are probably the coolest dude in the room, the lead singer in an international band with zillions of sales and adoring fans around the world. Have you any idea what the pressure would be like for me?

"I don't want to be on any stage. Look at the life you lead and the circus that follows you and Mum around? Would you really want that for me?" asked Bobby Bob Bob.

Mickey Grunge nodded sagely: "Yes, it's all a bit mad innit? But it's just like weird me sitting there listening to someone else's son sing when I was thinking why isn't it our Bobby?"

Chrystal Rox dug her husband in the ribs: "Are you deaf? He's just explained it, hasn't he? Our son is good with his brains. He's an athlete, loves football and is the school rugby captain. He don't want to sing and I don't blame him. We're hardly perfect role models, are we?"

Bobby Bob Bob laughed and said: "Hey guys, don't get so heavy. You know I love you both to bits and you are the coolest parents at Sweetheart. C'mon old man, lighten up." Mickey Grunge nodded enthusiastically and patted his son on the back and as he did so, he looked around catching Jane Rooke's eye.

"Hey Bobby, if you're so clever, why's that peeler giving me the evils?"

He looked around and caught the policewoman quickly glance in another direction. "I dunno, maybe she's a fan, Dad. Ever thought of that? But erm, you haven't brought anything into the school, have you?" Both parents shook their heads looking quite guilty and leaving their son a little bit unconvinced.

The awkward silence broke when Dr Collins announced festivities had come to an end as had the term and he wished everyone a seasonal farewell. "Those boys who are staying overnight should make their way back to their houses and we'll see your parents tomorrow. Everyone else, have a safe journey and we will see you in the New Year."

Dr Collins stood by the entrance shaking hands with each set of parents as they left. Lord Thornberry walked down the steps with Lady Jemima and Cecilia by his side and waved over at the Sparrows who were about to get into their *Range Rover* when, out of the shadows a policewoman carrying a large box walked over to where his Bentley was parked and shouted: "Who does this motor belong to?!"

Lord Thornberry raised his voice slightly: "Oh, that's mine officer. Is there a problem?"

The tall, willowy blonde policewoman strode over and said: “There most certainly is. The tax is out of date and I suspect you’ve been drinking, sir.”

His lordship looked aghast and horrified as by this time the focus of pupils, parents and teachers were on him. “Now look here, officer. I want your name, rank and number. Do you know who I am?”

The policewoman marched up to him, put down her box and put her hand on her hips: “So you want to know who I am? Well, I’ll tell you. I’m Rookie Blue and you are so busted!” She then pulled off her cap to reveal a mop of long, blonde hair and ripped off her uniform exposing an ample bosom trapped inside a silk and lace black and red basque, stockings and tartan garters. Bending down in a theatrical way, she pressed a button on the wireless box with her extremely long, red acrylic nails and suddenly the rap music of KRS-One’s ‘Sound of Da Police’ started pumping out.

While the lyrics and music might have been alien to stunned, onlooking staff and parents – with the exception of Mickey Grunge who by this time was dancing on the steps and waving his arms in the air – boy gamers familiar with the computer game Battlefield Hardline recognised the track immediately.

Lord Thornberry stood motionless like a rabbit trapped in the headlights, open-mouthed, as Rookie Blue then proceeded to crack a long leather whip she pulled from one of her garters and said: “Come on then, your Lordship, who’s been a naughty boy then?”

Cecilia Thornberry shouted: “Daddy, what’s going on?!” Lady Thornberry followed up with another question, demanding to know: “Who is this woman? Why is she doing this?”

Mickey Grunge, still swaying and rocking, turned to his wife and said: “This is quite a floor show Rox and we’re not in it but I think I quite like being on the sidelines for once.”

Eugenie Sparrow looked horrified and whispered to her husband: “Do something, George. You’re his lawyer,” but he snapped back: “She’s not a real police officer, you silly woman. She appears to be a strippergram. This is supposed to be a prank but it’s in extremely bad taste.”

Crispin Sparrow and Jacob Thornberry both rose slowly from the side of Mr Petrie's Austin Cambridge which was parked next to the Bentley. Peering wide-eyed over the bonnet, Crispin Sparrow wailed: "Oh my God, something terrible has happened. That is not the tart I gave the money."

"No, the tart you gave the money to was me, young man! PC Rooke not to be confused with the curvaceous WPC Rookie Blue and her wireless beat box!"

Sparrow turned around and saw Jane Rooke standing behind him. "You bloody muppet, Crispin!" screamed Jacob Thornberry. His hysterical loud outburst coincided with the very second the music was switched off and so was heard by everyone.

Now all eyes were on the real policewoman and the two guilty schoolboys as Rookie Blue shouted: "Will someone tell me what the hell is going on?! This is the last time I'm coming here. You're all a bunch of bloody freaks. First I'm told to go for the guy with an Austin Cambridge and then there's a last minute call to say dance for the Lord bloke with the Bentley. Well, I don't care anymore. I just want paying."

Pulling the brown envelope out of her bag, Jane Rooke said in a terse, commanding tone: "Here, Crispin! Take this and pay the woman and then you can explain why you wanted to humiliate the father of your best friend."

Dr Liam Wallace tilted his whole body slightly towards Dr Gideon McKie from their position near the entrance and said: "This is not a great day for Pythagoras House. Are you going to tell Professor McIntosh, or should I?"

Dr McKie retorted: "I think we both should but not just yet; in the interests of accuracy, I think we have a duty to remain just in case any more salient facts emerge."

Just then, Dr Jones emerged from The Caledonian Suite with Svetlana, Viktor and the twins and all looked on with bemused expressions as rugby master Mr Swain shouted: "I think the floor show is over for now and there's nothing more to see! Safe journey home, everyone."

Dr Jones looked around asking: "What have we missed? What was that awful screeching noise?"

Dr Collins turned to the choirmaster and said: "You've missed nothing but allow me to congratulate you once again for producing a concert beyond comparison. I think we have all been given a reminder tonight that exceptional music is a joy to the ears. I'm sure the choir will do us proud in St Petersburg and hopefully make our benefactors equally proud they chose to invest in such a way."

Svetlana beamed at such praise coming from the fearsome master while Viktor Volkov remained po-faced. His eyes were on the policewoman Jane Rooke who by this time walked back up the steps and headed towards the ladies washroom.

"Well, Sweetheart was never like this in my day, Mr Petrie. What just happened?" Sporting a mischievous look on his face and catching Duncan's eyes, he said: "I will tell you the whole story over a glass of single malt in Dulce Cor. Let's say goodnight to your grandson. It's been an eventful day and an interesting evening."

Crispin Sparrow was still frozen to the spot when Dr Wallace went over and snatched the brown envelope out of his hand, whispering: "You've got some explaining to do to your father, young man. I suggest you get to it now and in double quick order."

He then looked around and saw the angry Rookie Blue glaring at everyone. "I think this belongs to you, my dear," he said handing her the envelope. "Follow me and I will see you off the premises. This has been a most unfortunate incident."

As they walked towards the driveway, she said: "Hang on a minute, buster. I'm not walking home in these heels. You better get me a taxi."

Dr Wallace smiled and said: "I can do better than that, my dear. Let me take you home. Follow me. My car is just over there." The Plato head looked over his shoulder and caught Dr Andrew Collins staring back. The headmaster then nodded very slightly as if to signal his relief and approval that someone was taking the initiative to remove the strippergram quickly and without fuss.

Back in the female cloakroom, Chrystal Rox emerged from one of the toilet cubicles and began to wash her hands when she developed a series of sneezes. Jane Rooke emerged from the adjoining cubicle just as Chrystal gave one last violent sneeze.

As she recovered her poise, she asked Jane Rooke about what had happened. "Trust me, you really would not want to know," smiled Jane as she dried her hands. She then looked strangely at her and gently put her arms around Chrystal positioning her back in front of the oval mirror.

"See anything unusual?" Chrystal looked at her reflection and was about to say no when she saw something long and white literally hanging by a hair from her beehive.

During the coughing fit, she had managed to dislodge the giant spliff. "What the…well, I really don't know where that came from. It's certainly not mine. Here, officer, you take it for safe keeping." And with that, Chrystal beat a hasty retreat from a mildly amused Jane Rooke.

Later that evening, Jane regaled her elder brother with the whole story of her last forty-eight hours at Sweetheart. "I can't believe you met Mickey Grunge. He's like the coolest man in the whole world."

Jane laughed and pulled on her brother's hair: "Unlike you, bro! Aren't you a bit old for dreadlocks and a rainbow beanie hat?"

Ignoring her jibes at his hipster looks, he said: "What an exciting life you lead, sis, and I thought it would be all paperwork, parking tickets and persecuting the people. The only mystery now is what happened to the spliff?"

"Well," said Jane: "I thought I'd save the best till last because I know you like to recycle." And with that, she produced the cannabis joint from her bag.

Chapter 16

As promised, the Volkov blue and gold liveried jet flew into Edinburgh Airport two days before New Year's Eve and taxied to an apron near the VIP lounge. The jet was being prepared and refuelled to take Sweetheart's choir to St Petersburg when the excited boys arrived in a series of chauffeur-driven limousines at the terminal normally reserved for VIPs.

When it came to expense, Svetlana Volkova appeared to have a blank cheque as nothing was spared for the school choir which, over the years, had been last in the queue when it came to grants and handouts.

Dr Geraint Jones waited anxiously outside the VIP car park to supervise the unloading of the luggage and musical instruments from the Sweetheart Abbey bus. Douglas Sinclair, the school gardener, had volunteered to load and drive the mini bus and its precious cargo including the choir's traditional tartan dress.

"It all has to clear security first but I'm told it will be just a formality," advised Dr Jones as the gardener unloaded the bus contents onto some large security trolleys. "Well, all the instruments are in hard-backed cases so they'll be well protected in the hold and I've put the Skhean Dhus in that box over there to be checked-in as they are classified as restricted.

"I'm sure everything should go smoothly to clear security," added Sinclair.

Dr Jones looked at the gardener with mild surprise: "It seems there's more to you than lawns and flowering perennials."

The gardener, a handsome man in his forties, smiled: "You could say I've had some experience of the airline industry and maybe I'll tell you about it one day."

The choirmaster was curious but not enough to divert his attention from the forthcoming trip to Russia, although he was polite enough to enquire: "Did you have a good Christmas?"

The gardener responded: "Very quiet, I spent it at the cottage I have in the grounds; quite close to Mr Petrie and I think he was home alone too as I bumped into him on Boxing Day taking a walk to the village. Let me know the exact time of your return and I will be here to collect the luggage. Season's greetings to you and the boys."

Inside the airport, the choir members were chattering excitedly as they queued to go through security. Joining them was Duncan Dewar's grandfather, Gordon Buie, who was looking slightly apprehensive.

"He's never flown before and neither have I," said Duncan. "So this is all new to us," he told John Russell.

"And I thought it was because you were leaving Ninian Swithers behind," retorted Russell who then looked around and asked: "Where are the Bogofs?"

Duncan smiled: "We are meeting the Volkov twins in St Petersburg along with their family.

"Apparently this Gulf Stream jet can only carry fourteen passengers and since there's a dozen of us plus my granddad and Dr Jones, they decided they'd meet us over there. They were already in Moscow for Christmas, so it's no big deal," said Duncan.

Unlike the usual slightly chaotic festive scenes in the general airport area, the atmosphere in the VIP lounge that morning for those boarding private jets was much more sedate and calm. Dr Jones summoned the Sweetheart party together and bellowed: "Our luggage is going through security now, so follow me boys. Take off your coats and jackets and anything loose like scarves and put them in the plastic boxes along with any phones, tablets, computer games and laptops. Now form an orderly queue and walk through the scanner when the security officer beckons you.

"Hold on! Someone's missing. Has anyone seen Willie Carmichael?"

The boys all giggled and shouted in one voice: "Where's Willie?!" Just then, he emerged from behind a bookstand with an extraordinarily large gobstopper in his mouth and opened his arms in a begging expression as if to ask what all the fuss was about. Dr Jones scowled at him and muttered: “My final words on this godforsaken planet will probably be: ‘Where’s Willie?’ Now get in line, boy!”

All twelve boys stood behind Dr Jones and Gordon Buie. The old man walked through first feeling deeply uncomfortable as he’d overheard pupils claiming that security officers could see right through passengers’ clothes on their screens. Just in case they were right, he cupped his hands in front of himself like footballers do to protect themselves when trying to block a free kick.

As Duncan walked through the scanner, the machine emitted a loud bleep and he was told to remove his shoes and go back through. Again another loud bleep and so he was asked to stand to one side while a hand scanner was swept over his body.

Feeling deeply self-conscious by now, the portable scanner emitted a loud bleep as it passed over his head, prompting James Darling to shout: “I see you’ve found the zip in the back of his head, then!” Dr Jones glowered at Darling and again the scanner emitted a bleep.

Gordon Buie called over: “He was in hospital recently and an X-ray showed a metal chip from a previous car accident was lodged in the nape of his neck. You can see the area if you look closely but it’s not bigger than a freckle.”

Reassured by this news, the airport security allowed Duncan through, but by this time his face was several shades of red with embarrassment. “Granddad, did you have to tell everyone I’ve got a chunk of metal in my head? Russell will have my life for this,” he whispered.

Dr Jones rounded up the pupils and said: “Who here has heard of the buddy system?”

Most hands shot up as he replied: “Good. Pick your buddy or your partner and make sure you don’t lose sight of them.”

Some of the boys looked slightly lost so an exasperated Dr Jones said: “Do I have to do everything myself? Okay. Russell, Darling you’re a couple. The two gingers are also a pair as are you two.” He then went through the remainder of the group in the same brusque manner pairing off the boys and then added: “If you have any problems, see me or Mr Buie. We will be given an additional two Russian-English-speaking guides in St Petersburg, but the general rule is: 'Stick with your buddy' and you won't get lost."

None of the boys had been on a private flight before and gasped at the luxurious interior of the Volkov's jet with its deep pile carpets and soft, creamy leather seating with solid walnut panel surrounds. As they took their seats, they were offered a variety of freshly squeezed fruit juices and some small nibbles including caviar and crème fraîche-topped blinis.

John Russell turned to James Darling and asked what they were. "I think it's caviar, which is a posh word for fish eggs. Thornberry and Sparrow probably bathe in this stuff. Imagine if they could see us now, I think they'd be green with envy."

Russell retorted: "Even if they did sing in the choir, I reckon they'd be grounded after that stunt with the policewoman. I'm sorry James but your 'soapgate' is starting to look like amateur night at the opera after their Oscar-winning stunt. 'Rookiegate' will go down as one of Sweetheart's legends; that's for sure." Russell and Darling curled up laughing as they recalled the stripper ripping open her bodice in front of Lord Thornberry.

"Do you think old Petrie set them up?" asked Darling. "That was the rumour going around."

Russell laughed out loud: "Oh, come of it! That old fossil? I'm telling you now there's no way Mr Petrie would have got himself embroiled in a stunt with a stripper. No, I reckon the real policewoman got wind of it and set up Thornberry and Sparrow."

Overhearing the conversation, Gordon Buie looked at his grandson and gave a knowing smile. "It's a pity Mr Petrie's not on this trip. I would've enjoyed his company," he whispered to Duncan. The boy gave his grandfather a weak grin as his mind was on his maiden flight and he was nervous.

After a few minutes, they were over the skies of Edinburgh and marvelled at the view below. "Such a beautiful city, although I'd rather be walking down Princes Street now than flying over it," said Gordon.

Once it was safe to remove their seatbelts and relax a little more, one of the two male stewards with a lapel badge marked 'Sergei' began dispensing gifts to all of the boys as well as Dr

Jones and Mr Buie. Each was told: "A small token of appreciation from the Volkovs." There were whoops of excited chatter as the parcels were ripped open followed by gasps and silent admiration before more whoops of joy followed.

Inside each box was a *Vertu Mobile Handset* covered in a blue lagoon calf-leather skin with titanium grade sides. All the latest technology including a built in clock face, front facing and rear camera and unique alert tones performed by the London Symphony Orchestra were contained within the phones.

As most of the boys began assembling and disassembling their new phones and add-ons, Duncan and his grandfather sat back and neatly unfolded the wrapping paper. Like two peas in a pod, they opened the box and removed the start-up guide and warranty booklets to study in detail. Dr Jones leant over to Gordon Buie and said: "You know this would cost me more than two month's salary. I'm flabbergasted and normally I'd have to refuse such an extravagance, but I would hate to cause offence to our Russian hosts."

Mr Buie raised his eyebrows in surprise and confided to Duncan: "I'm still not sure what it is. Is it a travel clock, a mobile phone or is it a camera or a video recorder?"

His grandson grinned and said: "It's all that and so much more but I don't think I'll be taking this to school. Imagine if I lost it, or it got broken," he added.

Sergei knelt before the two and said: "Here, let me set it up for you, young man, because I know Mrs Volkova wants the phones powered up and ready to go for when you land. There, now when we arrive, just switch that button on and this one off and you are ready to use it."

As the air steward rose to his feet, he told the others: "You can use your phones freely during your stay in St Petersburg and the bill will be paid for by the Volkov Corporation, so there's really no need to worry about phone usage." As he returned to the small luxury on-board kitchen, he told his colleague: "Everyone has their phone and by the time they land, they'll be in full use. I guarantee it. I've switched on the old man's mobile and the grandson is up and ready as well. They won't be able to travel anywhere without us knowing about it first."

Thanks to the luxury gifts, time passed very quickly on board the jet and, after a substantial lobster and steak meal, the six-hour flight was nearing its end. Each boy took his turn visiting the flight deck for selfies before it was time for landing at Pulkovo international airport. The landing was smooth and as the passenger door swept open, a red-carpeted portable staircase leading down to the tarmac was wheeled alongside and attached to the jet.

As the boys and adults disembarked, they were hit by air so cold; it was like a slap across the face however, unlike the Scottish climate, the temperature was well below sub-zero but not damp. A fleet of blacked out limousines awaited at Pulkovo International to take the group off into St Petersburg and on to the luxury, five-star Kempinski Hotel overlooking the frozen Moika River.

The journey would normally take about fifteen minutes without traffic, but by 2 pm the roads to St Petersburg were congested. As the small party from Sweetheart was ushered into the vast, elegantly decorated lobby, an hour later the boys gasped and gawked in awe of their surrounds. Each was given a glass of non-alcoholic mulberry punch and handfuls of caramelised almonds as they were urged to sit down while Dr Jones went through the check-in procedure.

However, when Willie Carmichael spotted a great gingerbread miniature of the hotel, he instantly scrambled to his feet and ran over to inspect the edible model structure. “Dewar, return to your seat and sit still until I’m finished,” ordered Dr Jones.

“But sir, I’m over here,” protested Duncan who was sat on a sofa next to Darling, Russell and his grandfather. They all looked in Carmichael’s direction as he was about to do a taste test on the elaborate structure.

“Carmichael! Hands off and back to your seat, now!” ordered Dr Jones who muttered to himself: “I didn’t realise we had two gingers in the choir until today.”

By this time, Russians Sergei and Vlad, the stewards on the jet flight, joined Dr Jones at the reception desk informing him they had been assigned to the party to act as guides and translators.

"If there is anything you want, no matter how small, please Dr Jones, do not hesitate to ask. I am on the speed dial 1 and Vlad is on 2. Pass over your cell and I will show you how it works," said Sergei on seeing the choirmaster's flustered expression. "Mrs Volkova will host a dinner this evening on the ninth floor which is the Bellevue Brasserie. It would be nice if your choir dressed smartly for the occasion. I will furnish you with the full details later."

The boys were given rooms on the eighth floor with panoramic views of the city overlooking the Hermitage Museum, a former winter palace for the czars. Most could see the spires for the Church on Spilled Blood from where they would perform their concert at the event sponsored by the Volkov Corporation on New Year's Eve.

Three of the rooms – all adjoining – contained two sets of twin beds each, while Duncan and his grandfather had their own, larger deluxe suite and Dr Jones had a room nearby. Bowls of fruits and sweets and arrangements of fresh flowers adorned every room to make the Sweetheart choir feel welcome.

"Slacks, white shirts and school blazers tonight, boys," instructed Dr Jones. "Our host Mrs Volkova has invited us to dinner on the ninth floor in an hour's time. I want everyone on their best behaviour. Tomorrow we'll hold rehearsals in a room on the ground floor of the hotel and, by late afternoon, there may even be time to enjoy the sights."

That evening, there was a flurry of activity as the hotel manager greeted the Volkov family as they swept into the reception area along with more than half a dozen surly looking men in the security detail.

The boys were all seated in the brasserie awaiting their host when two burly looking men arrived at the restaurant entrance and two more stood by the lift. Just then the glass elevator glided into vision, stopping at the ninth floor to allow Svetlana, Viktor and their two sons to disembark.

Dr Jones rushed forward and the boys all took to their feet and began applauding the family as they walked to their table as a show of appreciation. Svetlana beamed and smiled at all of the boys, holding their gaze with her almond-shaped eyes while

Viktor, less effusive, nodded curtly before taking a seat next to Duncan.

"I'm told you will be the star of the concert on New Year's Eve," said Viktor in a low voice as he leaned towards the boy. Duncan replied: "Oh I don't know about that, sir. But I will do my best." Svetlana sat next to Dr Jones while the twins took seats with the rest of the choir. "We're also staying at the hotel tonight," Andrei told James Darling. "By the way, did you like your phones?" he asked. James responded: "O-M-G Andrei, you have no idea! Such a sick gift, insane, just insane." The young Russian laughed: "Alexei and I thought you'd be happy. You're such a poser we knew you'd like it."

Across the table Viktor was asking Duncan the same question and he replied enthusiastically: "An amazing piece of technology. I'm still reading up on the specifications and maximum potential before I activate it and familiarise myself practically with the multi functions." Viktor looked at Duncan in despair and rattled his fingers anxiously across the table, then added: "Use it, just use it and find out how it works by trial and error. It's no use having a phone if you're not going to use it."

Although the meal was informal Dr Jones still managed not to miss an opportunity to squeeze in a speech in praise of the Volkovs and thanked the Russian hosts for their sponsorship. At the end of the meal the party vacated the restaurant and chose to walk down to the next floor to their rooms.

Viktor pulled Andrei aside and said: "Make sure Duncan Dewar has his phone switched on and in his pocket by tomorrow morning."

As everyone went to their rooms half a dozen security officers spread across the eighth floor which was reserved exclusively for the Sweetheart Choir and their hosts. "Well so much for midnight adventures and sneaking out. It's like being in a five star prison," moaned James Darling. "I'm going to have a word with Alexei and Andrei tomorrow to see what the chances are of escaping. I'll go stir crazy if I'm trapped in here for the entire trip with The Drak!"

Chapter 17

The boys awoke early the next day due to a combination of excitement and wrestling with the two-hour time difference following their journey from Edinburgh. Although the temperature was below six degrees centigrade outside, the warmth in the bedrooms felt almost Caribbean by comparison.
James Darling, wearing a plain grey t-shirt and striped pyjama bottoms, popped his head around the room door before slamming it shut and returning to his bed. "Crikey! Those goons are still outside. We're definitely going to have to work out a plan if we want to explore the city. The Bogofs will have some ideas, I'm sure." Most of the others had gathered in Darling's room as he was regarded as one of the school's 'populars'.

"Yes, but we have guides and we'll be taken around on a tour bus so we don't get lost," said the studious-looking Andrew Richard Sinclair-Edwards. "That's the whole point. We don't want to see the touristy version of St Petersburg. I want to see the red-light district. You know all the naughty bits that Drac is going to do his utmost to prevent us from seeing.

"Remember last year's trip to Amsterdam? Tulips, clogs, Anne Frank's house and the Van Gogh Museum. The naughtiest city in the world and we were treated like choir boys!"

Sinclair-Edwards, adjusting his tortoiseshell and gold round glasses, said loftily: "Well, I found the Keukenhof Gardens inspiring and an illustration of Dutch orderliness and precision. Where else could you see millions of tulips, narcissi, daffodils, hyacinths and bluebells blossom, all in such perfect order? And I felt the tour at the Delftse Pauw factory particularly instructive…" Poor Williams didn't get a chance to finish as several of the others barked their favourite refrain: "Shut up,

Arse!" The boy was used to such verbal abuse and just soaked it up; his father Sir Anthony Richard, a Westminster MP, once reassured his son that while the acronym produced by his name was unfortunate, there was a family tradition to uphold, pointing out he came from 'a long line of Arses!' Most of whom had distinguished army careers followed by a stint in the London parliament before 'retiring to the House of Lords'.

The Volkov twins arrived unseen in the middle of the increasingly heated debate but they all fell silent as Alexei interrupted: "You have to remember you are choir boys. We're all choirboys! This is typical of you and your disruptive behaviour, Darling. You come to the most beautiful city in the world, the cultural centre of Russia, the greatest country in the world and you want a hooker! There is no red-light district here, although admittedly there are escorts.

"But be warned! If you break the law in Russia and are caught, it could prove difficult even for a guest of the Volkov family," added Andrei who adopted a more serious tone.

James Darling shook his head and said: "How can I break the law? Prostitution is not illegal here. I've checked it out. What is a problem is the security your parents have given us. We can't move without them."

Andrei laughed: "Sex under sixteen is illegal and if you don't have one of these, you'll be stuck," he said, pulling an ID card from his jeans pocket and waving it in the air. "Furthermore, if you blunder in to the less glamorous clubs, you're likely to get a knock out sedative slipped in to your drink so if you did lose your virginity, you'd probably not even remember!"

Everyone started laughing out loud as the Volkov brothers high fived each other followed by double fist bumps. Darling, who wasn't used to being so publicly undermined and upstaged, felt decidedly uncool and was grateful when Duncan Dewar tapped gently on the inter-connecting door and walked in to announce: "Dr Jones wants us at breakfast by 8:30 am with rehearsals beginning an hour later."

Duncan and his grandfather were already seated and eating Russian Kasha, a version of porridge, when the rest of the group tumbled in with Dr Jones bringing up the rear. As they ate their way through assorted croissants, cheese and fresh fruit, most of the boys were preoccupied with their new phones, snapping pictures and posting them on the social networks.

"I was going to ban the damned things but then Alexei Volkov told me his mother might be upset if the gifts were hidden away. It's quite a dilemma and a fine balance but they're definitely not coming in to rehearsals," said Dr Jones as he saw the look of disdain and despair on Gordon Buie's face. "We're divided, aren't we, from those who read newspapers and watch TV on the box to those who communicate via mobile phones, tablets and computer screens," sighed the old man.

"Well, it comes in handy some times," said Dr Jones as he pulled out a computer stick from his pocket. "This little devil has the sound of a full orchestra and will be used to support our concert. It's like travelling with a full compliment from the Royal Scottish National Orchestra. So, not all bad, eh, Mr Buie?"

Throughout the morning and early afternoon, the choirmaster put the Sweetheart choristers through their paces and finally let them go, with the exception of Duncan, for a late lunch. Vlad and Sergei were sitting at a desk outside the rehearsal room when the door swung open without warning and the boys stampeded out heading for the restaurant.

As their official escort, Gordon Buie was caught slightly off guard in the rush for the door and only just managed to grab Willy Carmichael. "Just slow down, young man. Let's go in an orderly fashion."

Carmichael grimaced, announcing: "You only grabbed me because I've got ginger hair. We always stand out in the crowd. It's not fair."

Mr Buie laughed and said: "Don't be so daft, laddie. The others were too slippery and you weren't quick enough, but you are Duncan's buddy and in his absence, I'm yours! Anyway they can't start without us, so just be patient. I'm not as quick on my feet."

Vlad and Sergei were apprehensive as they scanned the restaurant trying to count the boys but looked more relaxed on seeing Mr Buie walk in with Willy Carmichael. "There's the grandfather and the kid. No slips-ups as we cannot afford to let them out of our sight," urged Vlad.

After lunch, Sergei stood up and announced: "Dr Jones is keen for you all to see the Church of the Saviour on the Spilled Blood where the concert will be performed. Who would like to go?" he asked, and immediately all hands went up.

The two Russians led the way with Gordon Buie positioning himself at the end of the Sweetheart crocodile alongside Willy Carmichael as the boys walked to the Moscow-style church a few minutes from the Kempinski. As it loomed large before them, the richly coloured onion domes looked slightly incongruous in the very European setting of St Petersburg.

The boys sniggered every time Sergei mentioned the name of the church because it sounded so awkward. "Why doesn't he just say the church where Emperor Alexander II was murdered?" asked Darling.

Andrei Volkov snapped: "Because he didn't die on that spot but his blood was spilled in the attack. Not everything has to have a western tabloid headline, James.

"Anyway, most of the locals here call it 'the mosaic church' because the interior is covered with the most magnificent mosaics. You'll see when we get inside."

Gordon Buie admired his knowledge and added: "Who needs a guide when we have you Alexei, or is it Andrei? Either way, I'm impressed."

Meanwhile back at the hotel, Dr Jones told Duncan Dewar he was satisfied that, after spending the last hour going through the lyrics to the seven verses of Walking in the Air, his precious soprano was word perfect. By the time they got to the hotel restaurant, the rest of the choir had left for the church where the concert would be held the following evening.

"Let's eat anyway and then we'll catch up with them," said Dr Jones and Duncan, who was really hungry, nodded in agreement.

Once inside the church, the Sweetheart group agreed to meet back at the entrance thirty minutes later, giving them enough time to explore and marvel at the riches on offer. Each of the magnificent mosaics on the walls had a Biblical theme but all the boys gravitated to the spot where Czar Nicholas was fatally wounded by revolutionaries.

"It seems they built this church on top of the spot to commemorate him. It's a pity Duncan's not here to see this, although I'm sure he and Dr Jones will catch up later," Gordon Buie said to Willy Carmichael. Reading from an English guidebook, neither Mr Buie nor Carmichael noticed they were being followed around the building. The two drifted towards the tourist booths looking at the souvenirs on offer.

A small group of American tourists were led in to the church by their English-speaking tour guide as he explained how on March 13, 1881 an anarchist threw a grenade at the Czar's passing carriage. "Czar Alexander was a little shaken but he jumped out of the carriage and challenged the bomb thrower. While an argument developed, a second conspirator took the opportunity of throwing another bomb, killing himself and fatally wounding the Czar. He died a few hours later in the nearby Winter Palace," explained the guide.

Mr Buie grabbed hold of Carmichael and whispered: "We may as well try and earwig this, since he's speaking our language and then we'll go and find the others." As they moved in closer to the gaggle of Americans, the guide explained how a temporary shrine emerged on the site of the attack.

"It was decided to build a permanent shrine on the exact spot and a freestanding canopy, called a ciborium, was erected at the end of the church opposite the altar."

The group moved towards the shrine which was embellished extravagantly with semi-precious stones. "See, look here. There is quite a contrast as you can still see the original cobblestones of the old road on which the Czar's carriage travelled."

The group moved in closer and Gordon Buie turned around and said: "Can you see, Willie? Willie, laddie, where are you?"

His young buddy had disappeared causing the clockmaker to purse his lips and then utter: "That wee rascal has given me the slip. No doubt I'll find him with the others."

Meanwhile, outside the entrance Vlad answered a call on his mobile: "All the boys are inside enjoying the mosaics. There's really nothing to worry about." He then returned inside the church and nodded over to Sergei who responded with a knowing glance.

Within minutes, the Sweetheart group reassembled and Vlad motioned to count everyone. He looked slightly puzzled and, pointing his finger at each boy, proceeded to count again and then turned to the approaching Mr Buie and asked: "Where is your boy?"

The old man looked mildly surprised: "I thought he was already here."

Just then, Dr Jones arrived with Duncan and said: "Oh, are we too late to grab a quick look around?"

Vlad said: "We are missing Duncan Dewar. He's somehow disappeared."

An expression of puzzlement crossed the choirmaster's face as he said: "Here he is. The lad is with me." As soon as he saw Duncan, he breathed a sigh of relief and began counting again but once again the number fell short by one.

"It's not Duncan that's missing. It's Willy, Willy Carmichael. He was with me one minute and gone the next. He has to be here somewhere," said Mr Buie.

"Oh, he'll have his nose in something that doesn't concern him. Everyone scatter with your buddies, look around and find him. Meet back at the entrance in ten minutes," said Dr Jones. Ten minutes later, there was widespread alarm as it was becoming clear Willy Carmichael had vanished.

No one was more panicked than Vlad and Sergei who began making phone calls to Svetlana Volkova to raise the alarm. Although speaking in Russian, it was clear to onlookers that they were deeply concerned.

Vlad and Sergei worked for the Volkov Corporation's security wing, a euphemism for the dark forces or enforcers who ensured the smooth running of what Viktor Volkov described as 'external matters'. They had been detailed to keep the Sweetheart choir under surveillance and, in particular, safeguard Duncan Dewar.

"I was told to watch out for the boy and that he would be in the company of the old man. We followed your instruction, Mrs Volkova. How were we to know that there were two boys with red hair? Even so, the one who disappeared today was with the old man," insisted Sergei, who was protesting and defending his position.

In all the chaos, the local St Petersburg police were informed and alarm bells were sent ringing through the system as they would for a missing overseas visitor, especially a child.

While everyone's attention had been focussed on the spot where the murdered Czar had bled, a team of undercover officers in the Federal Security Service of the Russian Federation, known as the FSB, had moved in swiftly and kidnapped Willy Carmichael in plain sight. Using a hypodermic needle, one had administered knockout drops on the boy and quietly removed him from the church. Two of the agents, either side of Willy, supported him as they moved swiftly from the historic building and in to a waiting black *Mercedes Gelandewagen*.

Less than an hour later, the missing boy was lying unconscious on an operating table hooked up to a respirator and heart monitor in an anonymous building nearby. "I'm telling you, I have scanned his body and there is no metal chip, computer chip or any foreign chip in his neck, head or anywhere else. Believe me, we have gone over every centimetre and there is nothing," said a woman wearing surgical clothing. She was speaking directly in to a monitor.

"I don't care if you have to skin the boy alive and put him through a mincer. Find that chip Dr Mikhailov or it will be the last time you pick up a scalpel," boomed a voice back from the monitor which was a two-way camera.

Giving a sigh of reluctance, Dr Eva Mikhailov repositioned her facemask and asked the team around her to put the boy facedown. Giving another instruction, a surgical male nurse picked up an electric razor and shaved the back of Carmichael's head in a straight line down to the nape of his neck.

Addressing the surgical team in Russian, she said: "First we will remove his scalp and then, methodically remove the rest of the epidermis. Never let it be said we ever disobeyed an order." Slapping a scalpel into her outstretched latex-gloved palm, Dr Mikhailov grasped the instrument and then lifted her right arm. The atmosphere in the operating theatre was tense and each face of her surgically masked team reflected that in their eyes.

"Switch off the respirator and monitor, now. Double the morphine, there's no reason now why we should revive him," said Dr Mikhailov in an unnervingly calm voice.

"STOP! HALT!" ordered the mystery voice from the monitor. "There has been a development and it appears we have the wrong boy. Return him at once to the hotel with a minimum of fuss. We need total damage limitation on this." Dr Mikhailov looked at her team, removed her mask and afforded herself a smile before biting into her bottom lip.

"That was a close call," she said before walking purposefully out of the theatre.

Less than half an hour later, a drowsy Willy Carmichael was bundled into a hotel laundry basket and driven in the Mercedes Gelandewagen to the underground car park of the Kempinski. From there, he was taken by service elevator to the eighth floor. It was, unusually quiet, as Vlad and Sergei had urged Dr Jones to reconvene a meeting with the choir in the master's room.

"We have no news update to give you but I would urge you all to retrace your steps in your mind and try and think again of anything strange you might have seen when you were inside The Church of the Saviour on Spilled Blood," said Vlad.

John Russell sighed: "I thought you were going to give us some positive news."

Dr Jones, trying to remain upbeat, responded: "Look it's been less than two hours since Willie Carmichael wandered off. I refuse to accept anything else at this stage, so we must remain upbeat. But Vlad is right. Retrace today's events and try and think of anything out of character, anything unusual."

Disheartened and downbeat, the boys returned to their rooms. "Did Willie have his phone with him?" asked James Darling.

John Russell's eyes lit up: "Well, if he did the cops should be able to track him down. Let me check his room." He opened the adjoining door and shouted: "O-M-G! He's here. He's in bed. Willie! Willie, where have you been? Wake up, wake up. I think he's drunk."

Looking a ghostly white and rather dishevelled, Carmichael opened his bloodshot eyes and tried to focus. His pupils were barely visible, just tiny little pinpricks surrounded by bright blue irises.

"Where the hell have you been? Quick, someone get Dr Jones!" shouted Darling. The boy tried to get up but slumped back in the bed as Dr Jones and a relieved Gordon Buie arrived. The hotel doctor was called and, after a thorough physical examination, said it was clear Carmichael had either been drugged or had taken drugs.

"There's no sign of a sexual or physical assault," he told Dr Jones. "It's a bit of a mystery, possibly even a schoolboy prank which may have backfired. He is suffering from amnesia and says the last thing he remembers was standing near the spot where the Czar was assassinated. I'm confident, however, by morning he will be as right as rain, as you English say."

Dr Jones breathed a sigh of relief and called the Volkov twins to his room. "I don't want anyone leaving the hotel after the Carmichael fiasco, so tell everyone that they're confined to the eighth floor and can order whatever they want from the room service card.

"I can't be doing with any more excitement this evening and nothing, but nothing must interfere with the concert tomorrow night. We owe it to your wonderful mother."

Andrei nodded in agreement and said: "Mother is having one of her migraines, so I doubt we'll see her until tomorrow evening's event. She's just so relieved Willie turned up."

"Yes, we all are. Now hopefully we can draw a line under this whole matter," sighed Dr Jones. But if he thought the drama was over he was very much mistaken. In fact it was only just beginning. It seemed the Sweetheart Choir was about to be caught up in a game of international espionage and intrigue.

Chapter 18

Svetlana knocked back a shot of vodka and went to pour herself another. "It seems you can take the woman out of Nekrasovka but you can't take Nekrasovka out of the woman! Here, let me pour you another drink. It might be the last you have for some time. Today has been a disaster," roared Viktor Volkov as he brought his giant fist down on the cocktail bar.

"We cannot be blamed Viktor. We have done everything those swine have asked of us and it has cost us a small fortune. Why won't they let us go?"

Viktor paced up and down the presidential suite and screamed: "I'll tell you why Svetlana, because they have my balls in a vice, that's why! We've left ourselves exposed and if we don't deliver that boy, they will tie up the business with a tax investigation which will financially destroy us".

Again Svetlana cried: "But why, Viktor, why that boy? What is so special about him?"

Viktor heaved his giant shoulders and shook his head. "I've no idea. The twins say he has a good brain and an amazing voice but he's otherwise invisible, his parents are dead and his grandfather is a nobody; but whatever it is, the FSB has an interest and if he has attracted the attention of the chiefs in Lubyanka Square, then you can rest assured this goes all the way to the Kremlin. I can handle most things but even I am out of my depth with this.

"I can't reach Mama or Grandmama. I swear if anyone has harmed one hair on Babushka's head, I will kill them. Tomorrow, after the concert, whatever happens, I may want you and the twins back on the jet to Scotland with or without the choir. I've put some measures in place, nobody but nobody can do this to me and get away with it."

Equally baffled by all the drama was Gordon Buie and he also had a growing premonition of unease about the whole trip. While the boys were in the adjoining rooms eating burgers ordered via room service, he picked up the gift box from the plane and examined it thoughtfully for some time. The phone was still inside, powered up but otherwise untouched. He picked it up, tapped in a number and waited for a response: "Ah, Mr Petrie, it's Gordon Buie here. How are you? I hope this is not an inconvenient time." Mr Petrie was relaxing at home with a book and was surprised to hear from Duncan's grandfather.

"I'm not sure what you can do but I want to share my concerns with you because strange things are happening out here and they simply do not add up. May be I've watched too many old movies on Russian espionage but one thing I do not possess is an overactive imagination. I have a logical mind and some events simply do not add up."

Mr Petrie listened carefully to the old man's concerns and, after more than twenty minutes, he responded: "You were right to call me and of course everything you have relayed to me is in confidence. Let me ponder on this and I'll get back to you."

Mr Petrie sat back for a few minutes and then jumped from his seat. Gordon Buie's instincts had served him well, he thought, and he set off for help from the Council of Anam Cara. Down through the secret passages of his home, he headed for a meeting with Salar.

He relayed the conversation he had with Gordon Buie and expressed his own concerns and fears.

Salar nodded and gave an intriguing smile. "You're fond of the boy, aren't you? All this time and you've not allowed anyone to come near you but that young man has opened your heart, has he not?" Mr Petrie shrugged and admitted there was something 'endearing' about Duncan Dewar and then added: "You know fine well we go back a long way, Salar, for it was you who sent me to Melivich, the night of the so-called accident. I never knew why and I'm still uncertain. Are you ready to tell me?"

Salar smiled and said: "He carries a secret and perhaps now is the time to tell you why you were sent there. Duncan Dewar is in possession of an unusual electronic key to a safe which we believe contains the work of the boy's parents, Moira and Douglas Dewar."

Mr Petrie grimaced and then said: "But when I handed the child to the police and said he'd been found wandering around the roadside, he was wearing just a romper suit. There was no baggage or anything with him, not even a toy."

Salar said: "Like all secrets, the truth eventually comes out and some very powerful people in powerful places have done terrible things to get their hands on the work of the Dewars. Nations, dictatorships and international crime syndicates have come together – and on occasions clashed against each other – to unlock the secret work of the Dewars. I've instructed Merrick to give you the long view and equip you for this mission.

"Life is a jigsaw, Mr Petrie, and you have been given some pieces but not the whole picture. The time has now come to reveal the whole canvas and bring this to a conclusion."

Mr Petrie retraced his steps through the tunnel until he was standing at the entrance to the doorway marked 'Merrick'. On entering, he walked in to a rather gloomy, oak-panelled room with several oil paintings hanging on the wall. There was little furniture and compared to Salar's opulent space, this was rather dull and spartan.

'Merrick' emerged from behind a fading red velvet-curtained entrance. "Time is of the essence. Follow me. You have a tricky assignment and will need the full protection the council has to offer," instructed Merrick in a very deep but smooth, sensual voice. Tall, ebony, bald and very toned, Merrick was almost Amazonian in stature.

She wore a grey, sleeveless cat suit which highlighted her powerful, muscular but slender arms while a wide dark-jewelled leather belt exaggerated a tiny waistline.

They sat down in a circular room with two large cinema seats and a shiny black coffee table. Merrick's right arm glided towards the domed ceiling where an intriguing sculpted chandelier hung and she clicked her long, elegant fingers. The lights went out and a large section of the curved wall illuminated. As his eyes became accustomed to the dark and focussed, he saw a 3D view of what looked like a windowless laboratory. A white-coated couple came into view and were identified as Moira and Douglas Dewar. Douglas was holding a baby in his arms in a protective manner and said in an alarmed voice: “There has to be another way, Moira. We cannot do this. It brings a whole new meaning to the word child abuse.”

Moira was armed with some sort of heavy metal hypodermic syringe and, as she moved towards the baby, said: “There’s no other way. If what you suspect is right, then we are in danger of losing this altogether. Until we know exactly who we can trust, the Infinity Cell must remain secret.

“I don’t know who we can trust and I am not boarding that helicopter flight tomorrow with the others. If our suspicions are right, then someone inside Whitehall is leaking information and it’s exposing us all. We can’t go ahead with the demonstration in Caithness; somehow we have to stall.

“I’ve destroyed all the files and corrupted the ones left in backup. The prototype is secured in a place I know you’ll approve but let’s keep this on a need-to-know basis. The only evidence of our work on the Infinity Cell is safely stored and cannot be accessed without this Radio frequency identification or RFID. Let me slip it into Duncan’s hand because it is the last place anyone would think to look.”

The protective father tried to resist but Moira was too quick for him and, in an instant, she nipped a piece of skin in the nape of his neck and inserted a tiny chip carrying a unique radio frequency. The child winced and emitted a yelp as Moira stood back: “There, it’s done. We can trust no one, Douglas, and now only our son holds the key.”

Just fifteen months old, Duncan was quickly calmed and resumed to gurgling and spluttering like any other contented baby. “I’m sorry, little one,” said Moira as she reached out to hold him and used an antiseptic wipe to remove the small bloodstain on his neck. “There, you see. Barely a pimple.”

The laboratory door opened and an imposing man in a pinstripe suit walked in. “So it is true, Moira!” he declared. Professor John Dawson looked severe as he said accusingly: “You are turning my laboratories into a nursery, Moira.” She looked slightly flustered until her superior’s face broke into a warm smile.

“If having the baby nearby keeps you happy and doesn’t distract you from your work, then why should anyone care,

Moira? You two are my golden couple, my secret weapon in Whitehall."

Moira relaxed and said: "I'm surprised to see you. I thought you had already left for the conference."

As she placed Duncan in his Moses basket, Professor Dawson responded: "I will be part of the advance party to Caithness but I just wanted to make sure you have everything in order for the presentation. Scotland will be a rehearsal before the really big unveiling in London next month.

"There are quite a few sceptics in Whitehall and in these cost-cutting times, they want to know they're getting value for money. If this Infinity Cell is all you claim, then all manner of allies and enemies are going to be interested, the world and its dog really!

"The fact we are stealing a march on the Americans in terms of research and development will raise eyebrows. The Americans will want in, that is certain, and no doubt they will want to bring in their own people. No more reliance on Middle East oil or Russian gas for energy consumption will certainly change absolutely everything, especially on the geopolitical landscape."

Moira smiled, adding: "Let's not get ahead of ourselves on this. We've completed the theory and have some models to put into practice. Dounreay will be the perfect backdrop since decommissioning is well underway. I have to commend you on your perfect choice of location, Professor Dawson. The Infinity Cell could certainly herald the final curtain on the nuclear age and all the bad that comes with it."

The timeline crackled and the video ended and then reopened on the same day, in Professor Dawson's office in Wiltshire. He had just taken a phone call and responded: "They say they have all they need for the demonstration, so one has to assume the prototype will be on the Chinook as well. We can't let the demonstration go ahead. It's as simple as that."

There was a slight pause in the conversation as he listened to the caller and then responded: "Just do what you have to do."

The video crackled again and this time, the panicked voice of a pilot could be heard talking to his co-pilot: "We've lost contact with base and something has electronically jammed the controls. Someone or something else appears to be in control.

I'm no longer flying this machine. We are no longer in control. What the…" Mr Petrie watched in horror as the Chinook helicopter spiralled out of control through the swirling mists of the Grampians as it crashed into a craggy rock face. As smoke and flames rose into the descending mist, half a dozen commando-style soldiers wearing aspirators appeared on top of the crag and abseiled to the wreckage below. They then began checking the bodies. There were no survivors. One of the soldiers said on his radio mouthpiece: "They're not here. The bodies are not here. Check the flight details again. They can't have boarded."

A few minutes later, he again spoke in to his headset: "We have thoroughly searched the ground zone for passengers of interest and cargo. Neither is in evidence. We can only conclude the POI and cargo were never on board in the first place."

Merrick turned to Mr Petrie and said: "And this is where it really gets interesting." The screen's sizzling horizontal lines disappeared to show a car being driven by Moira coming in to focus. Douglas, sitting in the passenger seat, was talking. "Your instincts were right, Moira. Thank God we did not fly with the others. The Chinook down, the research team gone…who the hell is behind this? The Russians? The Americans? The Chinese? I thought when we set out on this research, we would be doing some good."

Moira agreed, adding: "But if we invent an alternative to fracking, gas, oil and other fossils fuels, then a lot of wealthy and powerful people suddenly lose their source of money, power and influence overnight. What we have discovered will completely devalue the Middle-East dynasties. It could bankrupt the energy producers and suppliers in Russia, China and America.

"All we imagined was a world that produced clean energy with little or no cost. We thought we were creating a safer planet for the benefit of billions. No more famine and wars would come to an end. I can't believe we were so naive. Instead, we've created a perfect storm of evil and made ourselves the bloody targets!"

Mr Petrie turned to Merrick: "This is the road from Melivich, right?"

Still focussing on the blank screen, she said: "Yes, you are right. You don't need to see the rest unless you really want to…" He nodded slowly: "I need to see this."

As the Dewar family car turned a bend on the narrow road with Moira Dewar at the wheel, they were confronted by an emergency checkpoint and forced to stop. There was no way out and as masked commandos moved forward, the Dewars sat there helplessly until they were dragged out of the car to a panoramic viewpoint twenty yards away.

Professor Dawson emerged from the mists and looked at the two: "I'm sorry it has come to this. For the record, you are the two most brilliant minds I have ever had the pleasure of working with, but I'm afraid your misplaced idealist outlook was always going to hamper this operation.

"You thought the Infinity Cell would save the world but whoever holds its secrets will control the world. Now let's make things easy. Hand over the hard drive and tell me where the prototype is hidden and you will be spared. Resist and I am afraid what you are experiencing right now are your final minutes on this good earth."

Moira grabbed hold of her husband's hand and said defiantly: "Whatever you think you are looking for is not here. Nor are there any traces of our work in the car. I suspected your motives last week, professor, when I saw you in the company of a member of the FSB. As soon as I saw the Russian connection, I realised what you were planning."

Professor Dawson laughed and said: "My dear Moira. You do possess one of the brightest minds I've encountered in four decades of serving my country. Since this is our final conversation, I will afford you the luxury of seeing the bigger picture. Yes, that man you saw was from Russian intelligence. However, he was a double cross who actually worked for the Americans. He was going to report back to his CIA handler the outcome of our conversation. Sadly, he died in a mysterious climbing accident… I think the local Kendal newspaper revealed another story of another Lake District tragedy, another climber and another fall.

"I've no doubt your story will also make headlines. Another tragic car accident, another Highland Road, another tragedy. But rest assured, life will go on much the same.

Goodbye, dear Moira. It's been a real pleasure," and as the professor moved forward to give Moira a farewell kiss on her cheek, she stared contemptuously into his eyes. Suddenly her own eyes widened and her pupils dilated as she looked down to her left just in time to see a large needle being withdrawn from her chest. Seconds later, she fell to the ground, dead.

Douglas knelt down by his wife's body and looked up angrily, with hate in his eyes, at the professor and said: "You will pay for this." He then physically lurched at his boss but was restrained by the commandos and while a violent struggle ensued, a familiar figure crept stealthily unseen towards the car twenty yards away and opened the rear passenger door. The struggle only lasted thirty or so seconds, before Douglas was also given a lethal injection, but it was time enough for the stranger to remove Duncan Dewar from his baby seat and vanish into the night.

"Put them back in the car, roll it over and set it alight. Our work here is done," said Dawson who then walked away.

The screen went blank and Merrick said: "You did well to save the boy. But now it seems he has inadvertently re-awakened interest in the Infinity Cell. You need to get to St Petersburg and bring him back safely. Here is the time coder and locator. The skelwarks will give you travel documents, money and anything else you need. Any questions?"

The pair rose to their feet. Merrick towered over Mr Petrie who looked up and said: "It's all falling into place now and that poor boy simply has no idea."

As Merrick walked away, she replied: "Probably better he never finds out."

Chapter 19

Mr Petrie followed the skelwarks as they exited from Merrick's quarters leading him deep inside the Caledonian Drift, a well-worn secret passage used by the privileged few who knew of its existence. It opened up into a cavernous underground space where a vast loch of unknown depths spread out before them.

As they navigated a hairpin bend on the path, a giant waterfall came into view. The purest mountain water tumbled from a rock face in the corner of the magnificent cave. Heading towards the powerful force of nature which provided a spectacular fifty-foot drop of crashing water, the sound of the party's footsteps were engulfed by the deafening roar as the bubbling liquid crashed onto giant stones at the edge of the loch. As the path snaked its way behind the waterfall, Mr Petrie braced himself as the lightest and most refreshing spray doused his face in the most pleasing manner.

Once behind the waterfall, the path wound its way through a stone tunnel which was illuminated by a bright light. Mr Petrie had reached the end of the Caledonian Drift and he turned to the two skelwarks and said: "You have set the right coordinates, haven't you?" The skelwarks responded with nothing more than a blank stare as one handed him a battered old leather briefcase. Completely expressionless, they stood back and watched him walk towards the blinding light.

The truth is he hated using the Drift which could transport him to any place or time in the world with pinpoint accuracy. It wasn't the huge leap of faith he had to make each time he walked towards the light that bothered him. It was reaching the destination at the other side and stepping out of an electronic wormhole into the unknown.

For someone grounded in pure logic, he had an irrational fear stemming from a recurring nightmare, that one day the coordinates would be wrongly programmed in, and he would emerge dressed in the wrong clothes for the wrong century at the wrong location into a crowded room.

Seconds later, Mr Petrie, having arrived at his destination, tentatively opened the door of the male cloakroom and stepped into the grand foyer of the Kempinski Hotel in St Petersburg. Walking over to the reception, he introduced himself and handed over his passport. "Ah Mr Petrie, yes, we have been expecting you," said a pleasant young man at the check in desk.

As he filled out his registration details, there was more drama on the eighth floor as a blood-curdling scream erupted from the shower cubicle. Willie Carmichael emerged gasping for breath and grabbed his striped, towelling hooded dressing gown before screaming again. The first to hammer on the bathroom door was Vlad: "Open up, open up."

The door unlocked and Willie ran out into Vlad's arms. It was hard to tell if he was crying or the water trickling down his face was from the shower. Either way, he was clearly in a state of shock and on the verge of hyperventilating.

"Quick, sit down and put your head between your legs. Give him space boys," said Vlad as by this time the entire choir had gathered in the room.

Dr Jones burst in: "What the hell is going on now?"

The boys stood back and revealed Carmichael sitting with his head between his legs. Dr Jones looked around to try and catch someone's eyes and connected with Vlad. "Well, what is it?"

Vlad shook his head and said: "I heard a scream coming from the bathroom. When he emerged, he was trembling and looked as though he was about to go into shock. You know it could be an aftershock or flashback from yesterday."

Dr Jones marched in to the bathroom but it was empty. He saw steam coming from the shower which was still running and opened the cubicle door but there was nothing there. After turning off the running water, he returned to the bedroom ordering everyone out before sitting next to a shaking Carmichael.

In uncharacteristic, soothing tones, he tried to coax the boy into an upright position. "Was it a bad dream? No one will think any the worse of you. You had some sort of ordeal and there's bound to be a reaction. What is it? Please Willie, you can trust me."

Carmichael looked at the choirmaster and then slowly removed the hood from his head and turned to face away from the master. Dr Jones gasped at the neatly shaved bald patch leading from his crown to the nape of his neck… 'A sort of Mohican in reverse,' he thought.

"Who did this to you?"

Carmichael was still trembling. "I don't know, sir. I was just showering and when I went to shampoo my hair, I felt this whole bald patch. Is my hair falling out with shock? Am I going bald? Do you think I've been abducted by aliens?"

Dr Jones smiled: "No, not at all. I think we need to look closer to home. I think you may have been pranked. What we do know is that you disappeared from the church and suffered from extreme food poisoning and, by some miracle, found your way back to the hotel bedroom. Dr Sasha did a thorough examination yesterday, so I'm sure he would have noticed something awry on the back of your head.

"Maybe one of the choirboys thought it would be a laugh to shave your head. How does a crew cut sound? I'm sure Mrs Volkova can arrange a barber or…you could sport it as a badge of honour. A tribute, if you will, to your courage in overcoming adversity.

"I will have a word with the rest of the choir and try and find the culprit. Worry not, I will make sure they see this for what it is and don't turn this into a cause for mockery. Carmichael, above all, know that I am proud of the way you've handled yourself so far."

Carmichael smiled as he began to regard his bald patch in a new light and wondered how he could exploit it. He nodded at Dr Jones and thanked him for his words and asked if he would have a word with the rest of the choir on his behalf.

Dr Jones called the boys in to his room and explained what had happened. There were a few sniggers which he abruptly silenced and added: "If I find the prankster responsible, there will be severe repercussions. This trip has been a challenge but we have shown there is unity in adversity and we will triumph. All our focus must now be on tonight and we must forget the traumatic events of yesterday, for now."

After breakfast, the boys were taken on a river tour of St Petersburg on a luxury glass topped boat hired by the Volkov Corporation. As an added precaution, another half dozen security accompanied Vlad and Sergei while a guide gave a running commentary via the radio system of the sights on offer in Russia's cultural capital. The boys were unusually compliant and well behaved which probably had more to do with what had happened to Carmichael and his shaven scalp.

Svetlana, nursing a hangover and wishing she hadn't indulged in so much alcohol the night before, picked up a checklist and handed it to her long-suffering personal assistant. She conducted most of her business that day from a king-sized bed with an icepack strategically planted on the top of her head.

A rather stressed Anastasiya Petrova shouted: "What do you mean the carpets have not arrived?! The concert cannot go ahead unless there are carpets over the marble flooring before we can put in place the hired pews." She had worked as Svetlana's PA for more than a decade and was reflecting the job was becoming more difficult: "Do you really want me to disturb Mrs Volkova and tell her why you've let her down? Aha, Okay. Before 1 pm will be fine."

"Anastasiya, how is my checklist?"

She lifted her eyes skywards and responded: "Yes, it's all in hand. You just relax and let me take the strain." By early afternoon, a small army of beauticians set about Svetlana with manicures and pedicures, shaping and re-doing her French polished nails. Another gave a shoulder, scalp and body massage while a hairdresser began re-styling her mop of blonde hair.

Viktor had left before dawn for an important 'business meeting'. Promising Svetlana he would return to the hotel no later than 6 pm that evening, it would be a tight call, he mused, but he adored his wife and would never let her down.

He sat at a large round conference table and scrutinised the other thirty or so attendees. Nearly all of the leaders of the crime syndicates which controlled Russia and beyond had assembled. Three of the most notorious gangs from St Petersburg were there; the Solntsevskaya Bratya sat next to Leningrad's Malyshevs who were staring solemnly at their sworn enemies and rivals the Tambov Gang.

Other mafia chiefs included the overall leader, a Ukrainian-born godfather called Ivan Voloshin, who scanned the faces around the room as if making mental notes. Some were still raking in money from drugs, extortion, crime and prostitution but others had become more sophisticated and invested in property, business and industry throughout America, Europe and Australia while setting up elaborate money laundering operations and offshore accounts.

The chair announced: "We have several lines of influence in the Duma now and are essentially in control of some major corporations and fuel trading businesses. This is the way forward and we must divide the cake evenly – there's enough for all of us, but why are we fighting among ourselves, eh? Today we should swear an allegiance to each other and our community and stop the infighting, gentlemen. United we are strong but divided we will weaken.

Several hours were spent horse-trading between districts and boundaries and eventually everyone seemed happy with his 'slice of cake'. At the end of it all, Viktor stood up to leave and the chair called him over: "There has been a misunderstanding between you and the Malyshevs, Viktor. This bad blood has to end now, so I don't want any reprisals. Your mother and grandmother are on their way to St Petersburg." He stopped, looked at his Rolex Oyster, adding: "Actually they should have arrived at the Kempinski by now and, I am assured, they are none the worse for their experience, in fact I gather they rather enjoyed their river cruise from Moscow to St Petersburg."

Volkov inhaled deeply through flared nostrils and, exhaling slowly, he said through gritted teeth. "On a boat, my mother and grandmother on a boat?"

Ivan Voloshin said: "Not just any boat. It was a luxury family yacht and I'm reliably informed they had a wonderful vacation.

"Look, Viktor, a foolish mistake was made over shares transactions in some Spanish property and it is now sorted. No reprisals, please. The Malyshevs accept full responsibility. They saw your jet in Barajas airport, put two and two together and came up with five. Okay?"

Viktor grunted: "Huh! They were never any good at maths. My wife was spending a few days with her family in Madrid.

What am I to do? Ground her as well as my jet?" As he walked away, he resolved to pay back the Malyshevs two or three months down the line. He was also relieved that his mother's 'holiday cruise' had nothing to do with the problems he was encountering at the moment with the Sweetheart choir.

However, before he could reach the door, a senior member of the Tambov gang called him over. "Whatever it is, make it quick I've an appointment tonight," snapped Viktor.

"Ah yes, a concert I believe and it is that I want to discuss with you. Mama is most disappointed she has not been invited Viktor, an oversight surely?

"The family would hate to think they're not good enough to sit at the Volkov table these days Viktor considering we've discarded some of the older practices." Viktor looked sneeringly at Yury 'the knife' Barsukov, for as far as he was concerned, he would always be a hired thug, pimp and loan shark.

As if reading his mind, Yury said: "I know what you are thinking. You think that you're better than us but all of our businesses are now legal and legitimate.

"Even the western establishment seek our counsel these days and you, you Viktor should watch your back. My contacts in Chicago have back channels in to the US State Department and they tell me someone has information which could bring the oil industry crashing down around all of our heads. We were even asked if we could make the problem 'disappear' but as you know, we are no longer in the business of elimination. Sadly not everyone here is as honourable as me."

Viktor looked at Yury through squinted eyes and said: "I will make sure there is a pew for the Barsukov family tonight, but be warned, I may need you to come out of retirement for just an hour. This concert will go ahead. It should be a pleasant way to see in the New Year and I will not allow anyone to cause any problems. Do you understand? If you discover anything more from your American contacts, I will appreciate it. See you tonight with your mama, Yury."

By 5:30 pm that evening, Viktor walked in to the presidential suite and was instantly mobbed by his mother and grandmother. They thanked him for their wonderful holiday. "You are too extravagant, Viktor, really. Such luxury and the pampering! I would have phoned you but the captain said the navigation system was acting up and if I switched on my cell, it might add to his problems.

"He was such a timid pussycat; I even handed it over so he could have peace of mind. That's why we didn't call but he said he was in touch with you regularly but you were very busy, as usual. Oh, the food Viktor and the sauna and the views. Are you and Svetlana going to buy this yacht? Is that what the cruise from Moscow to here was all about? My Viktor, owning his own yacht, what would our neighbours say. I'm so proud of you these days, not like thirty years ago when you were a teenager," his mother reminded him.

"Leave my favourite grandson alone, Anna. God loves him and so do I," said Viktor's grandmother. He gave the tiny Russian a big hug and laughed to himself that they didn't even know they had been kidnapped.

"Come, show me the gifts you were given and tell me more about the cruise," he said but Svetlana appeared and pointed to her watch: "Viktor, no time. You must get ready. We have to be at the church in an hour. The concert is oversubscribed and, if all goes smoothly, we will have hosted the only New Year Party worth hosting," she said.

"Ah yes, my dear. About that. I need at least half a dozen seats for the Barsukov family." As he followed Svetlana in to the bedroom, the mother and grandmother looked at each other and switched on the TV, turning up the volume but it still couldn't mask Svetlana's anger as she shouted: "I am not having a load of low life thugs at my concert and soiree! They will lower the tone, Viktor."

An hour later, St Petersburg's finest had descended on The Church of the Saviour on Spilled Blood. Svetlana looked magnificent in a pale green coat with a raised shawl collar and bracelet length sleeves complimented by deep, bottle green accessories as she sashayed down the aisle with Viktor, his mother and 'babushka'.

Viktor looked around as he took his front row seat to see who had arrived and he nodded as he recognised various faces. He saw Yury arrive with his own family and saw their satisfied look as they were directed to seats close to the front after Svetlana's PA managed to get an extra row inserted.

As much as he despised him, Viktor knew he had to keep Yury sweet until he could work out who was posing the biggest threat to him and his loved ones. He was curious that Yury, through his American connections, appeared to know a little about Duncan Dewar and the plot to kidnap him in St Petersburg. He wanted to know how much else he knew and was troubled that someone like Yury appeared to be 'in the loop' while he was still very much in the dark.

To loud applause, the Sweetheart Abbey School Choir gathered on the raised platform in front of the great and good of St Petersburg and opened with a lively rendition of Scotland, the Brave. The boys smiled as they sang in their traditional tartan dress with kilts swaying and feet stamping. To the delight of the Russian crowds, Andrei and Alexei wore Scottish tartan trews combined with traditional red Russian military-style jackets.

Chinese cousins Bo and Kong Zhang captivated the audience with their Igor Stravinsky 'Suite Italienne' playing cello and piano. The pair, probably the most introverted in the Sweetheart choir, showed not one ounce of emotion as they performed.

As they finished their piece, there was almost a hint of a smile from Kong as he set aside his cello and addressed the audience: "This next song was written by a member of the MacGregor clan of Glen Endrick, who was jailed, along with a friend, by the British Government in 1746. Condemned to death for his support of Bonnie Prince Charlie, he was told his friend was going to be set free. The song reveals an old Celtic myth that the soul of a Scot who dies outside of his homeland will find its way back home by the spiritual road, or the low road."

One by one, the Sweetheart choir emerged from the wings singing the opening lines and by the time they were all re-united on stage they reached the chorus: "Ye'll tak' the high road and I'll tak the low road. And I'll be in Scotland afore ye. But me and my true love will never meet again. On the bonnie, bonnie banks of Loch Lomond."

Viktor turned and saw Svetlana's eyes fill with tears. He got hold of her hand and whispered: "What is it with these Scots? Forever fighting, forever dying and forever in trouble! Why, they're just like us Russians!" Just then he noticed some movement from the corner of his eye. It was Yury Barsukov rising from his seat, looking slightly tense and sweaty. Where was he going?

A sinking pit began to develop in Viktor's stomach but he was unable to move from his front row seat which would attract the attention of the entire audience. Nor could he reach for his mobile phone and text Vlad or Sergei to find out what was happening. He hated being so helpless and so, for the rest of the concert, he was unable to relax.

He would not have been so concerned, had he known that Yury only needed a toilet break however, as any tourist faced with a similar dilemma could have told him, there are no public restrooms inside The Church of the Saviour on Spilled Blood. As he blundered around near the entrance, he realised it was time for desperate measures and so, he forced the door on the little souvenir shop in the building. Using his cigarette lighter to illuminate the inside of the booth, he looked for a decent-sized receptacle in which to relieve himself.

He picked up a vase but, on seeing an image of Vladimir Putin, he returned it to the shelf choosing, instead, one bearing a saintly image from one of the mosaics. Having achieved his aim, Yury returned the full mug and then gently opened the door.

He hesitated for a second as he heard the choir launch into 'Silent Night', checked his watch and saw he had time for a cigarette. As he leaned against the metal railings outside, his attention was diverted by a sharp red light which appeared to be dancing on the ground by the entrance. Yury threw his lighted cigarette down, crushing it underfoot and looked around. He realised instantly a rooftop assassin was busy scoping a red dot laser gun sight.

Yury casually strolled across the cobblestone path leading to a footbridge over the canal. As he did so, he saw the Volkov's security detail sharing some jokes and cigarettes leaning against the waiting cars. "Amateurs!" said Yury to himself, shaking his head as he picked up a pace, heading towards the building from where he thought the sniper was positioned. For a large, ambling man around six feet tall, Yury was remarkably agile and in the cover of darkness, he crept up an outside fire escape towards the roof.

The night sky was clear and the church looked magnificent illuminated with footlights and moonlight. He could hear strains of music and song drifting through the air and, as he reached the roof of the building opposite, he realised his instincts has served him well. With some satisfaction and adrenalin pumping through his veins, he whispered: "Got you."

Meanwhile inside the church, there was much anticipation as Duncan Dewar was introduced as the school's 'remarkable' boy Soprano. "Not only were we, at Sweetheart Abbey, unaware of his great voice, but he was as well and he may have remained undiscovered, had it not been for the sort of support we have received from Svetlana Volkova," said Dr Jones.

The audience seemed to collectively hold its breath as Duncan stepped forward and cleared his throat. As his voice pierced the silence with: "We're walking in the air. We're floating in the moonlit sky," the first of three perfectly balanced, black stainless steel knives sliced through the ice-cold night air and found their mark in the back of the sniper's head.

As Yury rose to his feet, he playfully swung his right forefinger around the fourth knife's ring handle, letting it spin in the air and then in a sudden movement gripped the handle and threw it into the back of the gunman. He then ran forward towards the slumped figure and, through gritted teeth, asked: "How do you like my steel work, eh?" Lifting the dead man's head, he quickly followed through with a violent twist until a sickening crack could be heard.

There were gasps from the audience as a giant white screen emerged behind Duncan revealing the familiar animated Snowman film on the backdrop. Towards the final verse, imitation snowflakes, which glistened at certain angles, began to drift from the ceiling on to the audience. Duncan reached the final line: "We're floating in the midnight sky. And everyone who sees us greets us as we fly."

An eerie silence followed as the snowflakes continued to descend and then the audience erupted to give loud applause. Svetlana gave a sigh of relief as her art director had gone through quite a tussle with the authorities to get their full approval for the stage backdrop, lighting and, in particular, the snowfall. After a few seconds, everyone was on their feet and

Duncan was joined by the rest of the choir as they began singing 'Auld Lang Syne'.

The song, very well-known and much loved to Russians as the 'Drinking Song' won the approval of the audience who sang with gusto at the final chorus: "For auld lang syne, my dear. For auld lang syne. We'll tak a cup o' kindess yet. For auld lang syne."

Viktor Volkov stood up and asked Svetlana to join him on the stage but she feigned reluctance to share the limelight although somehow managed to reach the podium before he did! They both put their arms around Duncan who was overwhelmed by the attention as the audience continued applauding. "I want to thank everyone for coming here tonight and, of course, the night is still young and we have yet to welcome in the New Year." He hesitated slightly as he saw Yury walking back to his seat, adjusting his tie and grinning from ear to ear.

"As our valued family and friends, Svetlana and I would like to welcome you to the Kempinski to see in the New Year." The Volkovs stood at the head of the church and personally thanked their guests, urging them to join them in the hotel nearby. "Let's hope this will be a night to remember for all the right reasons," Svetlana whispered in her husband's ear as they left for the hotel.

Chapter 20

Mr Petrie had a very self-satisfied look on his face as he strode purposefully towards the Kempinski by the River Moika embankment. Since he was in St Petersburg, there was no way he was going to miss the Sweetheart Abbey school choir's historic concert and although he didn't have much time for Dr Jones' past efforts, there was a feeling of pride in what he saw and heard.

Although the concert had already started when he arrived, he stood at the back and remained enthralled throughout. As the audience rose to its feet for the finale to give a standing ovation, he seized the moment to slip out unseen, almost bumping in to Yury Barsukov who was walking back down the aisle. Once outside, he turned left and headed for the nearby Italian Bridge pedestrian crossing over the Griboedov Canal.

As he walked over the single span bridge, he began whistling the Bonnie Banks of Loch Lomond and put his gloved hands in his pockets for extra insulation against the cold. He stopped momentarily and pulled out a pen. Looking at it for a few seconds, he pressed a button and it emitted a powerful red laser dot as the beam hit the path in front of him. He chuckled out loud. Mr Petrie just loved it when plans came together and this one had worked perfectly.

Yury would have been shocked to know that the sniper he crept up on had already been immobilised by the history master. The assassin made an easy target for the Russian's knives because he was suffering from an advanced state of paralysis brought about by a poison dart. He could still breathe, but only just and would fall into a coma within hours, not that it would matter by then in any case, Mr Petrie mused.

The assassin had accepted a contract to kill Duncan Dewar and was planning to shoot the schoolboy as he arrived at the church. Earlier that day, he had collected a set of instructions from a safety deposit box in the rental apartment block opposite the world famous church. After reading the instructions, he accessed the roof via an internal fire escape and picked the best position from where he could target the boy.

Mr Petrie had also accessed the roof but he used an internal staircase from a restaurant below. He lay in wait patiently despite the sub-zero temperatures for the hired killer to arrive. Then, using a blowpipe barely the size of a straw, he fired a tiny poisoned dart into the assassin's neck causing instant paralysis.

The dart had been laced with a deadly snake venom provided by Merrick. She had handed him two darts from her laboratory as he prepared for the trip and when he asked: "Why two?"

Eyebrows arched, she said: "You might miss and want to use the other on yourself! Failure is not really an option, is it?" Merrick was indeed one scary woman, he reflected at the time.

He walked over to his target and set about him like a crime scene investigator by gathering all incriminating evidence. As an extra measure, he used the dead man's mobile phone and took a photograph of the assassin's face, profile shot and ears. He then used a mobile electronic scanner to take palm and fingerprints.

It was only when he stretched out the man's right hand, any guilt he felt about his actions disappeared as there, clutched between his middle and forefinger, was a photograph of Duncan Dewar. If confirmation was needed that the boy was the intended target; here was the proof.

Opening his battered briefcase, Mr Petrie pulled out an oblong metal case the shape of a large letterbox and not much deeper. Using his own unique palm print pressed against an electronic window, the box flap opened and emitted a sapphire blue glare. He then quickly uploaded the contents he'd taken and, in layman's terms, was posting the data to an electronic portal in Merrick's laboratory.

Seconds later, a waiting skelwark, alerted by a high-pitched bleep of its arrival, removed a passport, flight tickets and documents from the portal while another began processing the data from the mobile fingerprint monitor. The Skelwarks instantly began a global search of all the known criminal, intelligence and military databases. Mr Petrie knew by the time he reached his room in the Kempinski, he would be in possession of the available information he needed.

Before he left the rooftop, he went to the edge and, using a red laser pen, tried to attract the attention of the Volkov security team but they were in deep conversation. Mr Petrie started to look around and saw another man emerge from the church and light up a cigarette, so he pointed the laser down towards his feet. It did the trick. He'd caught Yuri Barsukov's attention, and so would let the Russian mafia deliver justice to the roof top assassin in their own way.

By the time Mr Petrie stepped into the hotel lift, he saw Dr Jones arrive with his kilted choir much to the curiosity and amusement of the New Year's Eve revellers gathering there that night. After some gentle coaxing and the promise of free midnight feast from the night manager, the choir was persuaded to give one more rendition of 'Auld Lang Syne' before retiring to the eighth floor.

To the delight of those present, the boys sang the chorus in Russian. They'd rehearsed it often enough but Mr Jones didn't think it was pitch or word perfect for the concert but, now that the pressure was off, he gave the choir a free rein and, to his amazement and delight, they delivered.

"Boys you were magnificent, all of you. For those of you who want to go, I will escort you to the Volkov's party and while there may be some partaking of alcohol by guests, remember it is not for you. I want everyone accounted for and back on the eighth floor by 12:15 and if you still have the energy, we can tuck into this midnight feast."

Anticipating Dr Jones alcohol ban, Svetlana had already arranged to keep the choir out of temptation's way by providing an adjoining room with soft drinks, snacks and some computer games.

A pyramid-shaped glass mountain offering a choice of plain or pink vintage champagne formed the centrepiece on a table near the entrance where Svetlana and Viktor stood to welcome their arriving guests. "Ah, Svetlana, you look so gorgeous," oozed Yury Barsukov's wife Olga. "Tonight was incredible. You must tell me about this Scottish school. Maybe

I will send my boys." Svetlana kept a fixed grin on her face to mask her disapproval at the very idea the uncultured Barsukov's could send their children to Sweetheart.

After Viktor greeted his guests, he walked over to Yury and said: "Follow me." The pair went outside the function room and stood against the rails overlooking the pitched glass ceiling of the Kempinski foyer. "So did you get bored with the concert? I noticed you leave after only ten minutes."

Yury smiled and replied: "You should be grateful I am more alert than your own security. You do know there was a hired gun on the rooftop opposite, don't you?

Viktor tried not to look surprised and said: "Continue." Yury enthusiastically regaled him with the events that had unfolded outside the church and how he located the assassin. He could not fail to be impressed, although listened with an expression bordering on mild disinterest.

"I don't mind telling you, Viktor, it brought back the old days. I didn't realise just how much I'd missed the feeling of pure adrenalin racing through my veins. Watching my stocks and shares perform on the MOEX isn't as much fun. By the way I'm feeling rather naked now," he said, lifting up trouser leg to reveal two empty knife sheaths.

"So who was this unfortunate assassin, then?" he asked. Yury looked furtively around and said: "I'm not sure. He didn't look Russian, more European but the thing is he carried no documents, only this key for a room in the apartment block below." After giving the key to Viktor, he added: "I've no idea what's in the room. I had to hurry back for the concert, you know."

Viktor called over one of his security men and whispered instructions in his ear before giving him the key. He then turned to Yury and put his hand on his shoulder: "I will not forget this Yury. By the way, have your American contacts come back to you?"

Yury shook his head, adding: "All I know is that some British government scientists were developing a top secret energy programme and they turned rogue against the state.

"They hid their invention and somehow it is all linked to one of the boys in your choir. I think the Yanks are irate that their English poodles had been holding out on them and, as usual, we Russians get the blame. If we're not hacking in to their computers and rigging their elections, they accuse us of destabilising their economies and laundering dirty money.

"If we did everything they said we did, we'd be ruling the world." Viktor laughed and slapped Yury's back. He then walked over to the side room where the choirboys were being entertained with mind-bending card tricks by Vlad and Sergei.

He looked at Willie Carmichael who was wearing a baseball cap backwards, no doubt to hide his bald patch. Carmichael was born on the Isle of Lewis in the Outer Hebrides, although his parents came from Edinburgh where they'd cornered a sizeable part of the market on renewable energy. 'A bunch of wind farms was hardly going to destabilise the Middle East,' he mused. Then he looked at Duncan Dewar, another ginger-haired boy.

"Duncan, come over here!" shouted Viktor. "I want to congratulate you again on a stunning performance. A pity your parents couldn't be here, but we will make sure they get a recording. In fact we could download and send it to them tonight."

Duncan Dewar looked quizzically at Viktor and said: "I'm sorry, sir. I thought you knew. I'm an orphan and my parents died when I was a baby."

Viktor feigned surprise and said: "I had no idea. I'm terribly sorry. That must be really painful for you, being all on your own."

The boy nodded sadly and said: "At least I still have my grandfather, over there," he said, pointing at Gordon Buie through the open door and into the next room.

"Can I ask you something? What happened to your parents? Do you remember anything about them at all?"

Again Duncan looked sad and hunched his shoulders: "Sometimes I think I remember my mother but I wonder if it's because the picture I have in my head is like the photograph I have of her at home. She was beautiful and kind, and that's where I get my colour from as my father was blond. They were killed in a car accident in Scotland and somehow, I survived.

"I feel very sad because I'm sure they would have been proud if they had heard me tonight," he added. Viktor looked down at the boy and said: "I'm sure they would have been proud. Did they sing? Exactly what did they do?"

Again Duncan hunched his shoulders: "I don't know where I got my voice from as I don't think either of them sang. I don't think they had the time. Grandad said they worked very hard on space travel and other projects like that. They were both scientists and I think that's why I love science so much."

Viktor patted him on the head and said: "In the spring, you must come back to Russia and join me and the boys to the Yuri Gagarin Cosmonaut Training Center in Star City. I bet you would love looking around there." Duncan nodded enthusiastically. He'd heard about the facility named after the first man in space.

Andrei walked up and grabbed Duncan in a bear hug, lifting him off the ground. "So papa, you've met Duncan, then? He's the little shrimp with the big voice and we are all very proud of him."

Viktor laughed and said: "Put him down. We were just making plans for the spring vacation. I'll let him tell you all about it." He then walked back in to the main room to rejoin the adult guests but was still left pondering about the Sweetheart Abbey pupil.

Meanwhile, in a small balcony room, Mr Petrie sat back in his armchair as an organised fireworks display marking the arrival of the New Year lit up the St Petersburg skyline. The intelligence file sent from Merrick revealed the dead man was a former member of a top-secret covert action group from the DGSE, France's top-secret military intelligence agency. He had left his elite unit under a cloud and began working as a 'freelance operator' for US intelligence in the Middle East.

Pascal Bernard's CV made grim reading. The thirty-year-old excelled in his deadly trade after honing his skills in Iraq where he ran a covert assassination team for a US contractor. However, he had also accepted work from several major crime syndicates operating out of South America, Western Europe and the Baltic states as well as a couple of Arab royals; in other words, his only loyalty appeared to be with the highest bidder at the time.

The last sizeable deposit to his Swiss account was made days earlier and came from an equally secretive account in the

Cayman Islands but the Cayman account was tracked back to another account in Switzerland, belonging to the corporate entertainment account of a major oil producing company with investments in Iraq, Saudi and Kuwait oil.

The same account was used to buy first-class flights from Bernard's home in Nice to St Petersburg and pay for the rented apartment. Both the French passport and driving licence were top quality fakes in the name of Leo Dubois and the Kalashnikov VSV-338 sniper rifle was reported stolen from a Russian military base in Crimea a few months earlier.

The kid leather wallet removed from his pocket contained currency in euros, rubles and dollars and only one platinum credit card also in the name of Leo Dubois.

Mr Petrie's head was spinning at the enormity of the so-called players involved and realised that Duncan Dewar would never be safe as long as he walked around with the RFID chip in his neck. His parents had unwittingly condemned their son to death by inserting the chip under his skin. Their intention was to remove it as soon as they were in a safer environment but their premature deaths brought all their future plans to an abrupt end.

But the other mystery was who had alerted such dark forces to come together to target the boy? It could only be someone close to Duncan, possibly someone at Sweetheart Abbey School. Opening his briefcase, he pulled out a mirror the size of a tablet and pressed the right-hand corner. Within seconds, he was staring into the face of Merrick. "Duncan Dewar's secret was safe until it became known he had an implant in his neck. The first hint was at the hospital when an X-Ray located an alien object about the size of a rice grain underneath his skin.

"On the second occasion, he was passing through the airport security scanner at the VIP section of Edinburgh Airport when all in the immediate vicinity knew he had a metal fragment of some sort in his neck. I believe someone has had Duncan under surveillance for years, gambling on the chance that one day he might lead them to the Infinity Cell.

"We need to check and crosscheck all communications. There has to be an electronic trail that will lead us to the individual or organisation which would rather kill him off than see his parent's work resurrected."

Merrick nodded: “In other words, you want my team to search through an electronic haystack looking for a needle which may or may not be there?”

Petrie sighed: “I know, it is hopeless but we have to try. I’m not sure when the next kidnap or assassination attempt is going to be made on the lad, but it is now a question of ‘when’ and not ‘if’. Keeping one step ahead is taking as much time and energy as a needle hunt.”

Merrick snapped back: “Consider it done. Keep the channel links open. Oh, and Mr Petrie…”

The history master looked and said: “Yes?”

“Happy New Year to you.”

The screen went blank and an amused look crossed Mr Petrie’s face: “Did I just see Merrick smile?”

Back at the Volkov’s party one of Viktor’s security team handed his boss and envelope. He whispered: “The room was clean, although the guy did leave a photocopy of a French passport at the desk. It’s in the name of Leo Dubois of Nice but who knows if that is fake or genuine and I’ve no idea where the original is. Who do you think he was sent to kill?” Viktor just shrugged and walked away.

***

Chapter 21

Mr Petrie's tablet began flashing and Merrick appeared on screen to inform him that a possible three suspects had been gleaned from those who knew about Duncan Dewar's implant but all possibilities were quite remote.

The most obvious candidates, she said, were the head of Plato House, Dr Liam Wallace and Sweetheart's choirmaster Dr Geraint Jones. Both were present when doctors informed Duncan's grandfather of the mystery object they'd located in the nape of the schoolboy's neck after his cross-country accident.

"But by that time the boy ended up in hospital, the choir's trip to Russia was already being planned and the only dramatic increase in mobile phone activity was between Dr Geraint Jones and Svetlana Volkov. She automatically called her husband after every call with Dr Jones but, again, it's not hard evidence of anything sinister," observed Merrick.

"Perhaps you need to look more closely at your Sweetheart colleagues. You will receive background checks on Wallace and Jones in the next few minutes but there's nothing that signals alarm bells. However, there might be something in there more obvious to you," she added.

Mr Petrie was becoming anxious. "Our time is limited. Whoever is targeting the boy will make another attempt soon and it might be easier just to get him out by other means," he told Merrick.

He then faltered, adding: "You said there were three suspects but you've only given me two so far."

Merrick nodded: "Yes. The third is only a remote possibility. The police officer Jane Rooke also knew about the hospital discovery, didn't she? Well, while she seems innocuous, we have found an interesting past belonging to her elder brother.

"He's a convicted eco warrior; works for some environmental groups and has been arrested several times including once by Russia. His data will also be posted to you but, again, be warned the links are very tenuous. We're still looking for other leads and we will not give up just yet."

Mr Petrie sighed as Merrick exited from the screen. 'There must be a link with the school,' he mused, before his thoughts were interrupted by the electronic signal of an inbox deposit. Checking his electronic portal, he found a sheaf of papers outlining the history and details of all three suspects.

To the annoyance of Merrick and other members of the Council of Anam Cara, Mr Petrie preferred to receive intelligence files as hard copies rather than electronically, reading from a tablet or computer screen. "Yes, I am a dinosaur, an old fossil if you will, but I think better when I have paper in my hands," he once said in an argument with Salar in a debate over a paperless society.

The first file was on Dylan Rooke who was a bachelor in his late thirties and had devoted his life to environmental issues resulting in arrests in South America, the Arctic, the Great Barrier Reef and in Dounreay. The last entry caught Mr Petrie's beady eye, for this was the site chosen where Moira and Douglas Dewar were going to unveil their Infinity Chip prototype.

A group of international eco warriors had gathered around the same time to highlight UK Government plans to move radioactive waste from the old test reactor which had been closed down in 1969. Four decades later, the problematic group of so-called 'exotic fuels' had not been resolved and the uranium comprising of radioactive powders, pellets and compounds were still being stored at the site in Dounreay.

Could his arrival at the protest be a coincidence or had the group heard about the unveiling of an invention which, in the right hands, could deliver free energy to the planet making fossil fuels virtually redundant overnight? 'The Infinity Chip would certainly rock Dylan Rooke's world and catch his group's attention,' thought Mr Petrie.

However, as he scanned Rooke's charge sheet which listed piracy, terrorism, espionage and the more mundane breaches of the peace, anti-social behaviour orders and resisting arrest, he felt the arrests and convictions revealed nothing more sinister than passive resistance and, whoever Petrie was looking for did not fall in to this category. While the contract killer Pascal Bernard appeared to hold no conscience and would sell his soul to the highest bidder, Dylan Rooke was quite different, a man with a conscience for whom money meant little or nothing. Nor did violence appear to be in his DNA.

Dr Liam Wallace, at five feet three inches tall, balding with a desperate looking comb-over and suffering from clinical obesity, hardly cut the figure of an international man of mystery. Graduating from Edinburgh University with a First-Class Honours in Geography, he joined Sweetheart Abbey the same year as Duncan Dewar was enrolled in the prep school. He became head of Plato House a year later in addition to being promoted to the head of the geography department.

Mr Petrie's bushy eyebrows visibly heightened as he continued reading. It seems his penchant for female sex workers and several police cautions for kerb crawling brought about two divorces and while his cell phone activity was extremely high in the week leading to Duncan's accident, the flurry of numbers he called were to chat lines offering live calls with Russian and Ukrainian ladies.

"The man is clearly a sex pest. Who did his criminal background record check? He shouldn't be working with children, at all," said Mr Petrie out loud, adding to himself, 'No wonder the geography master volunteered to offer his services to escort the school choir to St Petersburg.' However, he reasoned, while Dr Wallace's unsavoury lifestyle choices did not make him a killer, if his sordid past and chat line activities became known, it could expose him to blackmail.

The real question Mr Petrie needed to know was exactly how far would Dr Wallace be prepared to go to keep his sleazy, double life a secret?

Before joining Sweetheart, he worked at several other schools in Scotland but started out in the oil industry during the oil-boom years as a geologist for a multi-national corporation. Mr Petrie called Merrick and said: "I need more information on

Dr Wallace like who provided his last job references, who carried out criminal background checks and if these Russian women he likes to telephone have any links, no matter how remote, with any other persons of interest. In addition, is he still in touch with the oil company he used to work for and if so, can we check into the backgrounds of his colleagues?

"I'd drop Dylan Rooke for now. He just doesn't have the right sort of profile," said Mr Petrie.

"And what about Dr Geraint Jones, then?" asked Merrick.

"Oh, I'm going to see him after we're finished. I may come back to you, although I'm still inclined to get the boy out of here quickly and back to Sweetheart where we can protect him."

Mr Petrie ran through the contents of Dr Jones' folder and while there was no criminal record, he noted he had been investigated and charged with murder, although there was no indication of a trial or media coverage. The investigation coincided with his mid-term departure from a boarding school in Wales where he was head of music.

It was all very mysterious but if Dr Jones was capable of murder, then he was capable of anything. 'Who did he murder and, if guilty, how did he wriggle out of it?' wondered Mr Petrie. Serving as Sweetheart's choirmaster and music teacher for more than ten years, he was also curious as to how he'd managed to gloss over his departure from the previous school, since it was so obviously linked to the police investigation.

Rather predictably the volume of calls between him and Svetlana Volkov spiked in the run up to the carol concert and the St Petersburg trip but there were no overseas calls prior or even many calls on his private line and mobile phone in the ten years he'd been at Sweetheart. This absence of interest beyond the school served only to fuel Mr Petrie's curiosity about Dr Jones even more.

Several minutes later, Mr Petrie made his way to the hotel lift and went to the ninth floor where Dr Jones and the rest of the choir were having breakfast. The chatter across the tables almost ceased as he walked in and looked around. "Mr Petrie! What on earth are you doing here? What a wonderful surprise!" bellowed Dr Jones.

He looked around at the rows of curious faces and declared: "Do you really think I would miss out on such a historic occasion? I went along to the concert last night and I have to tell you all, it was an amazing, powerful performance and I have never felt so proud of our school."

The choir cheered and Dr Jones looked delighted. He stood up and invited Mr Petrie to join him over breakfast, pulling an empty chair alongside. "You have no idea how happy I am to see you, Mr Petrie. These have probably been the most rewarding few weeks of my life, and wait till I tell you about the dramas behind the scenes."

Mr Petrie looked around and caught Gordon Buie's eye. He nodded over to the old man and Duncan sitting by his side before turning back to Dr Jones who was regaling him about all the work that had gone in to the previous night's performance. He then went to the buffet table to help himself to some fruit and, on the way, put a hand on Gordon Buie's shoulder, whispering in his ear: "We will talk later. Do not leave the hotel and keep Duncan close. Use your health as an excuse."

Sitting down again, Dr Jones continued with his excited chatter and then said: "The boys are going on a private tour around the former home of Catherine the Great. Apparently it has ornately decorated ballrooms and was also home to many other Russian tsars who used the palace as their summer retreat. You know there is one room called 'The Amber Room', created in 1701 using six tons of amber, imagine that!"

Mr Petrie began laughing: "I can see Geraint you've digested the local guide book. Before you head off, can I have a few minutes of your time?"

After breakfast, the boys returned to their rooms and began to prepare for the tour at 10 am while back in Dr Jones' suite the choirmaster was making coffee for himself and Mr Petrie. "I don't think, in the time I've known you Geraint, seeing you so happy before. It's as though a great weight has been lifted from your shoulders."

The choirmaster laughed and said: "I know I'm not the most gregarious soul and some folk might think I'm anti-social but if life has taught me one thing, Mr Petrie, it is to keep my own counsel. However the rebuilding of the choir, the endowment from Mrs Volkova and all of this," he said, waving his arm around the room. “Well, it has restored my faith in life.”

Mr Petrie hunched his shoulders and began rubbing his hands as he moved forward in his chair, saying: “I feel that there’s something you’re not telling me. I know we’ve never really had a sit-down talk like this before. Perhaps we’ve both been too busy or maybe we both guard our private lives carefully.”

Dr Jones’ smile seemed to freeze on his face and he said: “You know, don’t you?”

Mr Petrie tilted his head to one side and also became serious. “Was it Dr Collins who told you? Nobody else could have… I always knew my past would come back to haunt me.” The choirmaster gave a huge gulp and then just seemed to explode into a heaving mass of sobs which produced uncontrollable tears.

His whole demeanour took Mr Petrie by surprise as this was not what he had expected. He got up and put both his hands on his shoulders and bent down to his eye level. “Geraint, I am not a gossip and Dr Collins has said nothing to me but, some information has come my way about your previous place of teaching and rapid departure. Is it something you feel you can share?”

The choirmaster shook his head in denial and then gave a big sigh and said: “Oh, you might as well know. I was investigated for the murder of my beloved wife, Caitlin. She died, you see, from an overdose of sleeping pills which I administered. Yes, I hold up my hands I killed my wife, my childhood sweetheart, my Caitlin.

“There is not one day that goes by I don’t think of her and there is not one day that goes by that I regret my role in her death.” Taking a deep breath and gathering his composure again, he told Mr Petrie about how their lives were turned upside down when his wife, Caitlin, was diagnosed with a brain tumour aged twenty-three.

“We hadn’t even been married two years when it was discovered, inoperable of course and the most aggressive form of tumour. Caitlin was a nurse and she knew what to expect and she was so brave and courageous and beautiful, but…she wanted to die before the tumour robbed her of her dignity.”

The tragedy of the case almost took away Mr Petrie's breath. He had not expected such a confession and as he continued with his story he reflected on how cruel fate can be. "There's a group in Switzerland called 'Dignitas' which offers euthanasia but by the time we'd made a decision, she was too sick to travel.

"In the end, she decided on a date when she was still sound of mind and, with my help, she took an overdose of sleeping pills and drifted off peacefully in my arms. Of course her doctor called the police and, while I expected it, I had no idea of what would unfold. Local gossips pointed fingers, and while the story didn't hit the media, the hate mail began to arrive.

"The police handled it the best way they could because the 1961 Suicide Act makes it an offence to encourage or assist the suicide of another. You know it carries upto fourteen years in prison, but this vile disease has given me a life sentence, Mr Petrie, a life sentence indeed."

While police in Wales dropped charges against him on the advice of prosecutors who said justice would not be served by putting Dr Jones on trial, the school where he taught persuaded him to hand in his notice. "Because of their flaming Christian values, they said it was incompatible for me to remain as a teacher and so, I jumped before I was pushed," he said.

There was an uneasy silence and then Mr Petrie added: "You thought Dr Collins had told me…"

The tearful choirmaster nodded and said: "People think he's a cold fish, but I thought honesty is the best policy and so, when I applied for the position, I told him the truth. I asked for his confidence and he agreed.

"You know for the first time since my Caitlin's death I've tasted happiness again through the boys' choir. Their singing has inspired me and I almost felt as though my wife was by my side as young Dewar sang his solo last night. But, now that my secret is out, I suppose the finger pointing will start again…"

Mr Petrie stood up and said: "Nonsense, Geraint! What you have told me today will remain between us. I, too, lost my beloved wife and I can tell you the pain will ease, but hang on to the memories and treasure them forever. We have both been blessed by experiencing a love that some will never taste."

Rubbing his hands over his tearstained face, he looked quizzically at Mr Petrie. "I'm sorry, I never knew. I always assumed you were a bachelor, not sure why. I suppose we both keep our own counsel but perhaps now we can be friends and allies."

Just then, there was a knock on the door and both men composed themselves as Duncan Dewar walked in. "Please sirs, my grandfather is feeling unwell, so if you don't mind I think we will remain in the hotel for today and skip the tour of the royal palace."

Dr Jones smiled and said: "Yes, of course. Does he need a doctor?"

Mr Petrie intervened and said: "I'll pop in and see him, Geraint. You have a wonderful day."

As he reached the door to follow Dewar down the corridor, he turned back to the choirmaster and said: "Enjoy your triumphs and successes; they are well-deserved. You can stop hiding now and start living again.

"Your story today has reminded me of the pain of losing someone dear, but it has also told me that you are a man of great courage and moral fibre and for that, I will always hold you in great respect. Your secret is safe with me."

As he walked towards Gordon Buie's room, he realised he was no further to solving the immediate dilemma of who wanted to harm Duncan. However, he was confident that the finger of suspicion no longer pointed at Dr Jones, and since he'd also eliminated Dylan Rooke, the eco warrior, that just left the head of Plato, Dr Liam Wallace.

***

Chapter 22

Mr Petrie knocked on Gordon Buie's bedroom door and as it opened, the old man held his finger to his lips, nodding in the direction of the sofa where Duncan was lying fast asleep. "I think the events of the last few days have finally caught up with him.

"I couldn't believe my eyes when you walked in to the breakfast room. You must have ran straight to the airport and jumped on the first plane to St Petersburg after we spoke," he said in hushed tones.

"I can't go in to specific details, Gordon, but your instincts served you well and I am glad you called me, but I am going to ask you to take a big leap of faith and trust what I am about to say without question. Your grandson is in grave danger and is being targeted by dark forces, powerful men in powerful places who do very bad things."

The grandfather nodded in a resigned fashion and sighed: "It's his parents, isn't it? Their work has come back to haunt us. I've been in denial really since the time of their accident, the helicopter crash and the break-in. Some things just didn't add up, but I was too wrapped up in grief that I just wanted to focus on something good and that was Duncan".

"As I said Gordon, your instincts have served you well and perhaps your lack of curiosity has also acted as a self-preservation filter. My job now is to get us all back to Sweetheart as soon as is humanly possible, but I need you to feign illness in order for me to arrange an emergency flight to Edinburgh.

"A Learjet will be landing at Pulkova in around thirty minutes' time and an ambulance will collect us from the hotel at around the same time. There'll be a few flashing lights, sirens and a wee bit of drama, but this has to look convincing,

Gordon. Our lives depend on it. I remember you gave a brilliant portrayal of King Lear when you were a lad at Sweetheart, so I know you can do it."

Both men raised a smile at the memory of the performance. "I'm going to give you an injection which will send you to sleep and I promise you won't feel any pain. When you come around, we'll be well on our way to Edinburgh."

Mr Petrie reached inside his coat for the hypodermic needle which already contained the knockout drops needed to render Gordon Buie unconscious. As he administered the shot, Duncan Dewar had opened his eyes and witnessed his grandfather being injected and losing consciousness. He closed his eyes tight and pretended to be still asleep while he tried to understand what he had just seen.

So many questions were swirling around his head. Why was his history master trying to harm his grandfather? Had Mr Petrie just killed him? He heard Mr Petrie walk past him and leave the bedroom through the main door, but where was he going and how long would he be?

He jumped up and felt for his grandfather's pulse. To his relief, he was still alive and so he tried to shake him and wake him up. He didn't know when Mr Petrie would return and just then the door opened and it was the housekeeping maid.

"Quick, quick, you have to help me. We need to get my grandfather out of here. Someone is trying to kill him." The maid was surprised, momentarily, and felt for a pulse.

She looked around and asked: "Is there anyone else here?"

Duncan cried: "No, there's no one. We're all alone. We've got to get him out of here before Mr Petrie returns. Help me, please." Again the maid felt for a pulse, told Duncan to wait and then wheeled in her housekeeping trolley of sheets, towels and cleaning equipment.

By this time the boy was kneeling by his grandfather, urging him to wake up. "Don't worry, help is on its way," said the maid in a soothing voice. Suddenly he heard her gasp and then she fell clumsily on top of him before rolling on her back still clutching a hand towel. He turned around and saw Mr Petrie standing over him with what looked like a tiny, metal dart. The boy cowered and closed his eyes, instinctively covering his head with his hands.

"Hey laddie, what's wrong with you?" asked Mr Petrie in gentle tones.

Duncan sprang to his feet, trembling and shouting: "I don't know who you are anymore! You've tried to kill my grandfather and now you've just killed the maid."

Mr Petrie put down the dart and grabbed the boy by his shoulders, shaking him. "Stop this hysteria. It doesn't suit you. Your grandfather is alive and as for the maid, how many maids do you know who carry this is their cleaning bucket?" Mr Petrie bent down and removed a towel from the woman's right hand to reveal a revolver fitted with a silencer.

"If I hadn't walked in when I did, you would have a hole in the back of your head the size of a golf ball. Far from trying to kill you, I've just saved your life – and not for the first time either, laddie! All of this!" he exclaimed, waving his arms around the room: "all of this was done for you."

He then dragged Duncan over to the side of the balcony and, twitching the net curtain, said: "There are some very bad people out there who would do you harm. And if you look closely at the rooftop opposite, you'll see one of them. He has a gun and telescopic sights trained on this room and if he can get you in his crosshairs, he'll pull the trigger so stay away from the windows."

Kneeling down, Mr Petrie opened his briefcase and a puff of chilled air rose out of it before quickly evaporating. "Time is running out and I've one more thing to do now, which will probably cause further confusion in your mind. Duncan, do you trust me?"

The boy looked at his history master and stammered: "I'm not sure. I don't know who you are anymore. For all I know, you've killed my grandfather and just murdered a maid."

He plunged his hand inside the briefcase and pulled out a full-sized crossbow which, in itself, defied logic since it was three times the size of the case in terms of length. Putting his hand back inside the case, he seemed to be grappling or feeling around for something else and pulled out a pair of asbestos-coated gloves.

Duncan watched in silence as Mr Petrie donned the gloves before reinserting his left hand inside the amazing case to pull out a long silver container the size and shape of a thermos flask. He watched in silence as the flask was twisted open.

He couldn't quite work out the contents but noticed another wisp of chilled air rising from within the flask. He'd seen something similar in chemistry when the master had produced a block of dry ice as an illustration of what a solid form of carbon dioxide looks like. Still protected by the gloves, Mr Petrie picked up what looked like a bolt contained in the flask and slid it carefully into the flight groove of the crossbow.

Duncan asked: "What is that?"

He turned around with an enigmatic smile and replied: "Let's call it 'The Spear of Merrick'." He then gently said to the schoolboy: "I need you to remain calm, and you're doing an excellent job so far. Now when I give the signal, gently slide the balcony door back three or four inches which will be just enough to allow me to take aim."

The boy silently did as he was told and watched in amazement as his Scottish history master appeared to morph into a cold-blooded assassin. Focussing his eyes through the crossbow's telescopic sights, he took aim and fired the ice bolt across the canal. Moments later, a body plunged headlong in to the canal from the building opposite.

"The bolt was made from dry ice. By the time the police get there, it will have evaporated and all evidence gone," said Mr Petrie. He returned the crossbow inside the mysterious case which seemed to have an endless capacity before placing the silver flask inside too.

Scanning the room quickly for anything left behind, he then picked up the poisoned dart he'd used on the maid. Just then, the wails of an ambulance siren could be heard in the street below and Mr Petrie turned to the boy, saying: "The ambulance heading this way is for your grandfather. It's time to leave, but first help me drag this woman into the bathroom."

As they unceremoniously dragged her feet first across the floor, Duncan let out a gasp. "I've just seen her eyes move."

Mr Petrie replied: "She will make a full recovery in a few hours as the effects of the poisoned dart wear off. It contains a modified version of snake venom from the Common krait, also known as Bungarus caeruleus. Ever heard of it?"

Duncan looked incredulously at Mr Petrie. 'How could he remain so calm?' he wondered. Minutes later, having alerted the reception desk, paramedics came to their room and stretchered out an unconscious Gordon Buie accompanied by Duncan and the history master. In silence, they rode with the patient in the back of an ambulance as it hurtled towards the airport.

Once there, the ambulance was driven straight on to the tarmac to a designated area where the Learjet air ambulance was waiting. After a quick look through the paperwork and examining of passports, they boarded the plane and it took off almost immediately having been given special clearance by the flight tower.

The only others who remained on board were the pilot, co-pilot and a nurse. A few minutes into the flight, she appeared and gave Mr Buie an injection, reassuring Duncan: "He is fine and will gain consciousness in a few minutes. You're safe now, Duncan. Isn't that right, Mr Petrie? He nodded and smiled and then looked at Duncan with a more serious expression on his face.

"I suppose, laddie, you want some answers. Well, I should warn you to be careful what you wish for, but you are sensible and not usually given to histrionics, so brace yourself. What I am about to tell you is something far beyond your wildest imagination."

Mr Petrie then took Duncan through the whole, incredible history and timeline of his thirteen years. The boy experienced shock, anger, sorrow, rage and bewilderment and a few other emotions known to man in a period of about fifteen minutes. "I know it's a lot for anyone to take in, but you are capable and mature, Duncan. I would never have told you, had I not thought you could disseminate the information in a calm and rational way."

"You said back in the room that you'd saved my life before was that when I was in the car?"

He nodded and said: "You were belted in and asleep in a baby seat in the back of the car. You wouldn't have stood a chance in that inferno."

Duncan was trembling and his eyes welled up as he asked: "How, how much does my grandfather know?" There was a silence and then a third voice broke into the conversation: "Your grandfather knows as much as you do now, it seems." Both turned around in surprise; Gordon Buie had awoken from his deep sleep half way through Mr Petrie telling the story to Duncan.

"Welcome back, Gordon. You missed some excitement in the hotel room but I'll let Duncan tell you later. Suffice to say we are homeward bound and your grandson is safe for the time being, but for how long remains to be seen. While you were in the land of nod, there were two more attempts on his life, so whoever 'they' are, they are becoming more desperate and determined.

Duncan hugged his grandfather and said: "I thought Mr Petrie was trying to kill you!" They all laughed partly with relief and partly through a fear of the unknown that somehow brought them all together stronger and more solid than ever.

About an hour before landing, Mr Petrie turned to his fellow travellers and said: "I am still the Scottish History Master at Sweetheart and so, I would ask you both to keep my other activities a secret."

They nodded solemnly in agreement and then Duncan Dewar asked: "Who do you really work for, Mr Petrie? Are you like a James Bond?"

The history master chuckled and said: "Do I look like the sort of man who would drink a martini and have glamorous women falling at my feet? Gracious no, laddie. I'm no special agent but you can rest assured of one thing and that is, I do work for the good guys, which is why I am trying to keep you both out of harm's way.

"I've phoned ahead and the school gardener, Douglas Sinclair, will meet us at Edinburgh. Oh, and I've also spoken with Dr Jones and informed him of our dramatic exit but reassured him that Gordon is making a rapid recovery. I blamed the Russians for a misdiagnosis and said it was nothing more than extreme indigestion. However, it seems he's more concerned about you Duncan because the choir has been invited to perform before the local mayor but the show will now have to go on without you!

"Your absence will throw Mrs Volkova into deep despair," laughed Mr Petrie. This time, however, he could not have been more wrong. Svetlana Volkova and her husband were relieved to hear that Duncan Dewar and his grandfather were no longer in St Petersburg. “It is out of our hands now, thank God! They know we had nothing to do with the ambulance flight and we are off the hook,” Viktor told his relieved wife.

“Apparently, Mr Petrie organised the medical evacuation because the old man developed crippling chest pains which later turned out to be a chronic dose of indigestion and wind. I tell you Svetlana that schoolmaster is either a meddling old fool or a genius and I can’t work out which.”

***

Chapter 23

Gardener, Douglas Sinclair, loaded the luggage and the passengers on to the Sweetheart Abbey school bus. "Where to now, Mr Petrie?" He told him to head for Dulce Cor cottage and saw the look of dismay on Gordon Buie's face. "There is no way you can return to Stirling until this whole saga is resolved and your car is parked at Sweetheart, anyway."

As the bus pulled out of Edinburgh Airport, Mr Petrie moved forward to Duncan and said in a low voice: "The sooner we get that chip surgically removed, the better. If anyone makes mention of it again, no matter how well you think you know them, you simply tell them it worked its way to the surface and dropped out during a shower and down the plughole."

Mr Petrie, who was sitting with his back to Sinclair turned to the driver and asked him if there had been any unusual activity at the school. Sinclair, a handsome-looking, muscular man shook his head, replying: "Nothing that I have noticed. Apart from you and me, no one else has been at Sweetheart, although Dr Collins called to say he would be returning in the morning.

"I know the house heads are also arriving tomorrow night to prepare for the start of spring term next week. I have to go back to the airport for the school choir's return tomorrow evening but if you need me for anything else, I am at your service. You seem a little on edge, Mr Petrie. Is everything Okay?"

It occurred to Mr Petrie he knew very little about the gardener who had arrived at the school last summer after the previous gardener had retired. He looked at him thoughtfully and, on the surface, Sinclair seemed pleasant, polite and hard working. Standing at six feet two inches tall, he cut quite a striking figure and his long hair was usually scooped up casually in either a man bun or ponytail, neither trend of which he approved.

He made a mental note to have the skelwarks do a background check since it seemed the school's human resources department had not picked up on Dr Liam Wallace's extracurricular activities and they could have been just as sloppy when appointing Sinclair. It was becoming difficult to know who he could trust.

"No, you've done a grand job. I've got your mobile, Mr Sinclair, if we need anything else, but Mr Buie and young Dewar will be staying with me until the start of term," responded Mr Petrie. As they headed towards the city bypass, a blue *Audi* estate car with a driver and front seat passenger followed. This was quickly picked up by the old master whose sixth sense was tingling and on full alert.

About forty miles later, Mr Petrie shouted over to the driver: "Let's take the scenic route today, Mr Sinclair, and go to Sweetheart via Wanlochead! There's a small road on the right, the B797 I think, and it should make a pleasant diversion."

Sinclair looked puzzled and said: "You want to go via the highest village in Scotland when snow is forecast on the hills?"

Mr Petrie replied quickly and in a slightly terse voice: "Aye, I do."

Leaving no room for discussion or alternatives, the gardener, clearly not happy, did as he was told and indicated right as the turn off approached. Mr Petrie breathed a sigh of relief as the blue car continued on its route but his relaxed mode was short lived as a red estate carrying three people, two cars behind, also signalled right.

"It seems we have company," remarked Mr Petrie to his two travelling companions.

"Aye," piped up Sinclair. "I noticed them as we left the airport road." Mr Petrie looked mildly surprised and asked if there was any particular reason his attention had been drawn to the red car.

"I noticed two hanging around the VIP lounge, no luggage, nothing. At first, I assumed they must be drivers waiting for a pick-up but when you arrived, they left and jumped in to the red car which is behind us now."

"I'm very impressed," said Mr Petrie. "Are you one of life's keen observers?"

Sinclair laughed and said: "The only reason I'm driving a school bus today is because I didn't pay attention to my surrounds. Let's just say I've learned the hard way to be more aware of unusual behaviour and the people in the car behind fall into that category. Should I be concerned, Mr Petrie?"

Duncan turned to his grandfather and said: "Oh, no. I'm getting a bad feeling just now."

The old man agreed and said: "I wouldn't mind another of Mr Petrie's knockout drops and then you can wake me up when this is all over."

As the road narrowed and twisted and turned, the weather became more changeable and sleet soon turned to snow. "This bus does not handle well in this weather. I think it was a mistake to choose the B-Road as we'd have a better chance on the motorway. At least we could be in the public eye. Who are these people, Mr Petrie?"

He moved forward and sat in the passenger seat next to the driver. Shouting back at Duncan and his grandfather, he said: "Buckle up because I think we're in for a rough ride for a few miles!" Just then, the red car appeared to shunt the bus. "I'm not sure if that was deliberate or if he is losing control as well but the conditions are worsening, Mr Petrie."

"Look. I can barely see the road. It's almost a winter whiteout. There's a narrow hump backed bridge coming soon, if my memory serves me correct and…" Sinclair fell silent as he struggled to control the bus and its back end went into a spin, hitting something solid.

The engine stalled and there was complete silence inside as the driver looked at his three passengers. All were speechless as they rubbed past the condensation on the windows to see what was happening outside, but it was impossible to see anything. Sinclair wound down his window and was blasted with a howling wind and snow blizzard.

"Stay in the bus," commanded Mr Petrie. "If we can't see them, the chances are they can't see us. Start the engine, Sinclair, there's a good lad and let's see if we can't move forward."

Sinclair looked at him and shouted back: "Move forward, move forward?! What don't you understand about 'I can't see a bloody thing in front of me?'" Two loud bangs and a shattered side window persuaded the driver it was safer to drive than not.

"My God, we're sitting ducks. Was that gunshot?" he asked, as he turned the ignition key. The engine fired up and unable to move forwards, Sinclair put the bus into reverse. The wipers cleared enough snow from the screen to make them realise that the bus had crashed and wedged itself into the hump back bridge in the village.

Two more shots were fired which spurred the driver to twist and turn the wheel while accelerating before he manoeuvred the bus into a position to move forward. The next two miles were a series of slips and slides and then the weather began to clear enough for them to realise that the red car was no longer following.

They would find out later that it had overturned near the bridge and tumbled into the river, killing both driver and front-seat passenger. The Dumfries media would report it as the tragic deaths of two foreign tourists in a hire car caught up in a snowstorm. There was no news about the existence of a third man.

By the time they had descended from the hills onto the A76 for Dumfries, the sun was breaking through the clouds and the only sign of inclement weather was a bit of slush on the side of the road. "Next time we'll stick to the main routes, I think," said Mr Petrie out loud.

"Erm… Douglas, can you see that this quarter window and back window panel are replaced quickly. Here's some money which will more than cover it, but I'd rather no one knew about what just happened.

"Are we all agreed on this, then?" he asked out loud, but there was no response. An hour later, the bus pulled up outside Dulce Cor and Sinclair turned to Mr Petrie and asked what he would say about the bus. "Don't worry. I'll give you a report which should satisfy the headmaster. We just don't need to mention the red car or its unsavoury occupants, okay?

"I will take full responsibility for the drive through Wanlochead. Just replace those windows soonest, please. Once inside the cottage, Mr Petrie showed his guests to their twin-bedded room with en suite and while they unpacked, he went back downstairs to make some tea.

"Life always seems so much better with a good, strong cup of tea," he said to himself. As he went for the tea caddy, he noticed a note from Salar requesting an urgent meeting. Retrieving his tablet from his briefcase, he saw it was flashing with several messages from Merrick, each one terser than the previous.

The Council of Anam Cara was holding an emergency meeting and his presence was requested. As he handed his houseguests cups of tea and biscuits, he said: "I have an urgent meeting I must attend. You'll be perfectly safe here and I want you to make yourselves at home. Do not open the door to anyone and I will be back shortly."

Mr Petrie grabbed his briefcase and left through the front door. Normally he would have used the secret passage underneath Dulce Cor but he didn't want to share such an intimate detail of his life with anyone. Instead, he went to the chapel and, using a skeleton key, opened the door and followed the spiral stone staircase down into the crypt.

He pressed his hand against a stone panel and the sealed entrance opened up for him. Within minutes, he was travelling through a network of tunnels until he arrived outside the door of the Anam Cara Council's chamber. Several skelwarks stood silently and observing as was their habit. One opened the solid wooden door for Mr Petrie and he walked in to an antechamber waiting to be summoned.

After a few minutes, a skelwark emerged from the council chamber and beckoned him to enter. He took a deep breath and walked in to the ebony panelled circular room which was dominated by a large, round table of green onyx and gold. Salar, in flowing drapes of white silk sat on a majestic-looking ornate, golden throne and the rest of the seats were taken by the other five members.

Merrick sat in her trademark black catsuit next to Benyellary, a willowy, fragile-looking individual with strong pre-Raphaelite features framed by long, gently waving locks almost as flame red as the wrap around flowing gown. Kirriereoch was equally striking as an albino with short, cropped white hair, while Tarfessock with shoulder-length brown hair, looked exquisite in a gown of peacock colours and was the only one in the group to have facial hair neatly trimmed, almost manicured to perfection. Shalloch's olive skin had an almost translucent glow which clashed with the thick, wiry, layered and multi-coloured dreadlocks.

Each member of the council was striking, formidable and almost androgynous but their indeterminate sex only served to make them more awesome. One of the skelwarks brought a chair to the table and Mr Petrie was silently encouraged to sit down as Salar waved an inviting hand in its direction.

"The Council is deeply disturbed by recent events and so we've held an emergency session," opened Salar in Mr Petrie's direction. "We have known, for some time, the capabilities of the infinity cell and have deliberated its usefulness in the twenty-first century.

"Merrick and Tarfessock think it should be utilised for the betterment of the planet and, indeed, in some ways they are right. The third world would benefit greatly from the technology of the Infinity Chip which would do away with the need for fossil fuels. The environment would benefit instantly in terms of clean air, rivers and other waterways.

"However, other members of the council believe it would be hijacked by the stronger elements in society and be put to an alternative use to oppress and control populations. Benyellary and Shalloch think the human race is too immature to handle such knowledge and Kirriereoch is concerned that its power will corrupt this world even more.

"I want to know what you think, Mr Petrie." He looked around the table and sighed: "This invention would undoubtedly benefit the planet from the great oceans to the rivers, streams and waterways. It's hard to imagine any disadvantages until you factor in the human being.

"Already there are dominant nations, criminal syndicates and powerful politicians who have shown they are prepared to kill in order to get their hands on this advanced technology. Far from bringing peace, it seems in the wrong hands it will fuel wars, oppression and tyranny."

Salar nodded thoughtfully and invited the rest of the council to voice their opinions. It was clear from the questions and the debate that had preceded the meeting, the issue of the Infinity Chip had divided the normally harmonious Anam Cara.

"It is the majority opinion here today, Mr Petrie, that human beings cannot be trusted with the advanced technology of the Infinity Chip and so, until we think man has become sufficiently developed and mature, we may store it in the Cabinet of Secrets. The final vote will take place this evening after everyone has spoken.

"Kirriereoch will visit you in the morning and remove the chip from the boy's neck so it can be prepared for deep storage in the Cabinet, as I think it will be many decades before we can consider releasing this technology. Moira and Douglas Dewar were decades ahead of their time and these scientists paid with their lives for their brilliance. Enough blood has been spilled on this issue."

Mr Petrie left the chamber and hurried back towards Dulce Cor through the subterranean route which led him once again into the Chapel crypt. Making his exit, he arrived back at his cottage where his houseguests were waiting patiently.

"Apologies for being absent this last hour but I do have some good news. Arrangements are being made to surgically remove the chip from Duncan's neck. It's a minor procedure and will only involve a localised anaesthetic. Once that is gone, my boy, you should be able to resume a normal life and continue to make a nuisance of yourself in my history classes."

That evening Duncan had an early night in preparation for the operation the following morning while Mr Petrie offered his prized whisky collection for Gordon Buie to sample. As he opened the cupboard, he looked in amazement: "Why some of this whisky is more than hundred years old. Surely that wee green bottle can't be, is it? Is that whisky from the old Glenavon Distillery in Ballindalloch?"

Mr Petrie laughed: "I see, you know your drink. Of course the distillery is long gone but if you want a dram…"

Gordon Buie interrupted before he could finish the sentence. "No, no. You mustn't. I'll satisfy myself with a glass of Jura and toast my ancestors."

The two men sat back and talked over old times at Sweetheart, remembering masters and incidents that raised an eyebrow or two back in the day. As the whisky flowed, it seemed to relax their tongues and they chatted like old school friends. A knock at the door interrupted the jollity and Mr Petrie went to see who would be calling so late at night.

A small figure draped in a dark cloak stood at the doorway and a slender blue arm extended towards him with a note. Once passed on, the silent messenger vanished into the night. Mr Petrie went and sat down and opened the folded paper. It was a message from Salar informing him that the council had, as expected, voted 4-2 in favour of archiving the Infinity Chip.

"Is that bad news?" enquired his guest but Mr Petrie just shook his head and said: "Now let me charge your glass again, Gordon. It is not often I receive company, and so I am going to exploit the situation."

Feeling slightly emboldened by the single malt, Gordon Buie said: "I still do not know your first name and I looked at my old school records and I couldn't even find an initial." Mr Petrie looked down into his glass and swirled the amber liquid around until the scent of the whisky's caramelised orange segments and warming mulled wine filled his nostrils. Lifting his solemn face and looking directly into Gordon's eyes, he said: "The last person to call me by my first name was my wife and I vowed then no one would ever utter it again. Of all the precious memories I have, it was our final conversation."

The eyes of both men became moist as they sat back and reflected on the precious memories life had given them. "You know a secret shared is a burden halved, Mr Petrie. If these last few days have taught me anything, it is that you are not who you seem to be and the purpose of your life is far removed from keeping alive the flame of Scottish history."

Mr Petrie looked at his friend and deliberated if he should share his secret or not, a secret he had kept from his wife and one that he had held close for more than five hundred years. He finally broke his silence and said: "If I offered you the gift of immortality, what would you say?"

Gordon Buie reflected on the idea and then laughed shaking his head: "Good God, no! What a curse! I can't think of anything worse. Maybe if you offered me this when I was youthful, I would take your hand off, but now, having lived such a full life when my time comes, who knows? I may even embrace the Grim Reaper.

"There are two things we cannot escape in life, Mr Petrie, and that is: taxes and death. Everything else, as you know, is more or less in our own hands." The two continued talking until well after midnight before they retired.

***

Chapter 24

The next day, Duncan waited anxiously for the chip to be removed. He was told it was such a simple procedure that the doctor would perform the operation in the study in Dulce Cor. In solidarity, Mr Petrie and Duncan's grandfather decided not to have breakfast until afterwards. A sharp rap on the door signalled the arrival of Dr Kirriereoch, a startling-looking albino with white blond hair.

Once in the study, he asked Duncan to remove his shirt as his grandfather sat and looked on anxiously, firing several questions of concern, all of which Kirriereoch found irritating. He reached into his doctor's bag and pulled out a laser-style pen which he fired at both Duncan and his grandfather.

"Was it really necessary to freeze them?" asked Mr Petrie.

Kirriereoch responded: "I really don't have time for all this nonsense. It's a simple operation," he said as he took a scalpel to the boy's neck. "There!" he said, holding up a minute chip. "Now let's get this off to Merrick to download and analyse.

"Yesterday was a closer call than the 4-2 vote reveals, you know. Salar was dithering and keeping us all on the edge of our seats; of course the right decision was reached in my view. Until the wretched planet become civilised, wars end and famines become a thing of the past, your society will never advance.

"Still, it keeps us all in a job," he said, wiping the back of Duncan's neck with antiseptic. "There, no bleeding, a tiny little scar instead of a raise pimple. All gone. Is this the boy you want as an apprentice, then?"

Mr Petrie replied: "I'm not certain yet, not even sure if I could work with anyone else."

Kirriereoch nodded sympathetically: "We had great faith in your instincts and integrity when we appointed you guardian all those centuries ago and you were, by today's standards, still a child. You are valued but we also recognise you cannot do this job alone as the challenges of this world are becoming more difficult, not easier."

Kirriereoch put his equipment away and slipped the tiny chip into a small silver casket with a pair of surgical tweezers. "There, my work is done. Until the next time, eh, Mr Petrie?"

As Kirriereoch turned to walk away, Mr Petrie said: "I think you've forgotten something," pointing at the motionless grandfather and patient.

"Here, you can take the glory. I really can't be bothered with any more tedious questions. Catch!" said Kirriereoch on throwing the pen to the schoolmaster before leaving the study. Mr Petrie shook his head in dismay at such a cavalier attitude but was equally delighted to be the holder of an 'immobiliser pen'.

He pointed the device at the two human statues and watched them unfreeze. "There it's all done. Now let's get to the village for a slap-up breakfast at the hotel. I'll drive." Duncan rubbed the back of his neck and felt a plaster. Gordon Buie was baffled and thought he must have nodded off in the chair, blaming the excesses of the night before.

"Well, that's a relief, we can all breathe more easily now," he said. However, he couldn't be more wrong and as they left the cottage they were still being watched.

After breakfast, the three walked to the car park and discovered Mr Petrie's distinctive black Austin Cambridge had a flat tyre. What would have once been regarded as a case of bad luck today instilled a sense of foreboding and anxiety as all three looked around for any other signs of unusual behaviour.

Mr Petrie called Douglas Sinclair and asked for help. He arrived shortly with his tool kit and said he would change the tyre. Giving the school bus keys to the master, he said he would return the car as soon as it was repaired.

Dr Collins was walking across the staff car park as the bus pulled in with Mr Petrie at the wheel. "Where is Sinclair and what's happened to the bus? It's in a shocking state."

Mr Petrie disembarked and said: "It's all my fault. When he picked us up from the airport, I insisted on the scenic route and we got caught in a blizzard at Wanlochead."

"Well, welcome back from St Petersburg and I gather that wasn't all smooth running either. I've just got some admin to do but I think it would be worth a catch up Mr Petrie in, say about half an hour," said the headmaster.

Back at Dulce Cor cottage, Gordon Buie asked if the old Lantern wall clock he'd repaired was still keeping good time. "Yes, it is running like, erm, clockwork but you've just reminded me of something else. I found another old brass lantern clock in the attic which I'd forgotten all about. If you've a mind to, would you like a look at it? It's quite an interesting piece but in a poor state," said Mr Petrie.

Ten minutes later, he produced a brass lantern clock made in 1623 by William Bowyer. Rather spookily, it had a carved skeleton on one side of the face and Chronus, the Greek god of time on the other. Both figures carried a scythe illustrating the preoccupation with the afterlife during the reign of James VI of Scotland.

With a single hand, the square-shaped brass clock sat on urn-shaped feet and finials with a top mounted bell. It was barely forty centimetres high and while it didn't look too impressive, the clockmaker and his grandson were clearly excited. Mr Buie went to his car and pulled out his trusty Gladstone bag containing all the essential kit a horologist would need.

Satisfied they'd be kept occupied for some time, Mr Petrie went off to the headmaster's study, bracing himself for the barrage of awkward questions. As he walked in, Dr Collins' PA offered to make him some tea, which he gladly accepted. "Strong, no sugar?" said Jennifer Hunter.

"You have an excellent memory, Miss Hunter. That would be most pleasing."

She asked him to wait in her office. "Dr Collins won't be too long. I've just given him some additional paperwork which needs his attention. I hear there was some excitement for the choir in St Petersburg. Are all the boys back now?"

Mr Petrie replied: "Only Duncan Dewar. He's at my cottage with his grandfather. The pair of them is staying for a few days but the rest of the choir arrives tomorrow.

"How was your festive break, Miss Hunter? Did you go anywhere nice?"

She smiled and replied: “I just had a quiet Christmas, me and my cat at home in Dumfries. Incidentally Mr Petrie, did you ever find the original paper contract when you joined the school? I still need a copy for my personnel files.”

He shook his head saying: “I keep forgetting but it’s good to know you keep on top of everyone’s files.

“Of course there wasn’t a human resources department when I first joined Sweetheart and after the flood destroyed most of the archives in the seventies, I imagine you’ve got a much more rigorous procedure in order now,” he mused.

Miss Hunter nodded enthusiastically: “Oh yes, very little escapes our attention these days with checks, cross checks. We can’t afford to get sued. Accountability is the key.”

He was half tempted to ask about Dr Liam Wallace and his record as a kerb crawler, but thought better of it. Just then, Dr Collins buzzed through on his intercom, saying: “Please let Mr Petrie in. I’m ready for him now. Oh, and the rest of the papers are ready to collect. I’ve gone through them. They’re all signed, but frankly I’m not sure what the urgency was, Miss Hunter.”

He walked in to the study and sat down on a comfortable, leather armchair and proceeded to brief the headmaster about the trip to Russia. “Incredible as it seems, the boy’s parents had inserted a chip containing their work into the nape of his neck, and then of course they were killed in a terrible car accident. All an unfortunate coincidence.”

Dr Collins sat for a while and then said: “My God! His parents must have been desperate. I wonder what is on this chip. Can it be removed?”

Mr Petrie said: “That’s the irony. In all these years, it has slowly worked its way to the surface of the skin and must have popped out while he was drying himself after a shower in the hotel.

“It was only something the size of a grain of rice or a pea, either way it’s gone, probably down a Russian plughole, so we will probably never know,” he added, having agreed with Dr Geraint Jones not to mention the ‘Willy Carmichael’ episode. There was also no way he was going to mention the three assassination attempts and his role in dispensing with all three killers or the events in Wanlochead.

“What I can tell you though, headmaster, is that the choir performed magnificently at St Petersburg and the boys with Dr Jones were a real credit to the school.”

The headmaster smiled and said: “You know I am particularly pleased for Dr Jones. He’s suddenly come in to his own and is making a worthy contribution. I am contemplating making him head of music as the current head retires next year. What do you think?”

Mr Petrie looked over his half-moon spectacles at the headmaster and said: “I think that would be a fine idea and extremely well-deserved.”

The headmaster rose to his feet and said he had to leave for the day and picked up a couple of files and his car keys. As he walked into his PA’s room, he looked puzzled. “Hmm, not sure where Miss Hunter has gone. She made such a fuss about coming in today, insisting I had documents to sign but I’m sure another day wouldn’t have mattered. Still, I’m sure you know your way out by now.”

Mr Petrie smiled and said: “I just need to leave her a note headmaster and I’ll see myself out.” He waited until Dr Collins had left the building and then he quickly returned to Miss Hunter’s office and began searching through the staff files, removing confidential folders on the gardener and the head of Plato House, Dr Liam Wallace.

As he walked through the door at Dulce Cor, the kitchen table was covered in newspapers and the dismantled clock’s parts. “I can see you’re full of busy. I’m just going to my study for an hour and then we can work out where to go for lunch. Would you mind not disturbing me?”

Gordon Buie smiled and said: “You go ahead, Mr Petrie. This is so cathartic for the pair of us. We’re having a right royal old time. And don’t worry about lunch. We’ve had two doorstep cheese and pickle sandwiches which will tide us over for a few hours.”

Mr Petrie smiled and went in to his study. As he looked through Dr Wallace’s confidential file, he was unable to find any references to criminal records, English police cautions or details of his kerb crawling activities. He had two glowing character references from his previous employer. It was as though Dr Wallace had reinvented his past, or those who wrote the references wanted to forget his misdemeanours.

He then picked up the gardener's folder and was surprised to see he had a criminal record for insider trading and had spent several years in an open prison and was out on licence. He found a handwritten note from the headmaster to Miss Hunter informing her to offer the gardener's position and cottage to Douglas Sinclair. "Everyone deserves a second chance and I am confident, having interviewed Mr Douglas, he is a rehabilitated offender with a genuine remorse for his actions. Furthermore, I do not see his presence around children as posing a threat or conflict of interest.

"Please offer him the post with the usual 'subject to contract and references' etc. etc." Mr Petrie sat back and wondered if he did pose a threat to Duncan Dewar and pondered if he had any shady business connections. Certainly, news of an invention like the Infinity Chip could cause a global stock market tumble, he reflected.

He picked up his tablet and pressed a button putting him directly through to Merrick. She appeared within twenty seconds on the screen and said: "I suppose you're wondering if I've found that needle in the haystack, for you?

"Well, I double-checked the eco warrior Dylan Rooke and you were right to discount him. I've pulled the phone records on Dr Wallace and scrutinised them even further and the Russian ladies he's been talking to on these chat lines all have one thing in common… The multiple telephone number leads to two landlines at the same address."

Mr Petrie sat forward and urged: "Go on."

Merrick, seemingly enjoying the dramatic pause, continued and said: "Tatyana, Eva, Anka, Katerina, Anastasia, Ivana, Reza and Florentina are names used by Mabel Butterfield and her niece Nancy Potts of Scotswood Road, Newcastle. There's also been a flurry of activity on a Dumfries number to Tina Kirkpatrick of Dalbeattie Avenue who has several pseudonyms including Rookie Blue.

"Amusing as this has been, I'm afraid your three leads have led us to the bottom of the haystack. The only other item of interest is Jennifer Hunter for no other reason than I can't seem to find any record of her at all, not even a National Insurance number or tax reference. Everyone else seems to have a past, unsavoury or otherwise."

The conversation over Mr Petrie rattled the fingers of both his hands across his desk before clasping them together and pushing outwards resulting in a sickening crack of knuckles. He went back in to the kitchen just in time to see Gordon Buie carefully place his magnifying glass back on the table.

"I've just found a note for you from your wife, Clara. I'm sorry, I didn't mean to pry but it was wedged under the mounted bell. Mr Petrie, it's, it's…" Gordon Buie faltered and then said: "It's dated May 1665." Suddenly, the redoubtable Mr Petrie looked frail and began to tremble as he reached out for the note. He almost fell into his armchair as he read its contents.

It began: "My dearest love, by the time you have read this, I will no longer be here but I do not want you to mourn or grieve. Know that the last thirty years of my life have been blessed and I could not have wished for a better husband, so strong, so handsome and so kind and gentle.

"I think you should take up the appointment offered at Sweetheart for the teaching profession is a noble one and it will mean you can remain here, at Dulce Cor. I do not want you to spend a lifetime grieving or mourning, nor do I want you to spend your life alone and so, consider taking another wife. I am not afraid to meet our Creator and I am sure God will protect me and judge me kindly, for I have tried to lead a good and productive life.

"We will be reunited together one day, my love, and so we still have much to look forward to. Until I see you in the next life, please take care of yourself in this one. Your loving wife, Clara.

There was an uneasy silence, until Mr Petrie looked around and said: "Where is the boy?"

The old man, glad of the change of subject, said: "Oh, the school secretary came to collect him. She said Dr Collins needed to see him. It all sounded quite urgent and she was keen we didn't disturb you and I know you asked not to be disturbed."

Still clutching the heavily creased vellum paper in his hand, he said: "No, no! Dr Collins has left already. I watched him drive off in his *Rover*. Please look after this and I'll explain later," said Mr Petrie as he put down his wife's letter. He grabbed his overcoat and left behind the bewildered clockmaker.

He walked towards the school and on looking skywards, he saw Duncan Dewar standing on the rooftop peering over the edge. It was only after quickening his pace he realised that someone had hold of him by his jacket collar. He ran inside the building and went up three floors to the matron's room above Plato House.

There were drops of blood on the floor and in a kidney-shaped basin. Clumps of chloroform-soaked cotton wool also lay on the day bed and floor as though there'd been a struggle. By now Mr Petrie was working on pure adrenalin as he opened the fire exit in the school clinic and climbed up the fire escape and onto the roof.

"Tell me where it is or I will let go and you will drop like a brick. I'm getting tired, Duncan, and I could easily let you slip…just like this." Miss Hunter then pushed Duncan while grabbing his shirt collar and yanking him back to safety from the roof's edge. The violence of the movement and the boy's own weight as he kicked back sent a gargoyle plunging, smashing into pieces on the ground below.

"Next time I will let you go," raged Miss Hunter in the terrified boy's ear. Mr Petrie wasn't sure what to do or say. If he shouted at the raging woman, she might let go of Duncan in shock or even deliberately push him over the edge. He couldn't risk it.

And then he remembered how Kirriereoch had given him the immobiliser pen, but would it work over a ten-yard distance? There was only one way to find out. Still unseen, he reached slowly inside his jacket pocket and grasped the immobiliser.

"Please, please, Miss Hunter. You're scaring me. Whatever was in my neck has now gone and I don't know where it is. Please, I'm begging you." They were the last words Duncan uttered before Mr Petrie took aim and pressed the plunger which depressed the pen's back spring, activating the mechanism inside.

The movement was just loud enough to alert Miss Hunter who turned her head swiftly around to catch the gaze of the history master while maintaining her right hand's grip on the boy's bloodied collar. He could see from her murderous gaze she was more than capable of pushing the boy over the roof ledge…and she did.

Chapter 25

Mr Petrie ran forward to try and stop Duncan plunging to his death but, by some miracle, the immobiliser had kicked in just as Jennifer Hunter turned her head towards him. While she had gone to push the boy over the ledge, her hand had turned to stone and she still held him in a vice-like grip by the scruff of his collar. Since they were connected, Duncan had also been frozen in time.

He pulled the boy's legs back onto the roof and removed his jacket which was still being held by Miss Hunter. Pointing the immobiliser at Duncan, he unfroze the boy. "How are you? Do you know where you are? Speak to me, Duncan."

The boy was trembling by now. "When is this going to stop? She drugged me, Mr Petrie, and she tore at my neck with a blade and then dragged me on to the roof. She kept pushing me and pushing me. I—I—I…"

He then looked at the frozen Miss Hunter. "No! Look at me, Duncan Dewar, now!" ordered Mr Petrie. He clasped the boy's face in his hands and said again: "Look at me. Listen to me. You are fine. You are going to get through this. I now want you to go back downstairs and wait for me in The Caledonian Suite. Do you understand?" He nodded and Mr Petrie turned him around and pointed him back in the direction of the fire escape.

Walking towards Miss Hunter, he pointed the immobiliser at her and stood back. She unfroze and gasped as she looked at the jacket still in her hand. "Where is he? What happened?"

Mr Petrie moved forward: "You pushed him over the edge and I want to know why. I want to know who you are working for, Miss Hunter."

"Come one step closer, Petrie, and I will follow the boy. I'm not afraid to die, but you are, aren't you? You've been avoiding your demise for some time now, haven't you?" she taunted.

He shrugged his shoulders: "I've no idea what you are babbling on about woman, but I do know you aren't working for the school. Who is your real master? And why are you targeting Duncan Dewar?"

She threw her head back and laughed and then, looking at the jacket, dropped it by her feet. Turning towards the history master and moving a step forward, she said: "I had no interest in Dewar, well, not until you rescued him from the car crash, you old fool. I arrived at Sweetheart to watch you! That's why I was sent here. You are the real person of interest, you and your secrets. Who gave you your immortality and who are you working for, Mr Petrie?"

He was rarely lost for words and he felt his mouth go dry as he considered that for the last fifteen years, the quiet, conscientious Miss Hunter had been actively watching him, but for whom and why? How did she know he had rescued Duncan from his parent's car? Exactly how much did she know about his work, and was she a threat to the very existence of the Council of Anam Cara?

Since he still had the immobiliser in his hand, he thought he would reactivate it and turn her back into a living statue. As he raised his arm, she moved backwards. Catching her heel on Duncan's jacket, she stumbled and fell over the ledge. Her blood-curdling scream only lasted a matter of seconds but it seemed to rip through the school grounds.

Mr Petrie went down through the fire escape and back into the matron's room, past Plato House and down to the ground floor. Miss Hunter lay on the gravel motionless. A trickle of blood oozed from her ear and she was dead, concluded Mr Petrie after he failed to find a pulse. As he knelt over her body, he looked up and saw Duncan Dewar standing in the main entrance, completely traumatised by what he had seen.

Looking furtively around, he saw no one else and remembered the gardener had gone to collect the choir from Edinburgh Airport. Pulling out his mobile phone, he placed a call to Merrick using a speed dial she'd once keyed in for him. He explained briefly what had happened and, on closing the call, walked Duncan back into The Caledonian Suite.

“I didn’t want any of this to happen,” he explained to the ashen-faced schoolboy who was trembling with the shock.

“I am impressed with the way you’ve handled yourself and not many would have to cope with what you’ve endured, not in ten lifetimes.

“Let’s go back to Dulce Cor and try and make sense of recent events.” He pulled Duncan up to his feet and put a supportive arm around the boy as he led him out of the room.

Duncan faltered and shook his head looking upwards. “That’s you, isn’t it? You’re the man standing next to the king. It’s you. I know it’s you.”

They both gazed upwards to the large oil on canvas. “Yes, I do resemble one of the courtiers, admittedly, but…”

Duncan interrupted: “No more lies, please sir, no more lies.” Mr Petrie pursed his lips. He’d anticipated this day coming for many years but never dreamed it would be one of his pupils who challenged him.

“Come with me, laddie. You want the truth and you will get it, but I am not sure you will be able to handle it.”

As they stepped back outside of the building, Duncan gasped and turned his head in all directions. “She’s gone. Miss Hunter’s gone.”

Mr Petrie said: “All will be explained in good time. But first things first. We should go to the cottage because what I have to say to you should also be heard by your grandfather.”

As they entered the cottage, Gordon Buie stood up anxiously. Mr Petrie invited them to sit by the sofa since his table was still cluttered with the clock works the old horologist had dismantled and cleaned.

He brought three mugs of tea and some biscuits and after sitting down and serving his guests, he then said: “What I am about to tell you cannot go beyond these walls. It is a story spanning centuries and you will find it hard to believe but the time has come for the undiluted truth and if there is anyone left to trust in the world today, it is you Gordon and you Duncan.”

The pair sat in silence and partial disbelief as he took them through his journey from the sixteenth century to the present day. Without identifying the whereabouts or naming the Council of Anam Cara and its members, he explained how as a fourteen-year-old he had been offered immortality to work for the common good and development of Scotland and the wider world.

For each assignment or mission, he would be gifted with special powers to fight evil and make a difference to the lives of individuals without changing the course of history. "I should have read the small print," he laughed, trying to lighten what had become a very heavy and serious story.

"Of course one of the first things I wanted to do was cure cancer, stop plague and end wars and poverty, but I very soon discovered there were limitations to my work. I could make a difference but not make changes in history. Still, as a young man, there were irresistible challenges and great achievements were made by trimming the edges of our more brutal histories.

"Then I met my beloved wife, Clara, and we were married by the time we were twenty. Those two clocks you've been fixing, Gordon, were wedding presents we gifted to each other. Like you, we had a fascination for clocks and came to realise the importance of time."

He then told his incredulous audience how becoming a Guardian also had its disadvantages, too. Tears brimmed his eyes as he recounted the pain of watching his wife grow old and eventually succumb to plague and then the drops of salty water poured down his ruddy round cheeks as he spoke of watching his children, grandchildren and great-grandchildren die until there was no one left to carry on the line.

But he then spoke about the positive side of being a Guardian and added: "I would never have met you, Gordon or your wonderful grandson if it weren't for the path I'm destined to follow. I want no praise but your grandson wouldn't be sitting here today, had I not intervened on the night his parents were murdered.

"And if you hadn't called me when you did, he probably would not have left St Petersburg alive. There were some very powerful people, Gordon, who wanted the secrets of the microchip Duncan's parents planted in his neck. It was indeed a desperate measure but if they were to protect the secrets of the Infinity Chip, they felt there was no other alternative."

Gordon Buie said accusingly: "You didn't rescue, Duncan, did you? You were protecting the Infinity Chip. That was your reason to be on the road that night."

Mr Petrie let out a huge sigh and said: "Whatever my motives that night, I'm glad I did save his life.

"Your grandson is a remarkable young man and I want him to join me and help me in my work…if he's interested, but now that you are equipped with the facts, you must consider this carefully over days, weeks or even months."

Rising to his feet, the grandfather shouted: "Absolutely not! I forbid it! You've said yourself the gift of immortality is more of a curse and I don't want my grandson's life ruined before it even starts. I'm an old man and I love the life I lead but when it is time for me to go, I will not complain. You cannot meddle with God's laws like this.

"Look at yourself Mr Petrie. Can you honestly say you're at peace with the deal you made when you were Duncan's age? If it was offered again, what would you tell your young self? Eh, now be honest, man."

The two began talking ever more loudly over each other until their voices were interrupted by an even louder and more heart-breaking plea: "Stop! Stop it now! Grandfather, I love you and would never ever do anything to upset you but you cannot rule over my life. Only I can take this decision, no one else.

"Mr Petrie, I owe you a great deal. I am now losing count of the times you have saved my life. But I'm only fourteen and I have much to learn and years more to do at school and university and I have a grandfather I love dearly. Our time together is precious and I respect just about everything he says and does. But I am my own person and only I can decide. Mr Petrie, you will have my answer by tomorrow but in the meantime, let's see if we can't repair that clock."

Mr Petrie smiled and walked over to Gordon extending his hand, exclaiming: "We cannot fall out. We're Caledonians, man." Minutes later, all three were sat around the table, in silence, cleaning each part of the Lantern clock before Gordon Buie carefully reassembled and restored it to working order. Apart from a few furtive glances exchanged, there were no words around the table as each one focussed on the job in hand, although their minds were elsewhere.

That night, Duncan lay awake, thinking about his future and the astonishing offer Mr Petrie had made. He wanted him to become a Guardian and know the full secrets of what it entailed. The idea of immortality thrilled and excited him and he was confounded by his grandfather's hostility towards the idea. However, he knew the old man had his best interests at heart and trusted his judgement and wisdom.

As the boy tossed and turned, Mr Petrie was sitting with Salar and Merrick discussing the day's events and the mysterious Miss Hunter. "It's very disconcerting," said Merrick. "We've ran all known tests and records to get an identity and it's as though the woman never existed.

"All we can find from her DNA is that she is Eastern European, possibly from Chechenya. We are running more tests but I am fast running out of answers. Her DNA has the distinct J1 markers where auburn hair and blue eyes are prominent.

"So we know, more or less her place of birth, but how and where she reached adulthood is another thing. What are we trying to establish?"

Mr Petrie shook his head: "She spoke perfect English, too perfect perhaps. What we need to find out is exactly who she was working for and why. The skelwarks have downloaded all her computer files and she has a private apartment in Dumfries which is being forensically examined as we talk. What are we going to do with the body?"

Salar responded slowly and deliberately: "Well, until we find out more about her, we will hang on to it. After all, it is doubtless any relatives will come forward and report her missing. And, in the event they do, well, that in itself may help Merrick's investigations.

"We are also experimenting with some new pathology methods but it would be premature to talk about the Lazarus Project just yet.

"We could use the Gagultâ Stone as a last resort but I really do not want to go down that route ever again; it's neither scientific nor reliable, and resurrecting the dead always has negative consequences.

"The alarming thing is that she was embedded at the school with the express purpose of putting Mr Petrie under surveillance. Whatever intelligence she garnered, it is imperative we find it and also establish who she sent it to, why and for what purpose."

Salar then turned to him directly and asked: “Have you decided on your apprentice, yet?” The teacher smiled, nodded and said: “As we talk now, Duncan Dewar is deliberating my offer. His grandfather, and I had to let him know for reasons I’ll explain later, is very much against the prospect of Dewar becoming a Guardian.

“Should he say yes, I will, of course, ease the boy in gently. I think he’s probably not ready to meet you or the rest of the Council just yet. The next few months will reveal if he is capable of keeping secrets.” Salar’s long slender fingers tapped on the table, as if to display some angst.

“And if he’s not right for the role, what then?”

Mr Petrie replied: “Why then we revert back to default and put him and his grandfather under the Erasure Programme and life will continue as it has always. My main concern now is to get the message out that the boy is no longer of any value and the secrets of the Infinity Chip have gone forever.”

Salar enquired about his plans for that and Mr Petrie gave an intriguing smile as he stood up to leave: “I have an idea and will let you know by tomorrow evening.”

Chapter 26

Breakfast was an uncomfortably silent affair. Only the scraping sound of a mean little sliver of butter being thinly spread across a slice of toast by a dour-looking Gordon Buie could be heard along with the chink of china cups hitting their saucers. It was clear none of the three at the table had enjoyed a decent night's sleep and neither were they prepared to engage socially or even pretend to indulge in meaningless pleasantries.

Finally, Mr Petrie could stand it no more as he threw his linen napkin down and sighed: "Oh, for goodness sake. As Robbie Burns once said the suspense is worse than the disappointment. Duncan, have you made up your mind and if so, would you care to put us all out of our misery?"

Gordon Buie held up his hand as if requesting permission to speak and, without taking his eyes from the toast in his right hand, he said: "I want you to know, Mr Petrie, I have the utmost respect for you and whatever Duncan decides, I will not hold it against you nor will I take it personally. To be frank, I am exhausted with it all and my mind can barely turn. It's like an over-sprung clock."

The uncomfortable silence resumed for a few more seconds and this time it was Duncan who lifted his head and cleared his throat as he looked at the two men who were both huge influences in his life. "I have really considered the proposal, Mr Petrie, and I have taken in to account the words of wisdom offered by my grandfather, a man who has never let me down and offered me nothing but love and support.

"I am truly blessed to have both of you in my life and while I realise that I'm still too young to take full control, I would want some reassurances from both of you before I accept Mr Petrie's offer, for, despite your reservations grandfather, it does seem to be a wonderful offer."

Both men sat in silence, grim-faced, reflecting the gravity of the situation. "I want to become a Guardian and work as an apprentice under Mr Petrie, but I also want guarantees that my education at Sweetheart will continue and I will be able to go on to university, assuming I get the right qualifications. If there's one thing both of you have instilled in me, it is the importance of education."

Mr Petrie afforded a hint of a smile on his pursed lips and nodded before speaking: "Of course your education will be guaranteed and you will be introduced slowly into life as my apprentice. I don't expect it will be very exciting for you initially and certainly you will not be exposed to the sort of adrenalin-fuelled antics of the last few weeks.

"Well, I am glad that is sorted. You will make an excellent Guardian, of that I am sure. And Gordon, I promise you here and now you've not lost your grandson. Life will continue as normal for the foreseeable future and you will barely notice a difference."

Gordon Buie's eyes brimmed with tears as he said: "There can be no going back, no looking back in regret… Are you sure laddie? Are you…" He lurched forward and passed out. Mr Petrie jumped up and ran to support the old man as he said: "Help me put him on the sofa. Don't worry. He's just reacting to a sedative in his tea."

Duncan did as he was told and after putting his grandfather in a comfortable position, he turned to Mr Petrie and asked why it was necessary to drug him. "You have experienced, over the last few weeks, what life is like when you're being hunted because people think you know far more than you do. There is no way I want your grandfather exposed to any danger and I imagine you feel the same.

"In ten minutes, Merrick will come through that door and administer some very special medicine which will erase from his memory anything to do with 'The Guardians', your decision at breakfast and all the revelations that poured out recently. There are bad people out there, Duncan, and when we go into battle, we cannot leave anything to chance.

"Don't worry. He will still remember all the good things in St Petersburg, your singing and the sightseeing, but everything else will be gone as though it never happened. I could have done this much sooner but I wanted him to be part of your decision-making process. I love and respect your grandfather and would not want any harm to come to him now or in the future. Understand, eh?" Duncan felt uncomfortable but realised Mr Petrie was right.

Merrick, prompt as ever, arrived and without any acknowledgements to those in the room walked straight over to the sofa. Opening a small Gladstone-style leather bag, she produced a round disc the size of a pound coin and placed it firmly on a spot just above Gordon Buie's forehead. She then administered a blue-coloured liquid into the old man's left arm and whispered into his ear. Although his eyes were still firmly closed, he appeared to nod in agreement to whatever it was she had said. Duncan, who was chewing nervously on a forefinger and thumb, watched on silently.

"Job done. He'll wake up in five minutes and imagine he's had a catnap. I'll see myself out," she said brusquely before heading towards the door. As she lifted the latch, she hesitated and turned around to look at Duncan. Half smiling, she said: "Welcome on board. I'm sure we'll bump in to each other again."

As the door closed, Duncan gasped and said: "Is she one of…"

But he couldn't get his sentence out before Mr Petrie said: "Not now. There's plenty of time for questions later. Let's wake your grandfather and finish off our breakfast. There is one thing I'll say, Duncan," said Mr Petrie as he stretched out his arm placing it on the boy's shoulder: "I'm glad you agreed to join me. A whole new world is about to open up to you and every day will have the potential to become an adventure."

Duncan was excited, although he tried to contain his feelings. Gordon Buie awoke from his slumbers feeling quite refreshed and returned to the breakfast table. "I think I've just had one of those power naps, apologies for drifting off before breakfast." The others smiled as a fresh round of toast was produced by Mr Petrie. Mr Buie took a crust and lavished it with lots of butter which melted easily into the warm bread.

It was nearly the start of a new term and so, the school was bustling with activity as parents arrived to drop off their children while the school bus was on a constant shuttle between the airport and the train station. Duncan and his grandfather walked to the village while Mr Petrie went off to the main school building where new parents and arrivals were being greeted.

"I'm really sorry, Mr and Mrs Barsukov. I've simply no record of your boys being registered here, none at all. This is most peculiar," said Penny Jones who had been sent to the school by an Edinburgh recruitment agency. Mr Petrie strolled over and asked Miss Jones if he could help.

Pulling him to one side she said: "I really have been thrown in to the deep end here but the registration seems pretty straight-forward. However, I simply can find no record of the Barsukov boys. I'm really not sure what to do. Is there any news yet on, Miss Hunter?"

Mr Petrie shook his head and added: "It's a complete mystery. She seems to have vanished and has not left any messages, which is most uncharacteristic of her. Just soldier on, Miss Jones, and leave the Barsukovs to me."

Mr Petrie walked over to the Russian family, introduced himself and said: "There seems to be a misunderstanding and we will get this little matter sorted. In the meantime, would you care to have a look around the school and its grounds, Mr and Mrs Barsukov?" Glad of his intervention, the family agreed and one of the boarders was summoned to escort the family on a tour of Sweethearts.

The old Scottish history master smiled to himself and went outside by the steps just as the Volkov's chauffeur-driven car pulled into the drive. The limousine had barely stopped on the gravel when the twins jumped out and ran towards some friends they had spotted leaving the more graceful Svetlana and her husband, Viktor, to emerge.

There was a sharp intake of breath just behind Mr Petrie who was almost rudely swept aside as Dr Jones hurtled down the stone steps to greet the Volkovs. The Welsh choirmaster's beneficiary swept her white-gloved hand towards Dr Jones and linked his arm walking off as they both talked excitedly about their plans for the forthcoming term.

Viktor was unimpressed and began scanning the entire area as though he was a leopard looking for prey. "Searching for someone, Mr Volkov?"

He turned to see the Scottish history master walking down the steps and appeared slightly irritated he would have to engage in conversation. "No, I was just looking for my boys but they ran off as soon as they saw their friends, and as you can see Svetlana is already plotting with Dr Jones on how to spend my money."

Mr Petrie grinned: "Ah, yes, the burden of being such a generous benefactor. Still, you must have been pleased with the outcome of St Petersburg. It was such a success. By the way, some of your friends arrived about an hour ago asking for you." Viktor's leather soled shoes crunched through the gravel as he stopped suddenly and turned to face the smiling master.

"Who? Who is asking for me?" Mr Petrie gently touched the sleeve of his cashmere coat, as if to reassure him, and said: "Really, it's nothing to be concerned about but your acquaintance Yury Barsukov and his delightful wife, Olga, have arrived with their sons claiming to have registered for places at the school. May I be frank with you, Mr Volkov?"

Without waiting for a reply, he continued: "I get the feeling that Mr Barsukov intends to call our bluff. I don't believe he has registered the boys as I take a personal interest in all new arrivals and many of our pupils are registered years in advance. I believe they were so impressed with the choir in St Petersburg that they fell in love with the idea of sending their sons here, and who can blame them?

"What do you think?" Mr Volkov tugged on his crisp white shirt cuffs and smoothed down his tie. He was clearly ruffled but he wasn't quite sure what Mr Petrie was after. "I'm a simple man, Mr Petrie, and rather direct. It matters not to me if Yury Barsukov enrols his sons here, although Svetlana may not agree. However, it might suit my purposes if you can see your way to bending the rules and allowing them entry as long as they are made aware that, erm, it was I who intervened and made it possible. But what do you want out of all of this?"

As the two men walked towards the main entrance, Mr Petrie scratched his chin and this time he stopped and turned towards Mr Volkov: "It was not lost on me that you and some of your associates had more than a passing interest in one of my students. Duncan Dewar to be precise. They were under the impression that the boy was in possession of vital information which could be of value.

"I want it known that he is no longer a person of interest. I think that you could do that in your sphere of influence, Mr Volkov. This information needs to be spread far and wide so the boy can feel safe again. Is this within your gift?"

The Russian, who was twice as wide as the schoolmaster and slightly taller, looked at him and smiled: "Where is the microchip now? Who has it?"

Mr Petrie looked straight into the Russian's dark brown eyes and said: "You are indeed well informed. I can say in all honesty it is no longer on his person. It has gone. No one has it and whatever secrets it contained have also gone. The boy was not even aware he was carrying it until he dislodged it during a shower.

"I would like to tell you a glamorous, exciting story but the truth is it simply was washed away disappearing down some plughole, along with the secrets. A rather unspectacular and ignominious end, don't you think?"

Laughing out loud, Viktor responded: "And who is going to believe such a tall story?"

Shrugging his shoulders, Mr Petrie said: "I don't care what you think, quite frankly. You can walk away now with some information which will increase your standing in whatever shady world you occupy and, in addition, you can have the eternal gratitude of Yury Barsukov. Symbiosis, Mr Volkov, benefits both parties, not just the parasite."

Viktor Volkov's nostrils flared as he took in an amount of air so large that it seemed to increase his already massive chest and as he exhaled he seemed to expunge the anger that had been accumulating during his conversation with Mr Petrie. "We have a deal, Mr Petrie. Is there anything else?" The master held out his hand and both men exchanged forced smiles and shook on their agreement.

As Mr Petrie turned to walk away, the Russian leant forward towards his right ear and said: "Just who are you and who do you really work for?"

Mr Petrie stopped and turned his head without moving his body. "Me? Why, I'm a person of no consequence, Mr Volkov, just a humble teacher trying to interest teenagers in Scottish history which is quite a challenge, I can tell you."

He then continued walking towards the administration block but could feel Viktor Volkov's piercing gaze on him until he disappeared through the doors. Walking inside Miss Hunter's office, he went to a filing cabinet and pulled out two forms of registration which he backdated to the previous year in the names of Ivan and Dmitry Barsukov.

Clutching the forms, he then strolled in to the headmaster's office: "Dr Collins, how is your day progressing?" The head was sitting at his desk with his palms over his ears as if to block out all noise.

"I really do not know how I am going to get through today. Where the hell is Miss Hunter? Did she say anything to you? The woman's gone completely off radar. We've even had the police to her home in Dumfries but there's simply no sign of her, absolutely nothing.

"On top of that, the agency sent Miss Jones from Edinburgh, a very capable woman I admit, but there's only so much she can do and, on top of all of this, I've got some Russian parents threatening all sorts because we've no record of their sons and they assure me they registered them last year," moaned the unusually exacerbated Dr Collins.

"Well, I can't help with regards to Miss Hunter's whereabouts but I have found these forms in the back of her desk. I think she simply forgot to file them and, given the events of today, it is quite clear she did not have her mind entirely on the job. Are the Russian pupils called Ivan and Dmitry Barsukov, by any chance?"

Dr Collins breathed a sigh of relief: "Yes, yes. But what are we going to do now? I'm not even sure we have places…"

Mr Petrie interjected: "We have had one deferral in the first year which gives us an opening for Dmitry and we can easily slot in Ivan. I think I can smooth this out for you, headmaster, if you want." Dr Collins was in no mood for more problems that day and anyone offering solutions was gratefully received and so, with that, both the Barsukov boys were enrolled.

As anticipated, Yury and his wife, Olga, were eternally grateful to Mr Petrie, although the Scottish History Master told both parents that their gratitude should really be extended to

Viktor Volkov. He handed them both the backdated registration forms and asked them to complete the family details and pay two years of school fees in advance.

On seeing his friend in the school dining room, Yury Barsukov rushed over: "Viktor, Viktor, how can I thank you, my friend? How did you manage to plant the registration forms? How did you know we were even coming today?"

Viktor smiled at Yury: "I make it my business to know these things. You are one of my dearest friends, Yury, and if I can help you, I will, for I know you would do the same for me."

Leading Yury out of the room and into the corridor, he leaned forward and said: "As it turns out, there is something you can do for me." With that, the pair walked back towards the exit in deep conversation. By the end of the week, the Russian underworld had dropped all interest in the Scottish schoolboy Duncan Dewar. He was no longer considered a person of interest by them and news soon filtered out to other intelligence agencies.

The story of the lost Infinity Cell travelled well, and there seemed to be general relief all round that no one had its secrets. The news was welcomed by the Council of Anam Cara. "So, Mr Petrie, when will we get to meet your protégé in person?" asked Salar, as the monthly meeting was about to conclude.

"Oh, soon, very, very soon," responded the Scottish History Master.

After the first week, life at the school began to resume as normal and the mystery of Miss Hunter was no longer a hot topic with local police more than happy to file her as a missing person rather than the victim of a suspected crime.

"Dewar!" shouted Mr Petrie as Duncan and his friends walked across the courtyard. The gangly teenager ran towards Mr Petrie and followed him in to the classroom. "If you could meet anyone in Scotland's rich history, who would it be?"

Duncan thought for a while and said: "Burns, Robert Burns."

Mr Petrie smiled: "I thought you might say that. If you've no plans tomorrow. I want you to come to Dulce Cor for 10 am." Punctual as ever, Duncan was knocking on the cottage door at the appointed time.

Mr Petrie invited him in and said: "Consider this your first day as my apprentice. So young Guardian, follow me, keep your mouth shut and your eyes and ears open."

Wide-eyed, Duncan followed the master through secret doors and passages which led to a warren of dimly lit underground tunnels towards an old oak door from where shafts of moving light poked through the framework. "Where are we going, Mr Petrie?"

But before he could get an answer, Mr Petrie opened the oak door and the pair walked through.

"Welcome to the Black Bull Inn at Moffat," smiled Mr Petrie. Aghast, Duncan looked around and saw lots of men dressed in strange-looking heavy wool clothes. Some wore loosely tied woollen kilts and there was a heavy smell of damp and body odour in the air.

Duncan looked at Mr Petrie and then down at himself. Their twenty-first century attire had vanished and instead, the pair were wearing white shirts, waistcoats and knee breeches with heavy, long overcoats trailing their calves. "Follow me, laddie," instructed Mr Petrie as he pushed his way through the bar towards another room.

"Petrie! What a man! Why, I was just about to leave but I think I will change my mind. Come, sit down. Landlord, more ale! And who is this young callant?"

Mr Petrie turned to Duncan and said: "Allow me to introduce you both." The man, dressed like a country gentlemen, rose up from his seat in the back room. Looking striking with his black, wavy hair brushed and secured with a black ribbon, he pulled at his yellow and blue striped waistcoat before extending his hand to Duncan.

"Master Duncan Dewar, let me introduce you to this most handsome fellow. This is Robert Burns… Some say he has a way with words and poetry…"

<Ends>